MIDNIGHT SMOKE

BOOK THREE OF THE FIREBRAND SERIES

HELEN HARPER

BOOK COVER DESIGN BY YOCLA DESIGNS

❀ Created with Vellum

CHAPTER ONE

THE DOOR WAS EXACTLY THE SAME AS I REMEMBERED IT FROM my childhood. The varnish was a little more weather-worn, and there was more moss growing on the front steps than there used to be, but it was still the same familiar dark-blue colour with its old brass knocker and barely legible name plate.

I drew in a breath and raised my hand to knock. I'd barely made contact when the door swung open and my uncle's craggy face peered out. 'Saw you coming from halfway down the street,' he grunted. 'I suppose you'd better come in.'

There was no warm hug, brief peck on the cheek or handshake. He simply turned and shuffled into the house, leaving me to follow. I shrugged and wandered in after him.

He moved more slowly than he used to, and his shoulders were more stooped, but the glacial way he greeted me made me almost nostalgic. In a way it was comforting that some things never changed. I'd been meaning to make this trip for weeks but work had always forestalled my plans. When I'd finally found myself with a spare morning, the first thing I'd done was set off, leaving early to avoid the worst of the rush-hour traffic. I hadn't called ahead. Perhaps that had been a mistake.

My uncle settled into the same worn armchair that had always sat in the corner of the living room next to the overflowing bookshelves packed with biographies and treatises on global politics. Everything was the same, from the dusty rubber plant in the corner to the small flip calendar on the little table by the wall. I gazed at the date displayed on it in bold red letters: Tuesday 22nd June. It was hard to believe that it was summer already.

My uncle sniffed loudly. He didn't offer me a cup of tea or a glass of water, but I hadn't expected him to. 'Got your birthday card,' he said.

I nodded. 'You're welcome.' His acknowledgment of the card was his way of saying thanks.

He sniffed again and crossed his legs. 'How's life with the police?' he enquired. 'Bagged yourself any criminals lately?'

'Several. And, to answer your first question, I'm enjoying the job.'

His expression didn't change. 'Good.' Then, 'I suppose you're here because you're in some sort of trouble. Have you got yourself knocked up?'

I was thirty years old, hardly a teenager. If I did fall pregnant unexpectedly, not only would I be more than capable of dealing with it myself but he would be the last person I'd turn to for support. My uncle wasn't a bad man. He'd taken me in and ensured I was clothed and fed and had a safe roof over my head. The fact that he'd never shown up at school plays or read me bedtime stories wasn't his fault. He'd never asked to be saddled with a child and I certainly didn't hold any grudges towards him. I'd received plenty of warmth and attention from my schoolfriends' parents and various neighbours.

In his own way Wilfred Bellamy had done the very best

that he could and then, when I was eighteen, he'd sent me off, satisfied that his duty had been done. I'd kept in touch with him but only with the odd postcard or Christmas greeting and very occasional visit. We weren't close and never would be – but I'd come to terms with that long ago.

I smiled faintly. 'No,' I said. 'I'm not knocked up.'

'Good,' he said again. He fixed me with a beady stare. 'Why are you here then?'

We were two hours out of London in a small village on the outskirts of Brighton. There was no chance that I'd happened to be passing and decided to pop in on a whim to say hello. He knew it and I knew it. That was one of the things that I liked about the cantankerous old bastard – he didn't waste time bothering to maintain a facade. He liked it when people got straight to the point instead of faffing around with niceties and politeness. Unfortunately, in this particular case that was easier said than done. There were things about me that I was unwilling to say aloud, at least to my uncle, but I still had a lot of questions that only he could answer.

'I'm here about my parents,' I said softly.

'They're dead.'

I gave him a long, exasperated look. 'I want to know more about them. I don't remember very much.'

'You were five when they died. You must remember some things.'

Not the sort of things that were helpful. I remembered a warm, sunlit kitchen and a worktop strewn with flour as my mum and I baked together. I remembered running around a garden playing hide-and-seek with my dad. There were flashes of other memories – family meals, building a snowman, snuggling up together in front of a roaring fire. I knew I'd been loved. What I didn't remember was any mention of the supernatural, or the fact that I could die over and over and over again before being resurrected in flames. I didn't remember anyone ever telling me that I was a phoenix. No, I corrected myself, not *a* phoenix. *The* phoenix. *Infernal Enchantments*, the book that I'd come across during the course of an investigation, had suggested there was only ever one. And currently that was me.

'Did they ever have anything to do with supes?' I asked.

For the first time my uncle looked surprised. 'Vampires?' he barked. 'Werewolves? Those sorts of … people?'

I nodded.

'Your parents lived in Kent. We're talking English country garden stuff,' he dismissed. 'Not inner-city London shenanigans.'

'I know,' I persisted, 'but—'

'I'd be surprised if either of them ever met a supernatural creature. But I wasn't close to them, as you know. Mark, your father, was fourteen years younger than me. We didn't grow up together. I left home when he was two. He was a snotty-nosed child with a predilection for plastic trucks. I didn't spend a lot of time with him, even when he grew older. As for your mother,' his mouth pursed as he thought, 'well, I only met her two or three times. I seem to recall she enjoyed painting. She had brown hair.' He pointed at me. 'Same shade as yours.'

Neither of those two things were helpful, but all my grandparents were dead and my mother had been an only child. The only person in the world who could tell me about my parents was the uncle sitting in front of me. I wasn't going to give up yet.

'Do you have anything that belonged to them?' I asked. 'Any diaries? Or notebooks? Any old belongings at all?'

His brow creased. 'Why are you bringing all this up now? They've been dead for a quarter of a century. What does it matter?'

I didn't answer his question. 'Do you have anything of theirs?' I repeated.

He sighed and cast his eyes upward. 'There might be a box,' he said finally. 'Up in the attic.'

I sprang to my feet. 'Great. I'll go look for it.'

My uncle didn't move. 'There's a lot of stuff up there. I have no idea where it would be, even if it's still there. I certainly don't want you rooting around in my possessions.'

He wasn't making this easy for me. 'I'll be careful.'

He shook his head. 'I will look for it and send anything I find on to you. I am a private person, Emma. I don't like having my routine or my home disturbed.'

I was well aware of that. I considered arguing, but I didn't want to annoy him to the point that he shut me out completely. 'Okay,' I said finally. 'I appreciate the effort.'

He knitted his fingers together and gave me a dark look. 'What is this really about? He's not getting out is he?'

I knew who he was referring to – Samuel Beswick, the man who'd broken into my family home and murdered my parents, leaving me alone with their bodies. The crime had only been discovered when my wailing alerted the neighbours, although blessedly I remembered nothing of the event. Beswick had been arrested less than twenty-four hours after the double murder and had been in prison ever since. He'd never explained why he'd committed such a terrible deed, and he'd never admitted his guilt. But he was the reason I'd wanted to join the police in the first place.

'No,' I said quietly. 'He's not getting out.'

Something gleamed in my uncle's eyes. There were occasions when it seemed to me that he despised Beswick far more than I ever could. 'I'm pleased to hear it.' He stood up. 'I'll look out that box for you.'

I had the distinct impression that I was being dismissed.

'Thank you.' I paused. 'How are you?' I asked. 'Are you keeping alright?'

'A few aches and pains. Nothing serious.' He pulled a face. 'The worst thing about getting to this age isn't my health, it's the way everyone else treats me. I'm no longer seen as a real person. I no longer have a personality of my own. They see me as an old man who must be spoken to in a very loud patronising voice.' His lip curled. 'I used to be considered important. I used to be respected. Now I'm just seen as old.' He pointed to the door. 'I'll see you out.'

I opened my mouth, wanting to say more, but he was already moving towards me and ushering me out. I knew that the last thing he wanted was my sympathy. He'd view it as pity – and neither of us wanted that.

'There's no need to come back,' he told me. 'I'll post whatever I find.'

Translation: stop bothering me and interrupting my hermit-like existence. I sighed. Yeah. Some things never changed.

Then he surprised me. He reached out and took my hand, gripping it tightly. His skin felt papery and thin. My eyes flew to his but I couldn't fathom his expression.

'Dredging up the past isn't always a good thing, Emma. Sometimes it's better to leave matters where they are and move on. What happened to your parents is a tragedy. What happened to you is worse, and I know that I was not the best guardian for you. But you can't change what happened.'

I swallowed. 'I'm not looking to change it,' I said quietly. 'I only want to understand it.'

He held my gaze before nodding. 'Very well.' He released his hold on me. 'They would have been proud of you, you know.'

Unbidden tears rose behind my eyes and I blinked furiously. 'Thank you.'

My uncle shrugged. 'I merely speak the truth.' Then he nudged me out of his house and closed the door.

RATHER THAN APPRECIATE the opportunity to stretch her metaphorical legs on winding country roads, Tallulah had grumbled all the way to my uncle's house and all the way back. It wasn't until we reached the outer London limits that her engine stopped rattling.

The lurid purple Mini, which I'd inherited from my Supe Squad predecessor Tony Brown, had considerable merits despite her age and tendency to belch out black smoke whenever she felt like it. Unfortunately, performing well on long drives was not one of those merits. I was beginning to think that she might have a point; the entire journey south felt like it had been a waste of time.

We were crossing the river when my police radio crackled. It was so unexpected that I almost smacked Tallulah's bonnet into the rear end of the black cab in front of me. I was jerked forward and the edge of the seatbelt cut into my skin. The taxi beeped its horn loudly. I breathed out. That was close. London taxi drivers were not to be messed with. The driver shot his hand out of his window and flicked his middle finger ostentatiously in my direction. I scowled. Whatever. It wasn't like I'd actually pranged his taxi.

I glanced at my watch. Midday exactly. The morning had zipped by.

'DC Bellamy, this is Dispatch. Please acknowledge.'

'Uh...' I fumbled with the equipment. 'This is DC Bellamy.' I paused. 'Acknowledged.' I winced at my awkward phrasing. I was rusty with a lot of terminology. As the only Supe Squad detective, I didn't spend a lot of time around other police officers. There was Fred, of course, but he'd been in Supe Squad longer than I had. I was the only detective; he was the only police constable. Liza was counted as office support and didn't go out in the field. And although I'd made radio calls myself when necessary, I'd never received one before.

'What is your current location? Your presence is required at the London Eye.'

I glanced at the road. 'I'm less than ten minutes' away. What's the problem?'

'Suicidal vampire.'

My mouth dropped open. Huh. 'I'm on my way.'

I changed lanes to adjust my course. A vamp with a death wish was the last thing I'd expected. I'd never heard of such a thing before, and no doubt Lukas, also known as Lord Horvath and the leader of the London vampires, would be apoplectic at the idea. He was also sure to be on the scene both to help his vampire and to manage what could only be vast numbers of avid tourists.

I'd been avoiding Lukas for weeks but I knew it was only a matter of time before our paths crossed again. I quashed the butterflies in my stomach and focused on recalling my Academy training. Dealing with potential suicide attempts could be tricky. When such an attempt involved vampires and one of the most famous landmarks in the city … hell, anything could happen.

CHAPTER TWO

I PARKED AS CLOSE TO THE LONDON EYE AS I COULD BEFORE jogging the rest of the way. There was already a police cordon around the area but, rather than preventing onlookers from pausing to gawk, it was only encouraging them. Truthfully, I'd have done exactly the same if I had been a passer-by.

I'd never seen anyone perched on top of a gigantic observation wheel before. The vampire in question wasn't in any of the glass-domed pods which were slowly revolving, affording visitors a panoramic view of the city. He'd foregone them in favour of clambering up the outside of the metal structure. How he'd achieved such a feat, which must have included evading the Eye's security measures, was beyond me. Even for a vampire, it seemed nigh on impossible.

I squinted at the ascending figure. He was dressed in black and his hoodie obscured his face. I doubted that was by accident. I frowned and carried on towards the Eye.

I waved my warrant card at the first uniformed officer I came to, and he lifted up the cordon and gestured me through. I ignored the hum of curious questions from the crowd about my identity and walked quickly to the foot of the wheel.

A man with a shiny bald pate, who was wearing a tailored suit that hung around his slight paunch, was flapping his arms and yelling. It didn't take a genius to work out that he was part of the London Eye's management team; the dripping sweat on his brow and his obvious panic broadcast it. 'You have to get that idiot down!' he shouted. 'There are news crews here already. This isn't the sort of publicity we need right now!'

Lord Lukas Horvath was standing less than a metre away. He didn't flinch – in fact, as far as I could tell, he was the epitome of cool, calm and collected vampire poise. He looked relaxed, his expression was bland and his arms were held loosely by his sides. His confidence was such that he didn't appear remotely out of place, even though he was wearing clothing that made him look as if he'd stepped out of the pages of a Victorian romance. I'd seen him wearing ruffled shirts before, but I'd never seen him wearing one that was open almost to his navel with blood-red frills artfully sewn in so many places. His inky-black hair had been blow dried and was swept upwards from his face. On anyone else that hairstyle would have looked ridiculous but it suited Lukas perfectly. All he needed was a swooning woman in a corset hanging off his waist and the picture would have been complete. Fabio, eat your heart out.

I glanced down at my jeans and plain T-shirt. If I'd known this was supposed to be a fancy-dress party, I'd have taken more care. Truthfully, if I'd known I was going to be in Lukas's company, I'd have taken more care full stop. I couldn't deny my attraction to the vampire. And I couldn't allow it to go anywhere.

Lukas's priority would always be the vampires, and I

knew that vampires couldn't be trusted. They desired blood, power and sex, not necessarily in that order. After what had happened to me at the hands of my boyfriend, who had killed me twice, I wasn't willing to do anything that might jeopardise my fragile heart. But that didn't prevent the lurch in my stomach when I looked at the vampire Lord.

'Are you suggesting, Mr Hannigan,' Lukas enquired, 'that the pages of tomorrow's newspapers are more important than a person's life? Perhaps we should hope for a gust of wind to knock the poor fellow off his perch? Then you can clean up the bloodied mess of brains and splattered internal organs while the tourists get back on board for their selfies.'

Uh-oh. Usually Lukas could charm the pants off anyone he spoke to. The belligerent edge to his words spoke of his genuine anxiety about whoever was clinging to the observation wheel above our heads.

I jumped forward before an argument ensued. 'Detective Constable Emma Bellamy,' I said by way of introduction. 'I'm with Supe Squad. I need to know what's going on here, then we'll see about the best way of talking that man down. Who is he, and how did he get up there?'

Lukas turned to me, his black eyes searching my face. What he was looking for, I had no idea. 'Hello, Emma,' he said. He moved a fraction closer. 'How are you?' His tongue darted out and wetted his lips. 'You've been avoiding my calls.'

I pointed at the wheel, ignoring his attempts at pleasantries. My uncle would have been proud. 'Who is that?'

If Lukas was irritated, he didn't show it. 'We haven't been able to get a decent look at his face so I can't tell.'

'But he's definitely a vampire?'

'Yes.' Hannigan gestured towards a young woman wearing a London Eye T-shirt who was staring at Lukas with wide eyes. Considering the clothes he was wearing, I didn't

11

blame her. 'Paige,' he snapped. 'Tell her what you saw.' When she continued gazing at Lukas, Hannigan nudged her. 'Paige!'

The woman shook herself and focused on me. I estimated she was about twenty. She was probably a student working at the Eye during her holidays. No doubt it was a good gig – most of the time. She scratched her head and blinked rapidly. 'Er, I was getting ready to open up when he came past me. Half the security team were on his tail but they couldn't get close. I tried to stop him too but he was too fast. He's definitely a vampire. I got a good look at him and...' She opened her mouth and tapped her canines.

'Fangs?' I asked.

She nodded. 'Big ones.'

'How do we know he's suicidal?' I asked no one in particular. 'How do we know that this isn't some kind of stunt?'

'Stunt?' Lukas growled sharply.

I gave him a long look; just because he believed his vampires were above reproach didn't mean it was true. As their leader, he was powerful and he garnered considerable respect but at the last count there were almost two thousand vamps under his control. He couldn't possibly keep track of all of them.

'If someone wanted to commit suicide,' I said calmly, 'why would they choose such a public place? Any bridge would do. Picking a tourist attraction seems like vanity.'

Lukas's face darkened but he didn't answer, probably because he knew I was right.

'I don't care why he's up there,' Hannigan said. 'Just get the blighter down!'

Easier said than done. 'Tell me about the wheel. What do I need to know?'

'We've shut down the power,' Paige told me. 'Obviously.' She pointed at the immobile glass pods. Some of them still contained people; anxious faces were peering down at us then up at the precariously perched vamp. 'It's 135 metres high. It's not the tallest observation wheel in the world—'

Hannigan's expression soured further.

'—although it used to be and,' Paige continued, 'one revolution takes around thirty minutes.'

I scratched my chin. 'I suppose you've already considered turning it back on and waiting for our would-be jumper to rotate to the ground.'

'We don't want to do anything that might provoke him to step off.'

'Or,' Lukas added, his expression shuttered, 'fall off by accident.'

'He was halfway up before we managed to shut everything down,' Paige said. 'I don't think he'll fall by accident. He seems pretty nimble.' She cast another wide-eyed look at Lukas. 'Is that a vampire trait?'

He glanced at her then smiled slowly without taking his eyes away from hers. 'It is. Typically, we're more athletic and stronger than humans.' The intensity of his gaze increased. Paige was all but melting.

I frowned. What exactly did he think he was doing?

Hannigan's cheeks were turning a vicious shade of red. He was obviously immune to Lukas's obvious charms. 'Get that freak down from there!'

Lukas placed a hand on his arm. 'Don't worry,' he murmured, power vibrating through his words. 'Everything will be fine.'

The London Eye manager opened his mouth then closed it again, as his body subsided. 'Everything will be fine,' he repeated robotically.

'Lukas,' I warned.

He raised an eyebrow. 'What? You can't tell me that he didn't need calming down.'

I tutted.

'That's so cool,' Paige breathed.

Yeah, yeah. I sighed and looked up again. What comes up must come down, I decided. One way or another.

'Do you have any safety harnesses for climbing up the structure?' I asked.

'They're being collected,' Paige answered. 'They should be here soon.'

Soon might be too late. I nodded before moving away and examining the web of steel. It didn't look too difficult, and fortunately I had a head for heights. I raised one foot and tested my weight.

'Emma,' Lukas said, 'what do you think you're doing?'

I grinned. 'I've told you before, I prefer it when you call me D'Artagnan.' Then, without further ado, I started to climb. The watching crowd gasped loudly, a perfectly synchronised sound of excitement and horror.

I'd barely gone two metres when Lukas was by my side, climbing with me. 'I will ask the question again. What the fuck do you think you're doing?'

'I'm going to talk to your vampire and see if I can encourage him to come down of his own accord.' I reached for the next steel section and hauled myself up.

'Don't be an idiot. You might fall.' He was keeping pace with me. Higher and higher and higher.

'So might you,' I pointed out.

'I'm a vampire. I have preternatural abilities.'

'True,' I answered, without stopping. 'But if you fall, you'll still go splat.'

'So will you.'

'I'll wake up again twelve hours later. You won't.' I paused. 'And, as it turns out, the more times I die the stronger I become. So not only is this easier for me than you might think but, if I slip and fall, I'll be more powerful tomorrow. If you slip and fall, you'll be dead.'

'He's a vampire. He's my responsibility.'

'I represent Supe Squad,' I replied easily. 'The responsibility is mine. You head down to your new friend. I'll take care of this.'

There was a beat of silence. Lukas continued to match me step for step. I risked a glance down and estimated we were already about forty metres up. There was still no sign of the harnesses. This had definitely been the best call.

'Paige does seem like a lovely girl,' Lukas said finally.

'Mmm.' A gust of wind rippled past, ruffling my hair and tugging at the frills on Lukas's shirt.

'I wonder if she's single.'

I didn't respond.

'You look annoyed, D'Artagnan. Are you jealous?'

'Nope,' I said. Forty-five metres up now. 'But you're trying to make me jealous.'

Another beat passed. 'Yes,' he said, 'I am. You were supposed to come round to my house for dinner. I was … disappointed when you didn't. I ended up being called to a meeting at Fairfax's place instead. It was very dull. If you'd kept our … date, I could have avoided his pointless attempts at friendship.'

'I called you about that. I had to cancel because I had an assault in Lisson Grove to deal with. A daft human bloke was trying it on with some of the Carr wolves and he ended up getting bitten. I had to make sure the paperwork was in order and double-check that all procedures were followed.'

One werewolf bite wouldn't turn a human into a furry beast but two might, and three separate bites would almost definitely do the trick. The werewolf clans were only permitted to turn a small number of people each year because their numbers were strictly capped by the 1901 Limiting Act. Accidental bites had to be carefully logged and communicated to all werewolves to avoid inadvertent repeats and accidental transformations. It was a process the clans took care of for themselves but this had been the first opportunity I'd had to witness it first hand. I couldn't pass that up. And, if I were honest, having an excuse to avoid dinner with Lukas had been a godsend. I was conflicted about him, both about my feelings for him and his activities as vampire Lord, so avoidance seemed like the better option. If that made me a coward, well then, so be it.

'You're scared of me.'

'No,' I answered. Sixty metres. Almost halfway. 'It's not you I'm afraid of, it's your job. Especially when it's compared to my job.'

'Being Lord is more than a job.'

'Yeah,' I said sadly. 'That's what worries me.'

'Emma,' Lukas began.

Something fell from above, clattering past us as it bounced off the steel structure of the Eye. I stopped moving and stared down, tracking its fall. 'What was that?'

Lukas frowned. 'I don't know.' He angled his head up. 'Shit,' he muttered. 'He's on the move.'

I squinted against the sun and spotted the vamp above us. He seemed to be moving across the top of the wheel towards the other side, away from us.

'Can you see his face?' I asked. Lukas had far better eyesight than I could ever hope for. 'Can you tell who he is yet?'

His voice was grim. 'No. He knows we're here – he wouldn't be moving away otherwise. But he's not once looked back in this direction. It's like he doesn't want to be identified.'

Suspicion nibbled at me. There was more to this than met the eye, I was sure of it. 'I have a bad feeling about this,' I muttered.

'Yeah.' Lukas's jaw was set. 'Me too. You should head down to solid ground.'

'So should you,' I retorted. I looked at the nearest pod. There was a large group of people inside, staring at us. I considered raising a hand to wave at them but I didn't want to tempt fate. We were rather high up now and, despite my newly enhanced strength and stamina, I was starting to tire. This climbing business was harder than it looked.

At the front of the pod was a young boy, perhaps seven or eight years old. His mouth was smeared with chocolate from the ice-cream cone in his hand. With all the excitement, he seemed to have forgotten that he was holding it. Rather than gazing at Lukas and me, however, his saucer-wide eyes were trained on the figure above us. All of a sudden he seemed to gasp. My head swung round, just in time to see the supposedly suicidal vampire leap down from the steel beam he was balancing on to the top of one of the other observation pods.

'Don't move!' I shouted, throwing as much force into my voice as I could. The wind whipped away my words and, even with the keen hearing granted to his kind, I doubted the vampire had heard me. By my side, Lukas cursed.

Then the vampire leapt down again, his hands catching another of the steel rods, and swung in mid-air for a moment. I was all but certain he was going to fall and plummet the hundred metres or so to his death. Instead he dropped and lowered himself further down with astonishing speed.

The wind gusted even harder. The vamp, who was still on the opposite side of the wheel, barely seemed to notice. He drew level with us but didn't once glance over in our direction. He seemed intent on getting to the ground. In theory that was a good thing because nobody wanted him to jump, but I wanted to talk to him and find out what was behind

17

this stunt. If he ran away before we reached him, there'd be a lot of unanswered questions to deal with.

I had to follow suit – if he was clambering down then so was I. I started to lower myself but, in my haste, my foot slipped. I let out a sharp cry. Within a heartbeat, Lukas was reaching for me and pulling me back up again.

His hand curved round my waist, gripping me tightly, and he looked into my eyes. 'I tried to warn you, D'Artagnan,' he murmured. 'It's dangerous up here and I don't want you to fall.'

I stared at him, my heart hammering in my chest. Then there was a clang and I looked away, towards the descending vampire. 'He's still heading down,' I said. 'We have to get to him.'

Lukas nodded. 'Be careful,' he warned.

This time I didn't offer any clever quips. 'I will.' I started to climb down.

Lukas and I moved quickly, mirroring the actions of the mysterious vamp, descending step for step, albeit on opposite sides of the wheel. The structure of the Eye heaved and groaned. I knew it would more than hold our weight, but my near fall had knocked the wind out of my sails and I felt less confident now.

It was harder going down than it was climbing up, and it wasn't long before the vampire started to pull away. Below us, various police officers and London Eye officials were positioning themselves. Someone would catch him when he reached the ground then we'd find out what the hell all this was about.

Lukas and I were about twenty-five metres from the ground and the vampire was about fifteen metres away. I tried to move faster to catch him up, but he suddenly stopped. He looked down, swinging his head first one way then the other. What on earth was he up to? Was he stuck? Attacked by a bout of vertigo?

I was totally wrong.

Lukas yelled down at the small crowd of police and Eye security officials. 'Left!' he roared. 'Go left!'

It was already too late. As we watched and clung helplessly to the Eye, the vampire on the other side jumped and sailed outwards from the steelwork. Instead of slamming into the ground and collapsing into a heap, he hit the tarmac and rolled. Then he sprang to his feet in one fluid movement and started to sprint. Security and police officers streamed towards him. but he paid them no attention as he pelted directly for the barrier to the far side. It was designed to keep out trespassers but the vamp scrambled up it easily, threw himself off the other side and disappeared. Well, fuckity fuck fuck.

We climbed down the rest of the way, first Lukas and then me.

'He's gone,' stated a panting policeman who rushed up to us. 'We tried to catch him but he was like a damned ninja. I've never seen anything like it.' He shot Lukas an accusing look as if it were entirely his fault that vampires had such acrobatic skills. If Lukas noticed, he didn't react; his expression was set like granite but his black eyes were flaring with rage.

'You've never had to deal with a suicidal vampire before, have you?' I asked quietly.

'No,' Lukas bit out. 'And I don't think we're dealing with one now, either.'

CHAPTER THREE

I'D ONLY BEEN BACK ON SOLID GROUND FOR A FEW MOMENTS when my phone rang. I checked the caller display and my heart sank.

Lukas leaned across and glanced down. 'Ignore it,' he said.

I shook my head. I couldn't do that. I pressed the button to answer. 'This is DC Bellamy,' I said.

'Emma,' Detective Superintendent Lucinda Barnes barked. 'What in bejesus' name is going on? Why am I watching the lunchtime news and seeing reports of a damned vampire climbing the London Eye?'

I winced. 'He's not climbing it any more,' I offered helpfully.

'Did he fall?'

'Er, he climbed down and ran away.'

Her voice rose to a screech. 'Ran away? What is going on? Where is Lord Horvath?'

I held the phone towards Lukas, suggesting that he take it and speak to my boss himself, but he backed away looking grimly amused. He didn't have to answer to DSI Barnes. Unfortunately I didn't have the same luxury. 'He's busy,' I said. 'But he's here and he was trying to help bring the man down.'

'Well, he didn't do a very good job, did he?' She hissed under her breath. 'He probably planned this. He probably wanted to remind the world of just how powerful the vampires are. I'm surprised he didn't arrange for a group to abseil down Big Ben at the same time.'

'Actually,' I began, 'I don't think that—'

There was the sound of muffled voices from DSI Barnes' end. 'What?' she said to someone. '*What?*'

I frowned, prickles of tension on the nape of my neck.

My boss came back on the line. 'Get to Tower Bridge,' she ordered. 'As fast as you can.'

My blood chilled. 'Why?'

Lukas was watching me, his eyes narrowed.

'Three werewolves have hijacked an open-top bus.'

My mouth dropped open. 'You're kidding me.'

'You have no idea how much I wish I were. Go. Now.'

I didn't waste any further time. I was already running for Tallulah.

'Emma!' Lukas called after me.

I waved a hand. 'Find that fucking vampire!' I yelled over my shoulder. And then I ran faster.

I'D STARTED KEEPING a loaded crossbow in Tallulah at all times. When I reached the edge of Tower Bridge and saw the commotion ahead, I grabbed it from the back seat before hauling arse. This time I didn't need to show my identification to gain access to the scene; Tallulah and the crossbow heralded my arrival. The relief on the faces of the police at my end of the bridge was unmistakable.

'What's happened?' I asked, wasting neither time nor breath on any unnecessary preamble.

'Tour bus up ahead,' stated a lanky male police officer. His voice was calm and his expression was studiously bland, but I didn't miss the faint tremble in his hands. It was understandable; very few police officers ever had to deal with supernaturals in person. Apart from yours truly, of course. 'It's one of those buses that you can catch on any street corner around here. It takes in the sights. Has its own tour guide. You know the sort of thing.'

The bus had come to a halt in the middle of the road and was sitting at an angle across two lanes. Both in front and behind it were scattered cars that had been abandoned by their drivers. There were also, by my count, at least eight armed officers with guns trained on it. The open top deck appeared to be empty. Whatever was going on was happening inside on the lower floor.

'We have reports that three men with large backpacks got on board outside the Tower of London. A few minutes later, they transformed into werewolves, grabbed the tour guide and several other tourists and threatened the rest. They seemed to want the bus driver to drive out of the city, but he crashed the bus instead and got away. Some of the other tourists managed to jump off the top of the bus when it stopped. We think there are seven people still inside, not including the werewolves.'

Okay. This was crazy. But okay. 'Any word on what clan the wolves are from?'

The police officer goggled at me. 'How would we know that?'

They wouldn't necessarily, but werewolves were loyal creatures. There was no chance that any of them had made a move like this unless it had already been sanctioned by their clan alpha. And, nutty as the four alphas were, I couldn't for the life of me imagine why any of them would have thought that bringing central London to a halt was a good idea.

'Has anyone contacted the clan alphas?' I asked.

'We thought you might do that.'

'Uh huh.' I nodded. 'Any word on the wolves' rankings? Did anyone spot any coloured tags on their arms before they transformed?'

He shook his head slowly. He was about as much use as a one-legged man in an arse-kicking contest.

There was a sudden commotion behind us from the police line. I turned and spotted Fred, who was waving his arms frantically in my direction. Finally, someone who could provide me with real back-up. I nodded at him. 'Let him through,' I instructed.

The police officer raised a hand and Fred was ushered over. 'Which clan are these idiots from?' he asked urgently.

'We don't know.'

'Has anyone spoken to the alphas?'

'Nope.'

'Do we know their ranks?'

I smiled slightly. 'No.' I passed him my phone. 'Get onto all four clan alphas straight away. Find out who these idiots are and which bastard ordered them to create this kind of havoc.' I paused. 'Start with Lady Sullivan.'

While I was currently on speaking terms with the Sullivan clan alpha, she was the most reckless. She'd once even tried to have me killed so she could examine my resurrections for herself. I guessed that she was the likeliest candidate for this kind of tomfoolery. If she'd sanctioned this attack, then her days were numbered. The public tolerated the supernatural community as long as they kept to their corner of London and didn't bother everyone else. Hijacking a damned tourist bus was not in that remit.

'What are you going to do?' Fred asked.

I bared my teeth in a nasty grin. 'I'll get closer and try to talk to these numbskulls,' I said. 'If they're low-ranking enough, I might manage to compel them to back down.' I crossed my fingers. It would be good to end this farce without any shots being fired.

I held my crossbow loosely at my side to indicate that I wouldn't aim or fire unless I had to, then I moved slowly towards the bus. Every eye was on me – and probably several cameras too. I didn't think about them as I focused on the bus. I could make out the flickering shapes of a few shadows inside, and every few moments a head bobbed up to stare at me. Judging by the long ears, the wolves were still in animal form.

When I reached the first armed officer, he pointed at a megaphone. I considered it for a moment then picked it up. 'This is Detective Constable Emma Bellamy,' my voice boomed out across the bridge. 'You know who I am. You will stand down, return to human form and leave the bus immediately.'

Every word thrummed with power and I could feel the compulsion I'd injected into my command reverberating through my body. I couldn't be sure, but it seemed that the megaphone amplified my power as well as my voice. I couldn't always compel supes to do my bidding; usually I needed their real names to boost my power and force them to my will. However, if the supes were weak enough, I could do it without their names.

I held my breath and waited, hoping that I'd done enough. When there was no immediate response from inside the bus, I cursed under my breath. Okay. If the mountain wouldn't come to Mahomet, Mahomet would go to the mountain.

I dropped the megaphone and walked forward. I was getting onto that bus.

'DC Bellamy!' one of the armed officers hissed. I glanced

at him. 'Protocol demands that no move is made to approach a hijacked vehicle until all other avenues have been explored.'

'That protocol is for humans,' I replied, 'not for were-wolves. Waiting them out might work in other circumstances, but wolves will react positively to a show of strength, not patience.' I gave him a look. 'You called me here for a reason. I know what I'm doing, trust me.' Then I continued walking towards the bus.

I'd barely covered ten feet when there was a flurry of movement behind the grubby windows. I stopped. Excellent. I waited two beats, then the bus door opened. But the person who stepped out, fear written all over his face, wasn't a wolf.

'Don't shoot!' he yelled in what sounded like a Kiwi accent. 'Please don't shoot!' He stumbled forward onto the road and the bus door closed again.

My eyes narrowed.

'Put your hands on your head!' shouted the same officer who'd tried to stop me.

The man did as he was told and staggered forward, his face paper white. I checked his clothes: khaki shorts, sandals and the bulge of a money belt round his waist. He was definitely a tourist. As soon as he reached the first police car about fifty metres from the bus, he gasped. One of the armed officers sprang up, grabbed him and hauled him behind the car.

I wasted no time in joining them and the three of us crouched behind the car. The officer took up position again, the muzzle of his government-issue gun pointing at the bus. I focused on the escapee. He was wheezing and his eyes were writhing wildly with panic.

I placed a hand on his shoulder. 'Breathe,' I commanded. 'In.' He heaved in a breath. 'Out.' He gasped. 'In. Out.'

He did as he was told. His body shaking beneath my hand but slowly the tremors started to subside. 'You're safe now,' I said. Then my voice hardened. I needed him to talk. 'Tell me what's going on inside that bus.'

'Three,' he said. 'Three werewolves.'

'Did you see them transform? Did you see what they looked like before they turned?'

He shook his head. 'I was upstairs – we all were. They must have changed before they came up top. I didn't see them when they got on board.' He reached into his pocket with a shaking hand and held out a sheet of paper. There was a message scrawled in messy handwriting.

I read it aloud: '*We have six hostages. Stay back or we will eat them. We will present our demands in one hour. Be ready.*' I frowned and looked at the man. 'One of the wolves wrote this?'

'I…' The man looked at me helplessly. 'I think so. One of them gave it to me and shoved me out of the door.'

No werewolf in animal form could write; their paws didn't allow for that sort of dexterity. 'They're still all wolves?'

'Huh?'

'They're still furry?'

He looked confused. 'Yes.'

They could have prepared the note before they got on board, but how would they have known how many hostages they'd end up with? Buses like this one were hop-on and hop-off, so sometimes they were empty and sometimes every seat was filled. It didn't compute. And I'd never heard of a werewolf wanting to eat a human. All the ones I knew preferred burgers, usually with lashings of tomato ketchup.

I scratched my head. First that vampire on the London Eye and now this. 'Describe them to me. Describe the wolves.'

He stared at me like he didn't understand the question. 'They have brown fur. And big teeth. And they smell musty.'

Musty? I frowned.

'One of them had blue eyes,' the man supplied helpfully.

My body tensed. Werewolf eyes changed colour to yellow or occasionally green when their bodies transformed. Never blue.

'Cavalry's here,' I heard someone mutter.

I glanced back and saw Fred at the far end of the bridge. Four identical black cars had pulled up – the alphas had arrived. The doors opened and the familiar figures of Lady Sullivan, Lady Carr, Lord McGuigan and Lord Fairfax stepped out. They were too far away for me to decipher their expressions, but they were all standing stiffly and staring at the bus.

I abandoned the man, stood up and marched towards them. Fred was already trying to talk to them but they were paying him little attention. Their focus was on the bus.

'Those cannot be my wolves,' Lady Sullivan said as I approached.

'Well, they're not from my clan,' Fairfax snapped.

Lord McGuigan folded his arms. 'Or mine.'

Lady Carr glanced at the other female clan leader. 'You are the only alpha with form for this type of action. Our wolves are accounted for.'

'You know what this means,' McGuigan snarled. 'The Sullivan Clan is officially dead. The humans will never stand for this! All the diplomacy and plea bargaining in the world won't let you off the hook this time.' He looked at me. 'We are innocent of this, DC Bellamy. You cannot tar every werewolf clan with the same brush. This is not our crime.'

'They are not my wolves!' The strain in Lady Sullivan's voice was unusual.

I pulled back my shoulders. 'Get in your cars and get back to Lisson Grove. Now,' I ordered.

'What?' Lord Fairfax jerked. 'You can't make us do that. If

werewolves are holding a bunch of humans hostage, we have a right to be here. You might be powerful, DC Bellamy, but you're no wolf.'

'Neither,' I said, 'are any of the people on that bus.'

Every pair of eyes blinked at me. 'What?'

'I might still be relatively new at all of this,' I said, 'but I know that no group of werewolves would do this unless they were under your orders. One lone wolf might be this stupid but not three together. And looking at you lot, it's obvious that none of you ordered it. You know what the consequences would be if you did and you're not that reckless.'

'Damn fucking right,' the petite Lady Carr muttered.

'Less than an hour ago,' I continued, 'a vampire was perched on top of the London Eye. Now three werewolves have hijacked a bus. Lord Horvath left Soho to deal with the vamp. You left Lisson Grove to deal with this.' I shook my head. 'These aren't real incidents, they're diversions. Someone is trying to distract you. I reckon that when the bus is stormed, it won't be three werewolves in there – it'll be three idiots in fancy-dress costumes pretending to be wolves.'

'What?' McGuigan's mouth dropped open. 'Are you sure?'

Not entirely, but I hoped I was right. A musty smell? A scribbled note? Blue eyes? Tourists wouldn't necessarily know what a real werewolf looked like, and fear could make you believe just about anything – even that someone in a costume was actually a supernatural creature.

'Why would someone want us out of Lisson Grove?' Lady Sullivan asked. 'If this is a distraction, what is it distracting us *from*?'

'I don't—'

A voice on Fred's radio, which was clipped to his belt, interrupted. 'I'm getting some reports of a robbery under way.' It was Liza, calling in from the office. 'At the Talismanic Bank on Grosvenor Street.'

Carr and McGuigan were running for their cars before she'd finished her sentence.

Fred stared at me. 'Shit.'

'That's my bank,' Fairfax whispered. He spun away.

'It's the bank we all use.' Lady Sullivan's jaw clenched. 'It's the bank the vampires use, too.' She glanced at the bus once more, her expression contorting. Her eyes had narrowed to slits and a dangerous yellow sheen was rolling across her irises. I glanced down and noted the fur springing out across the back of her hands and the sharp claws. Then she also turned and ran for her car.

Fred rubbed his forehead. 'All this is about a bank robbery? What the fuck? What do we do?'

'We get to the Talismanic Bank,' I said. 'Now.'

CHAPTER FOUR

Under normal circumstances I could have driven from Tower Bridge to the bank in less than twenty minutes but there'd been an accident on the main road. Ambulances, police cars and several diversions forced me to detour and I arrived far later than I'd intended, frustration boiling inside me.

I ignored the parking restrictions and pulled up Tallulah directly outside the bank before jumping out and heading in through the grand front doors.

The Talismanic Bank had been established for centuries. It was held in high esteem across the world. Unusually, it remained untouched by the disasters that befell other banks; as far as the Talismanic Bank was concerned, another financial crash was simply another day at the office. There were only six branches – New York, Beijing, Rio De Janeiro, Lagos, Sydney and, of course, London. Antarctica was the only continent it didn't cover.

Not anyone could stroll in and open an account. To be a client, you had to be a supe: vampire, werewolf or Other. Humans could wander in and have a look around the famous building but they weren't allowed to conduct business with the Talismanic Bank. That was as a result of the bank's own rules, nobody else's.

The London branch was located smack bang in the centre of the city between Soho, where the vamps resided, and Lisson Grove where the wolves were. As the crow flies, it was only half a mile from the Supe Squad office, although the busy London streets and one-way systems meant that getting there from my workplace took longer than it should have done.

The bank was an enormous building made out of Portland Stone. It had massive pillars and elaborately carved gargoyles and grotesques on the outside, and high-ceilinged rooms, steel-lined vaults and dramatic interiors inside. There was so much art hanging on its walls that it occasionally gave guided tours. I had never darkened its door before now. Gazing round the destruction on the ground floor, I wished I didn't have to do so now.

All four clan alphas and Lukas were already there. My feet crunched on the shattered glass that covered the elaborate mosaic floor. Several of the stained-glass windows had been shot out, as well as the glass that fronted the bank tellers' booths. I doubted the bank's administrators had expected that anyone would dare to attack them and had never upgraded to bulletproof versions.

'Two bank employees are dead,' Lukas told me grimly. 'And five customers – four wolves and a pixie. There are also two dead humans. One was killed on the steps outside and one in here.'

I looked at him sharply. 'Is there any indication that any of the victims were with the bank robbers?'

'Not so far – most of the dead were customers. The human outside seems to have been an unlucky bystander, and the human inside appears to have ventured inside for a quick gawk. He was in the wrong place at the wrong time.' Darkness flickered across his face. 'Everyone was.'

I swivelled round, sick to my stomach. From the amount of blood I'd expected worse, but it was still a desperately high body count. The supernatural community would feel the effects of this for years to come.

'Did they get away with anything?' I asked. Surely the security in a place like this would be ridiculously high? It was impossible to believe that anyone could gain access to the vaults and make off with wads of supernatural cash.

A tall man, with a body so thin it was almost skeletal, walked towards us. I looked him up and down. Since I'd been fooled into believing the worst of the ghouls while investigating the gruesome disappearance of a body from a grave, I'd improved my knowledge of the Others. The number of supernatural species who were not wolves or vamps was tiny, but that didn't make them less important.

I knew without asking that this man was a goblin. Caricatures made by humans usually portrayed them as squat, chubby creatures with avaricious temperaments. In reality, they tended to be quiet, thoughtful beings who were marked by their green eyes and gold-tinged skin. Most lived in mainland Europe, but a hundred or so resided in London. I already knew that this particular goblin was Mosburn Pralk, Moss to his friends. It wasn't his real name; as far as I was aware, not even his wife knew his real name. That was the price you paid when you were bank manager for virtually every supe in Europe.

There was a small cut on his cheek below his left eye but otherwise he appeared unharmed. He folded his bony hands together and regarded us solemnly. 'They stormed inside and shut off the power at the circuit box. That caused our back-up security system to kick in, and half the doors in the building locked automatically as a result. I was upstairs in my office. By the time I managed to over-ride the system and get down here, the robbers were already leaving.'

'Did you get a look at any of them? Did anyone see their faces?'

He shook his head. 'No, they were wearing masks. Of course, we have CCTV footage but I'm not sure what good it will do.' He gestured helplessly. 'We don't know if they were supes or humans.'

Lukas leaned forward, his black eyes inscrutable. 'DC Bellamy was enquiring about what was stolen.'

Pralk's skin took on an ashen tone. 'You'd better come with me and see for yourselves.'

We trooped through the destroyed room, following in Mosburn Pralk's wake. I noted several bodies, none of which were covered. Two dead werewolves lay in the centre of the bank's main hall and the third was near the exit, as if he'd either been trying to escape or had come in as the shooting started.

I looked away from the unnatural angle of the body of one of the golden-skinned bank employees, then the pixie's corpse drew my gaze. She was lying on her front with her arm outstretched towards the front door, as if she were reaching for it.

The robbers didn't have to kill so many people. Chilled, I wondered if it had been part of their plan from the beginning. Everything about today seemed designed to throw us off balance and these deaths compounded that feeling.

'I'm afraid it wasn't money they were after,' Pralk said. 'Not in the first instance, anyway. The vaults are on a timer, and our insurance would have more than covered any losses. And as I said, the power cut caused most of the other doors to lock automatically. But not all of them.' He spoke stiffly and I could tell that he took the robbery as a personal attack. The bank was his baby; no doubt he had sacrificed a great deal to rise to his current position. Whether he would still be manager this time tomorrow was another question.

'They went after the safety deposit room,' Lukas murmured, as much to himself as anyone. Lord McGuigan stiffened and shot him a grim look but nobody else spoke. Pralk sighed heavily and didn't disagree.

He led us down a wide corridor as impressively designed as the main hall. Paintings lined the walls; I was no art expert, but I was fairly certain I recognised some of them. Doubtless they were originals and worth a considerable amount but the bank robbers had ignored them. That sent a trickle of worry down my spine. If they hadn't stolen money and they hadn't stolen priceless artwork, what the hell were they after?

We turned left into a waiting room. There was another door at the opposite side and beyond it the Talismanic Bank's safety deposit room. Rows upon rows of narrow steel lockers lined the walls, each one with an identifying number and a small keyhole. To get to the contents, the lock had to be opened. As far as I could tell, most of the lockers were untouched – but not all of them.

Lady Sullivan took the lead, pushing past Pralk and banging into his shoulder as she stormed into the room. She knew exactly what she was looking for. She pivoted on her heel and stared and her nostrils flared. That was the only indication that the robbery had affected her personally. With her arms swinging, she marched straight out again into the corridor, her back to us. It was obvious that she needed a moment or two to compose herself.

The rest of us entered the room. Lord Fairfax's expression was like granite, while Lady Carr had turned pure white. Lord McGuigan was just the opposite; his cheeks were now a mottled shade of puce. Lukas's fists clenched and unclenched. Pralk made sure not to meet anyone's eyes.

I noted all their reactions and then slowly looked around the room. By my count, ten of the boxes had been stolen, their shiny metal doors hanging open to display their lack of contents.

'The robbers used violent threats to get hold of our keys,' Pralk said dully. 'As you all know, our keys on their own wouldn't allow access to the boxes' actual contents. We hold the keys to the lockers. The clients hold the keys to the boxes within. The bastards didn't waste time trying to break open the second locks for themselves, they simply slid the boxes out and dumped them into a bag.'

It made sense. If the robbers took the boxes with them, they could take all the time in the world to unpick the locks to open them.

'Exactly whose boxes were stolen?' I asked. I had a feeling I already knew the answer but I wanted to be sure.

Pralk pointed to a line of adjacent lockers. 'These three are held by Lord Horvath.' I sneaked another look at Lukas. He didn't so much as twitch, but I could feel the waves of rage emanating from his body. 'These two belong to the Sullivan clan. This one is Lady Carr's. The bottom two are Fairfax, and the locker in the corner is maintained by Lord McGuigan.'

'And the last box?' I asked, nodding towards the one empty locker that Pralk hadn't mentioned.

'That box,' Pralk enunciated carefully, 'is used by this bank.'

Huh? I gave him a long look as I tried to decipher his thoughts. Other than anxious despair, he wasn't giving much away. I pondered matters for a moment or two and then said, 'The robbers knew which boxes to go after. How is that possible?'

Every pair of eyes turned to Pralk and he swallowed. 'We

have very strict privacy protocols. I don't see how anyone could know who owns which box.'

'Unless they worked at this bank,' Lady Carr snapped. 'This is an inside job. It has to be.'

Pralk shook his head adamantly. 'That's not possible. My staff are beyond reproach. Two of my employees are dead, for goodness' sake! If you're suggesting that someone who works here cares so little about their colleagues that they'd risk their lives, you have no understanding of how we work.'

I sighed. I understood that Pralk didn't want to believe the worst of his staff but right now there was no other explanation for what had happened. 'You'll have to give me a list of all your employees and their details,' I said.

'Damn right,' McGuigan growled. Tufts of fur were springing out on his skin. First Lady Sullivan and now him. It was unusual for an alpha werewolf to lose control so openly but these were extraordinary circumstances.

Pralk looked defeated. 'Fine,' he whispered. 'I'll get you a list.'

'I also need to know the contents of each safety deposit box,' I said, addressing everyone else.

Nobody answered immediately, then Lady Sullivan turned to face us. She seemed determined not to enter the room again, as if she couldn't confront the facts of the burglary for a second time. Instead she hovered at the threshold and fixed me with a steely glare. 'I don't think that's necessary,' she said. 'The contents are immaterial.'

I spotted flickers of relief on both Pralk's and McGuigan's faces.

'Agreed,' Fairfax said. 'You don't need to know what is in each box in order to retrieve them.'

'That's ridiculous.' I stared at them. 'Once the robbers get hold of the contents, they'll dispose of them. I can't keep track of what ends up on the black market and track it back to the thieves if I don't know what I'm looking for!'

'I can't speak for the others,' Lukas said stiffly, 'but what is in my security boxes won't end up on the open market, no matter how black that market happens to be. It will be passed on in private sales to very specific individuals or...' His voice trailed off.

'Or what?' I prodded.

'Or used against us in some way.' He lifted his gaze and his eyes met mine.

I frowned. I hadn't particularly cared what was inside each box, other than to use the knowledge to help me track the robbers down. Now I was genuinely curious.

'Blackmail is a distinct possibility where we are concerned,' Lady Carr said.

Lord McGuigan's shoulders dropped. 'Yeah,' he mumbled.

Fairfax nodded in agreement.

I glanced at Pralk. 'What about you? What was in your box?'

'It would be better,' he stated firmly, 'if the contents were not advertised in any way, shape or form. They could prove ... embarrassing to the bank.'

Each of the supernatural leaders had been guilty of shady dealings in the past. I had no evidence of anything illegal, but I'd always known that they all – Lukas included – danced a thin moral line from time to time. From the way they were acting, there was far more to this than mere dubious possessions that might cast them in a bad light. None of them wanted anyone to know what they'd squirrelled away. No wonder someone had been desperate to steal their stuff; whatever had been nicked was obviously very valuable.

I hardened my expression into granite. 'I shouldn't have to remind any of you that there are nine corpses lying out there. Some of those corpses belong to your own people.

37

Whoever is responsible for those deaths did this because of what's inside those damned security deposit boxes. You *will* tell me what was in them.'

'You can't force us to speak,' Lady Sullivan said mildly. 'Even someone with your abilities can't compel the likes of us to talk.'

I turned a cold-eyed stare in her direction. 'Do you want these killers found? Do you want your possessions returned?'

'Of course, but—'

'There are no buts.' I glared. 'You will tell me what was stolen. All of it.'

Lukas folded his arms across his chest. 'We'll tell you privately. No one else is to know.'

'We can't tell her!' Lady Carr snapped. 'She's with the fucking police. This is exactly what she wants. It'll give the human authorities a hold over us that we won't be able to alter. Handing over this sort of information could affect us adversely for generations!'

Bloody hell. What was in the damned boxes? I drew in a long breath. 'I won't tell anyone other than the two members of my team about what has been stolen. They will keep their mouths shut. And none of us will use the information against you, as long as the items don't present a risk to the public either now or in the future. I give you my word.'

'With the best will in the world, DC Bellamy,' Pralk said, 'you can't promise that. You're a detective constable on the lowest rung of the police force. If your superiors demand to know what's been taken, you'll tell them.'

'No,' Lukas said, his black eyes trained on me. 'She won't. DC Bellamy is wholly honourable. If she gives us her word, she won't break it.'

Lady Sullivan gave a grudging sniff. 'I have to agree about DC Bellamy's honour,' she said. 'Reluctantly. And I want the fuckers who did this brought to heel. They can't get away with it. What happens if they advertise what they've stolen?'

Lord McGuigan blanched.

'If she doesn't find them—' Lady Carr began.

'She will,' Lukas said.

I nodded. 'I will.' It was a big promise but I wasn't sure there was anything else to offer. Safety deposit boxes or not, there were nine dead bodies outside. Given what had occurred at both Tower Bridge and the London Eye, and my belief that those events were a diversion for what had happened here, this robbery had been planned for a long time. But this was my home turf. And the perpetrators wouldn't get away with what they'd done.

CHAPTER FIVE

PRALK SET ME UP IN A SMALL ROOM ON THE SECOND FLOOR. While the werewolves from all four clans inspected it for any sign of listening devices, I located Fred who was taking statements from the shaken bank employees who'd escaped unscathed.

'There were three robbers in total,' he told me. 'All of them were armed and wearing what appeared to be body armour. They left in a florist's van that was parked outside. I've got uniforms trying to locate it through ANPR and CCTV.'

I suspected that these bastards were organised enough to have avoided being caught on camera or by the Automatic Number Plate Recognition system, but we had to start somewhere. 'That's good,' I said. 'Well done. Are you getting anywhere with the witnesses?'

He grimaced. 'Not yet. The gang entered the building at 1.34pm. They were inside for less than nine minutes and were wearing masks from start to finish. The best anyone has come up with so far is that two of them were male and one was female. Only the female spoke and her accent was pure Cockney. They've all remarked upon it.' He pulled a face. 'That's all we have in terms of identification so far. We won't get any fingerprints – they were all gloved up.'

Figured. 'And the CCTV footage from inside?'

'I've had a copy burned off and sent to Liza. She's going through it back at the office.' He paused and gave me a side-long look.

'What is it?'

'DSI Barnes has already been in touch. A team from CID are on their way.' He fiddled with the buttons on his jacket. 'I think they're planning to take over the investigation.'

I grimaced. There was no doubt that we'd require help to catch the bank robbers but I hated to think that I'd have to answer to someone else after being pretty much autonomous for the last few months.

'Okay,' I said. 'We'll deal with that if and when it happens. A lot of people are going to be very unhappy about today. That the supes have been targeted specifically is a no-brainer, but the diversions the robbers created to keep Lukas and the alphas away from here affected other parts of the city too. There won't be a lot of sympathy for either the wolves or the vamps – people think they're too wealthy so there won't be many who sympathise with them having had some valuables stolen. However, there'll be a lot of anger that a tourist bus was hijacked and a landmark shut down.'

'Mmm.' He pulled out his phone. 'On that note, I've got something for you.' He held up the phone and showed me a photo. 'This was found at the foot of the Eye.'

I squinted, then I remembered the object that had fallen past Lukas and me when we'd been attempting to clamber upwards. 'Fake fangs,' I said.

'Yep.' Fred sighed. 'The sort you can buy in any fancy-dress shop or market stall.'

So the would-be jumper hadn't been a vampire after all.

That was interesting. He'd certainly been acrobatic enough to pass for one.

'You were right about the werewolves on the bus as well. They've all been taken into custody and the hostages were released unharmed. The "wolves",' he drew air quotations around the word, 'were drama students. They thought they'd been hired by a film production team and it was some sort of televised prank. They're obviously not the sharpest tools in the box.'

'Do they know who hired them?' I asked sharply.

Fred shook his head. 'They're claiming it was all done online.'

'Great.' I sighed and pushed back my hair. 'Keep on with the witness statements. Something useful might turn up.'

'What did they steal?' Fred asked. 'What were the robbers after?'

'I don't know yet,' I said. 'But I'm about to find out.'

'Whatever it was, I bet it's valuable.'

'Whatever it was,' I returned, 'it's hush hush. I've agreed with the supe leaders that we'll keep the contents of the boxes to ourselves. You can't tell a soul what's been stolen.'

Fred's mouth dropped. 'What? How do we find what's been nicked if we can't speak to anyone about it?'

I grimaced. 'Yeah. I know.'

He would have continued to complain bitterly if Scarlett's figure hadn't come into view. Her stilettoes click-clacked across the floor less than ten metres from us and Fred's head jerked up. He watched her every move, his cheeks flaming red. He still wasn't over her even though their relationship, such as it was, had been little more than a game to her.

Scarlett didn't even glance at Fred but she did offer a brief, grim smile at a group of hovering wolves who were eyeing her up. Her smile was more crooked than it used to be, although her hip sashay was just as pronounced. She'd lost a fang when she'd tried to attack Ted Nappey, the grave-robbing bastard who'd caused so many problems a couple of months earlier. Scarlett had elected not to replace the tooth and oddly the gap made her more alluring. And she knew it.

My gaze drifted over to Lukas, who was frowning at a stray bullet hole in one of the bank's walls. Vampires liked to play, I reminded myself. I gave myself a little shake. 'I'll catch up with you soon,' I promised.

Fred gave me a distracted nod.

PRALK'S office was exactly what I'd have expected of a bank manager: dark-green leather chairs, mahogany panels, framed certificates and an expensive aroma. What surprised me was the wall displaying employee photographs and the small plaques beneath each one. Employee of the Year 2009 was a smiling female goblin who looked as if she were about to burst out into giggles at any moment. Employee of the Year 2010 was a bespectacled male goblin with a serious expression and a perfectly styled cravat. He'd gained the same accolade for three further years, most recently in 2019. Each photograph was unique but he had the same expression on each occasion, albeit with slightly more wrinkles.

I gazed at the wall. There was a photograph for every year of the last twenty. The fact that Mosburn Pralk displayed them in his office implied that he was proud of his staff. I passed a hand over my eyes. Heartbreakingly, I recognised the face from 2017. She'd received a bullet to her skull only a few hours ago. I sighed.

The first supe leader into the room was Lord McGuigan. Unlike the other clan alphas, he'd been born human and turned to a werewolf when he was twenty-two. He was now almost sixty years old, with a lined and scarred face that told the tale of every one of those thirty-eight lupine years. He was vain enough to dye his hair, keeping it a mahogany brown although it was cropped close to his skull. Of all the alphas, he was the one I knew the least about. He kept his cards close to his chest and rarely revealed anything about himself. I sincerely hoped that wouldn't be the case now.

I gestured to the empty chair in front of me. 'Have a seat.'

'I'll stand,' he grunted. 'This won't take long.' He glowered at me, as if all this were my fault. 'We're not as rich as the other clans. That's no secret. But if you tell any of them, or if you even hint to anyone else about what has been stolen from me, then—'

I held up my hands. 'I've already told you, I won't breathe a word unless I'm concerned that the objects are dangerous.'

He huffed; he still didn't believe that I'd keep my mouth shut but he didn't have a whole lot of choice. He had to tell me what was inside his box.

'Go on then,' I said, when it became clear that he wasn't going to volunteer the information unless I prodded him. 'What was inside your security deposit box?'

He crossed his arms and looked at me defiantly. 'Nothing.'

For fuck's sake. 'Lord McGuigan, we've been through this. I need to know—'

'I'm telling the truth,' he said. 'Nothing was in there. There used to be a collection of diamonds and some cash, but we've had a few problems with some of our investments lately so I divested a number of our assets to bring us into the black again. Including what was in that box.'

I stared at him. 'If there was nothing inside in the box, why make such a big deal about keeping it quiet?'

'It was the others who were protesting the most. Not me. Besides, do you think I want them to know that I had nothing in there?' he demanded irritably. 'They've all got expensive secrets to keep and I have nothing. They already look down on me because I wasn't born a wolf. I can't have them knowing that I'm as poor as a church mouse as well. I'm very aware that pride is my sin, detective, but I have good reasons for that pride. I have to maintain appearances. My *clan* has to maintain appearances.'

I licked my lips. 'Are you struggling for money?'

He held himself stiffly. 'We have recouped many of our losses. I kept the lease on the box because I planned to fill it again at some point with a proper insurance policy. It is fortunate that I hadn't got around to it yet.' His mouth tightened. 'But three of those wolves who were slaughtered out there were mine. All young. All zetas with promising futures ahead of them. They were good kids who'd done nothing to hurt anyone. I'm told Fairfax's beta was in the bank and she decided to fight back against the robbers. My wolves followed her lead. It wasn't their fault. She outranked them and, despite clan differences, werewolf hierarchy means they would have felt compelled to follow suit.' He gazed off into the distance. 'But they deserved better than to be cut down by some greedy idiots. If you don't find them, I will...' His voice trailed off.

'You will what?'

'I will not say it aloud.' He pulled back. 'Just fucking find them.' He turned and left the room, slamming the door shut behind him.

I remained where I was for a moment, staring at the closed door. It surprised me that his coffers were all but empty; the McGuigan clan had a veneer of respectability, and it certainly maintained a large number of smart properties. Not to mention that affluent humans who were bitten and then turned often bequeathed their money to the clans. I suspected that, unless he was telling the truth about recouping the wealth he'd somehow lost, I'd have to keep a close eye on the McGuigan clan. The supes cared a great deal about the face they presented to the world. Lord McGuigan would go to any lengths to appear on a financial par with his peers.

The door opened again and this time Lady Sullivan entered. She glided in, shaking out her full skirt before she took the seat in front of me. 'What did you say to McGuigan?' she enquired. 'He stormed out with a look on his face as if you'd threatened the size of his manhood.'

I leaned back in my chair. Of all the werewolf alphas, Lady Sullivan was by far the most dangerous. She didn't intimidate me, but she possessed a ruthless streak that I was wary of.

'The whole point of this set-up,' I said, waving a hand around the small room, 'is to keep the conversations private. I won't tell you what I discussed with Lord McGuigan any more than I will tell Lord McGuigan what I discuss with you.'

Lady Sullivan raised an amused eyebrow. 'I'm not asking you to tell me what's in his safety deposit box. I already know that. He has nothing. His entire clan is on the verge of bankruptcy and he came here last month and emptied whatever he had to sell.'

I kept my expression as blank as I could and said nothing. I wouldn't allow my expression to confirm what Lady Sullivan already knew. She watched me for several long seconds, then shrugged elegantly. 'Very well,' she murmured. 'You wish to know the contents of my boxes.'

'Yes.'

She smiled sweetly. 'The first one contains a number of valuables. Diamonds and the like.'

I sighed. 'I need you to be more specific.'

'Yes, I rather thought you might, though I don't see why. All you need to do is keep an eye on anyone selling large numbers of precious stones. Any thief worth their salt will be already breaking up the settings to dispose of the individual stones.'

Again, I refrained from speaking. There was no point in getting into an argument with Lady Sullivan because eventually she'd tell me what I needed to know. We both knew it. First, however, she needed to make this display of her power. I really wasn't in the mood to play ball and rise to her bait.

Her pleasant expression didn't so much as flicker. 'You are the most exasperating creature, DC Bellamy.' She leaned forward. 'And when I say creature, I mean creature. You are not human. Your DNA results proved that.'

This time I was forced to respond. Some time ago, I'd allowed her to swab my cheek for my DNA. I wondered how long she'd been sitting on the report. 'You promised to give me a copy of those results,' I said stiffly. 'That was the deal.'

'I will have them couriered to your office.'

'Great,' I said, without altering my tone of voice. 'I will expect them within the week.' I folded my arms. 'Now tell me – and in as much detail as you can – exactly what was in your security boxes.'

'As I said, the first box contained numerous valuables.' She ticked off her fingers. 'Two exquisite Fabergé eggs. The jewellery worn by Empress Alexandra during her execution, including several heavy rings and a quite wonderful necklace.' She passed over a photograph of the items and I studied it carefully.

'May I keep this?'

She inclined her head. 'You may.' She paused and I knew we were about to get to the important stuff. 'The second box contains a box of hair clippings, nail clippings and shed skin.'

Goddamnit. I *knew* it would be something icky like that. My stomach dropped as I remembered Ted Nappey, the crazed human who'd also had a gruesome penchant for body parts. His motives centred around a potion he'd discovered in an old book called *Infernal Enchantments*. Infernal indeed. I sincerely hoped that Lady Sullivan wasn't about to tell me she was planning something similar.

'Go on,' I said grimly. 'Tell me why you were keeping them.'

'You don't need to know why.'

I met her gaze. 'Tell me.'

Lady Sullivan clicked her tongue. 'If you insist.' She tapped her fingernails on the arm of the chair. I was convinced it was purely to irritate me. Then she smiled again. 'The samples all belong to a werewolf by the name of Bradford Carr. Before you get all hot and bothered that I'm storing DNA belonging to another clan, you can relax. He's long since gone. He died in the 1950s, long before DNA was ever thought of.'

I bit back a retort. I wasn't the fluff-headed cop she seemed to think I was. DNA was first isolated in the nineteenth century and the double-helix model was completed in 1953. We might not have had the means to test and track DNA until more recently, but it had certainly been known of for far longer than she'd said.

'Where did you get the samples from?'

She laughed, a crystal-clear tinkle that echoed around the small room. 'From his body, of course. Where else?'

I glowered and waited for her amusement to subside.

'You ought to have more of a sense of humour, Emma,' she chided.

'It's DC Bellamy.'

Lady Sullivan waved a hand. 'Whatever. To answer your question, one of my predecessors took the samples after Bradford Carr died. Nobody else thought to do it, not even the Carr clan. And nobody else knows that we have them.'

'Why?' I asked. 'Why do you have them?'

'There,' she said softly, 'we get to the crux of the matter.

I'm not supposed to have them. Lords Fairfax and McGuigan would not be pleased if they knew, and Lady Carr would be apoplectic.' She started tapping her nails on the chair arm again. 'In fact, it's quite possible she would declare war on us.'

I folded my arms. 'That explains why you don't want to reveal what you have. It still doesn't explain why you had such things in the first place.'

'If I lunged towards you and sank my teeth into your flesh, you would be incredibly unlucky to be turned into a werewolf as a result. Perhaps one in a million people are transformed because of a single bite. It's almost never happened. Receive two bites and your chances increase, especially if those bites come from different wolves. Three bites and your fate is sealed.' She paused. 'Unless you were Bradford Carr.'

I waited. She tapped some more.

'Like Lord McGuigan, he was originally human. He was bitten three times before he turned. As many like him discover, neither the biting nor the transformation are pleasant processes.' She shuddered delicately. 'Bradford was bitten four times, twice by Carr wolves, once by a Sullivan clan member and once by a Fairfax delta. He was the strongest werewolf we've ever known. Until his death, the Carrs ruled the roost. Even the vampires couldn't compete with his power. The rest of us bowed and scraped at his knee.'

I raised an eyebrow. 'Did *you?*' I asked, unable to help myself.

For the first time Lady Sullivan scowled. 'How old do you think I am?' she snapped. 'I wasn't born until several years after he passed away.' She realised I'd baited her deliberately and a spasm of annoyance crossed her face, this time directed at herself. She'd revealed more of her vanity than she'd wanted to.

Her eyes flashed before she returned to her story. 'Bradford Carr's feats and power are well documented. He is no secret, even to those outside the supernatural community. Google him, if you wish,' she sneered.

'Is that why you kept samples from his body?' I asked. 'Because he was some kind of super wolf?'

'We believe he was a ... super wolf, as you so crudely describe him, because he was bitten four times. Nobody else has been able to replicate that – every single wolf in every single clan has been turned by the third bite. We kept his DNA in the hope that one day science can explain how future Sullivan werewolves can also receive four bites before they are transformed. To use your own words, we're hoping to be in a position to create a super clan. We are unable to manage it now, but one day we will.'

No wonder she didn't want anyone else to know what she had in her possession. Lady Sullivan's ambition for her kith and kin was strong indeed, and it was potentially very dangerous. I had no clue as to the legality or otherwise of holding historical DNA or using it for experimentation, and I didn't know how much of a threat her plans were. Nor did I know what I could do about them.

'It's very important that Bradford Carr's DNA is recovered and returned to us,' Lady Sullivan said. 'I would be disappointed if it went astray, or if these thieves were never found.' Her tone of voice suggested her disappointment would stretch to dismembering my body and burying its various parts in the four corners of the world so I could never resurrect again.

I ignored the unspoken threat. I wouldn't reveal what she'd told me, but if the thieves were found and the contents of all the safety deposit boxes recovered, I wasn't sure I'd be able to hand the DNA samples back to her. It was a moral question I'd have to consider in more depth later.

'Thank you for both your honesty and your time, Lady Sullivan,' I said.

'You're welcome.' She rose to her feet. 'Before I go, and while we're on the subject of werewolf bites, there was an accident last night that you should be aware of.'

I passed a hand in front of my eyes. Of course there was. 'A bite?' I asked.

'Yes. Just one. It was only a nip and there is virtually no chance that the receiver of the bite will have any adverse lupine effects.'

There was more to this than she was telling me. 'But?' I prodded.

'But,' she answered smoothly, 'it was Devereau Webb who was bitten.'

I stared at her. 'What?'

'Devereau Webb was bitten by one of my wolves last night.'

'Devereau Webb? The Shepherd? The guy who runs a petty crime gang out of London and who was desperate for his niece to be turned into a werewolf?'

'That's the one,' she replied cheerfully. She dipped into a mock curtsey. 'Have a lovely day, detective.'

CHAPTER SIX

I CHECKED MY WATCH BEFORE LORD FAIRFAX CAME IN. IT WAS almost 5pm. No wonder my stomach was beginning to grumble – I'd not had anything to eat since my rushed breakfast en route to my uncle's house, and I wasn't convinced that a Ginster's pasty and a packet of salt and vinegar crisps counted as a proper meal. I sighed. There was too much to do for me to stop and eat.

I ignored the hunger pangs and nodded at Fairfax when he opened the door and peered in with a dark, questioning expression. 'Come in,' I called. 'Have a seat.'

He obeyed, although his body language indicated that he was doing so under duress. I looked him up and down, noting the dried blood on his shirt. He'd been helping remove the dead bodies from the ground floor. 'The werewolves who were shot,' I said quietly. 'One was from the Fairfax clan?'

He nodded, a jerky movement that wouldn't have looked out of place on a wooden marionette. His hands gripped the chair arms tightly, and I saw that his fingernails were shaped into claws rather than the perfect manicure that he normally favoured. Like the others, Lord Fairfax was struggling to keep it together. Under the circumstances, I could hardly blame him.

'Toffee. It appears that she was shot first. She probably tried to stop the robbers in their tracks,' he said. 'It's the sort of thing she'd have done. She always acted without thinking. The other wolves would have followed her lead, even though they were from the McGuigan clan.' He sighed heavily.

'Toffee?'

'She is one of my betas.' His shoulders dropped an inch. '*Was* one of my betas. Had been for years. I didn't know she was going to the bank today.' His voice dropped to a whisper. 'I didn't know. She wasn't supposed to be here.' He glanced away, staring at a spot on the wall until he composed himself again.

I waited until his gaze returned to mine. 'I'm sorry.'

'Don't be sorry, DC Bellamy. Be angry.' A muscle ticked in his jaw. Fairfax was doing well to keep his emotions in check but I suspected he was feeling the events of the robbery more deeply than any of the others. No doubt that was because of losing Toffee.

I nodded solemnly. 'You had two safety deposit boxes. What was in them?'

'The first is personal to me and unrelated to the Fairfax clan.'

Interesting. 'Go on.'

He gave me a defiant look. 'It contained around ten grand in cash. And three passports.'

I sat up. 'Whose passports?'

'Mine.' Fairfax folded his arms.

'Are they current passports?'

'Yes.'

As far as I knew Fairfax didn't possess dual – or triple – nationality. Getting full answers from him was like drawing blood out of a stone. 'Under your name?'

'They are my passports.'

I drew in a breath. 'With respect, Lord Fairfax, that is not what I asked.'

His expression was stony. 'Is all this completely necessary?'

'Yes. As I've already stated, unless the contents of the safety deposit boxes pose a danger to others, I won't reveal what they are. Neither will I take action against anything that is illegal.'

A muscle ticked in his cheek. 'There was a Swiss passport in the name Johannes Muller, an American one for Michael Hatt, and a South African passport for Arnold Steenkamp.'

Definitely illegal passports, then. Surprise, surprise. 'I take it that you don't legally possess multiple nationalities and identities.'

Fairfax sniffed. 'Your assumption is correct. I procured these documents at various points and for various reasons.' He folded his arms. 'Not because I'm some sort of international villain but because sometimes I like to travel without having to declare that I'm a werewolf.'

That made a lot of sense. It wasn't easy to take a holiday abroad when you were a supernatural creature. Few people were happy about sharing the confined space of an aeroplane with someone with the potential to turn furry and attack them, even though the likelihood of that happening was miniscule. But there was more to this; I'd lay money on Lord Fairfax having the passports as his own personal insurance in case he needed to make a quick exit from the country because his werewolves had decided to turn against him. Or for some more nefarious reason. I was learning more about each of the alphas than they'd ever have wanted.

'Very well,' I said. 'What about the second box?'

'It contains the only surviving copy of William Shakespeare's play, *Love's Labours Won*.'

I blinked. As far as I was aware, that particular play had been lost to the annals of history. 'Why would you keep that hidden?'

'The main character is a werewolf. The play is a nasty piece of propaganda against our kind and should never have seen the light of day. It's been hidden for centuries. To suddenly produce it now, like a rabbit out of a hat, would cause far more problems for us than we could handle.'

I remained astonished. 'But…'

Fairfax glared at me. 'You only wanted to know what was inside the boxes, DC Bellamy. I'm not here for an existential discussion about the contents. I'm merely informing you of what they are.'

He had a point. 'Very well. Thank you for your time.' I paused. 'And I am truly sorry about Toffee.'

He grunted and left.

The last werewolf to enter the room was Lady Carr. The petite alpha belched loudly as she sat down. I strongly suspected that she'd been saving it up until she was in front of me but I refrained from commenting; it wasn't worth it.

'I'll give you five million pounds right here and now if you tell me what's in the others' boxes,' she said, without preamble. 'We're in a bank, after all. It'll take me less than ten minutes to arrange the transfer and you'll be set for life.'

Wow. 'No, Lady Carr. I won't be doing that.' I gave her a long look. She matched it, unwilling to back down until she was sure that I couldn't be bribed. 'Tell me what was in your box.'

She sniffed. 'How do I know you won't blab about it to Lord Horvath? You and he are engaging in amorous congress, are you not?'

I felt my cheeks warming. Irritated with myself, I snapped, 'First of all, that's none of your business. Secondly, I think I've just proved that I'm trustworthy.'

She settled in her chair. 'Ah, I see,' she said. 'You haven't yet thumped thighs with the fanged freak.' She smirked. 'It's only a matter of time, you know. Once you have, you'll do whatever he wants. Look at your boy – Fred, is it? If that Scarlett crooks her little finger, he'll do whatever she wants and he'll also tell her whatever she wants to know.'

My temper rose. 'I can assure you, Lady Carr, there is a definite line between our professional and personal lives. Everyone else has played ball so far. I must insist that you do the same.'

'Alright, alright. Don't get your knickers in a twist over a tiny tease,' she tutted. 'He'll make you scream though, you know. He'll run his fingers down your body, cup your breasts and lick your...'

'Lady Carr!'

She smiled.

I inhaled deeply. 'Just tell me what was in your safety deposit box and then get out of here.'

She shrugged. 'If you insist. My box contained the original Hope diamond. The one used in the Crown Jewels is a fake. A good fake,' she added, 'but a fake. And there's also the only surviving copy of William Shakespeare's play, *Love's Labours Won*. The main character is a vampire. If I'm honest, it's quite titillating.'

'A vampire,' I said slowly.

'Yes.' She leaned forward. 'One day I might exchange it with Lord Horvath in return for something I want. Or I might not. It's priceless, you know. Nobody else knows it exists.'

'Alright,' I said faintly. 'Thank you.'

She smiled again and left.

I ran a hand through my hair. This was getting crazier by the second.

Pralk marched in and fixed me with unhappy eyes. His skin was grey instead of the typical golden lustre of his kind, and he looked to be on the verge of collapse. 'Are you alright?' I asked, alarmed.

He answered shakily, 'I'm fine. I just got off the phone with the board of governors. It wasn't a pleasant conversation.' He smiled weakly. 'It will be fine.'

It didn't look as if it would be fine. It looked as if he was about to have a nervous breakdown.

'The board is not made up of particularly forgiving people,' he continued. 'Once you find the culprits, it will not go well for them regardless of who they are and their ethnicity.'

I liked that Pralk believed I would find the bank robbers, but I didn't like the explicit threat. 'I'll do everything I can to bring them to justice,' I said carefully. I stressed the final word. The last thing anyone needed was a vigilante bank.

Pralk nodded then passed over a brown envelope. 'Here. Inside are the names and addresses of all the current bank employees, mine included. I still can't believe that anyone who works here is involved. I have full trust in my staff – they've all worked here for at least a decade.'

Nothing about his tone or his expression suggested he was lying. I thanked him and took the envelope. 'How did you get the cut on your cheek?' I asked. 'You said you were inside your office when the robbery occurred and that you missed it.'

'I was. When I ran across the floor to check on the people who'd been shot, I trod on some broken glass. I don't know what happened, I guess I slipped and one of the shards from the floor flew up and hit me in the face.' He shook his head dismally. 'I have two dead bank employees and the rest are shaken beyond belief. And the worst I have to show for it is a damned cut that I got by accident.'

'None of this is your fault, you know.'

A muscle jerked in Pralk's cheek. 'Tell that to the families of those who died,' he said. He looked away. My heart went out to him and to the victims. 'I won't waste any more of your time, detective,' he told me. 'Inside the box that was stolen from us are the details of almost every supernatural creature in the country. Names, addresses, birth dates, that sort of thing.'

I breathed out. That didn't sound so terrible; every British supe lived in London and their names and identities were a matter of public record.

'As I'm sure you are aware,' he said, 'not every supe lives in London, despite what the law demands.'

I blinked.

'And,' Pralk continued, without noticing my reaction, 'a lot of them hide from the world at large. But they all need a bank and they all bank with us.' He glanced at me. 'Apart from the odd supe such as yourself, of course. There are exceptions to every rule. There are also supes who don't know they're supes, if you take my meaning.' He fiddled with his cufflinks. 'So, *almost* every supe is a customer of the Talismanic Bank. We try to take precautions – for example, we don't register their real identities on computers in case we're hacked or our records are subpoenaed. If the government discovered there are supes who conceal their existence from the authorities, it would go badly for them.'

I tried hard not to look shocked. 'Uh…' I licked my lips. 'How many hidden supes are we talking about?'

He frowned. 'About a thousand, give or take.'

I swallowed. Good God. 'I can see why it would be a problem if that list fell into the wrong hands.'

'Indeed.' He looked even more defeated at the thought. 'Do you think you can locate the culprits?'

'I'll do everything that I can,' I promised, still reeling from his revelations.

Pralk's head drooped. 'Please do,' he whispered as he left.

I pressed the base of my palms into my temples. If I hadn't been feeling out of my depth before, I certainly was now. I sighed deeply and closed my eyes. Then, when the aroma of cooked food wafted up to my nostrils, I opened them again. Sitting on the table in front of me was a large burger and chips.

'It's vegetarian,' Lukas said, gazing down at me with a crooked smile. 'I thought you might be hungry.'

'I shouldn't be,' I told him. 'Those are dead bodies downstairs.'

'The bodies have all gone. The world doesn't stop turning and your physical needs don't disappear even in the face of tragedy. You're allowed to eat, Emma.' He paused. 'Sorry. D'Artagnan.'

I smiled faintly. 'Thank you.'

'For the burger?' he enquired. 'Or for using your nickname?'

'Both.'

His black eyes crinkled. 'Eat it up before it gets cold.'

I needed no further encouragement. I flipped open the box and heaved out the burger. It looked delicious. I took a large bite and murmured happily to myself. Lukas grinned and settled down in the chair. I noted, however, that this time his smile didn't quite reach his eyes.

'I don't need to tell you how serious this is,' he said. 'This bank robbery is a personal attack on every supe in London.'

Not just London. I nodded.

'You have to find the bastards who did it. I won't stand for these deaths or for the robbery.' His voice hardened. 'I won't stand for any of this.'

I swallowed a mouthful. 'You know I'll do whatever I can to find them.'

'I know.' He held my gaze. 'And you know that I'll help you in any way possible. Where will you begin?'

'The key to all this is the safety deposit boxes. Gaining hold of them was the robbers' ultimate motive and we need to know why. If the gang were merely after money, they'd have taken the bank's cash and run. That would have been far easier than going through the rigmarole of selling the contents of your boxes. The people who did this want to sow chaos.' I grimaced. 'And they're prepared to take considerable risks to do so.'

'Agreed.' Lukas leaned forward, his inky dark hair falling artlessly across his forehead. He was still wearing the ridiculous frilly shirt, and it still looked ridiculously good on him. I kept my eyes trained on his face, rather than glancing at his exposed chest. Go me. Self-control in spades.

'What was in your boxes, Lukas?' I questioned.

'The first contained details of all the assets we own around the world. There are many of them, including several which we don't want to advertise.'

'Such as?'

He shrugged. 'Let's just say we possess the deeds to some famous landmarks.'

At my look, Lukas smiled slightly. 'We've been around for a long time and we live for twice as long as the average human. That gives us considerable opportunity to amass land and wealth.'

And then some. Lukas, and indeed all the vamps, were as careful as the werewolves about the face they presented to the world. They acted like hedonistic partygoers. This was concrete proof that there was far more to them than that.

'The second box,' Lukas continued, 'held a range of priceless jewels. Specifically, the Florentine Diamond, that went missing about a hundred years ago, and which we acquired rather than see it cut up into smaller stones by the original thieves. There is also Llywelyn's coronet, the crown belonging to an old Welsh ruler that was supposedly destroyed by Thomas Cromwell in the seventeenth century, and a small dagger called Carnwennan that belonged to King Arthur.'

My mouth dropped. 'The real King Arthur?'

'Oh, yes.'

Okay dokey. I swallowed. 'And the third box?' I reached for the burger again and prepared to take another large bite.

'I only opened it with the bank recently. It contains all the information I've uncovered so far about the existence of the supposedly mythical phoenix.'

I froze, then slowly returned the burger to its box. 'Why?' I asked.

'You know why.'

'Actually,' I said, 'I don't. The only person that information is relevant to is me. Are you searching for my weaknesses? Planning to blackmail me with what you know? Control me?'

Lukas's eyes glittered. 'None of the above, D'Artagnan. You know me better than that.'

I wasn't sure that I did. I folded my arms.

'If you hadn't been avoiding me for so long, this wouldn't have been in question,' Lukas murmured. He reached into his pocket and drew out a bunch of keys, selected a small golden one and held it up. A number was etched onto it, a number that corresponded to one of the plundered safety deposit lockers.

'You are named as the second holder of the box,' he went on. 'The key is useless now, but I'd been planning to give it to you so you could keep track of everything I'd found and access it yourself. If you don't believe me, you can check with Pralk. All the paperwork is there. It's signed and dated.' He gazed at me for a long time. 'I'm not your enemy. That couldn't be further from the truth.' Something in his pupils flared. 'I promise.'

I looked away. 'What have you found so far?'

'There is no limit to the number of times a phoenix can die and be reborn. Only old age and death through fire can halt the cycle, or so the old stories say. With every death, a phoenix grows stronger and more powerful. And there is only ever one. You are unique, Emma.' He smiled. 'But I already knew that.'

'Have you found anything to explain who becomes a phoenix? Is it hereditary? Does it happen by accident or design?' I lifted my eyes to his. 'In other words, why me?'

'I don't know. I have no information on that.'

That figured. I sighed. It was tempting to forget everything else and focus on myself but that wasn't why I was there. There had been a serious robbery with several vicious homicides. I'd deal with Lukas and his investigations into my ethnicity later.

He spoke again. 'I'm sorry about your parents.'

I stared at him.

'I knew they were dead,' he said. 'You told me that much yourself. But I didn't know how they'd died, or that you were so young when it happened.'

'So it's not just facts about the phoenix that you've been investigating,' I said flatly. 'It's facts about me.'

'Not for the reasons that you think.' He reached across for me but I pulled back.

'What reasons?'

Lukas opened his mouth but before he could speak there was a knock at the door. It opened and Fred appeared, his expression grim and forbidding. 'You'd better finish up quickly,' he said. 'CID is here already. And they're causing problems.'

I raised my eyes heavenward. That was all we needed.

CHAPTER SEVEN

THERE WERE MORE CID OFFICERS THAN I'D ANTICIPATED – there had to be at least a baker's dozen. My gaze swept around the ground floor and the numerous police officers who'd taken up their positions and I felt my stomach tighten. This was supposed to be my turf; it felt as if they were invading. Then I spotted Molly, my old friend from the Academy. She gave me a bright smile and I relaxed slightly. That was one friendly face, at least.

One of the detectives, a muscled chap with a bald patch and a shiny suit, had cornered Mosburn Pralk. I watched for a moment as the bank manager wrung his hands and shook his head in vehement denial at something the detective had said. When the detective gestured to two others, who immediately marched over and started to lead Pralk away, I interrupted. 'I'm DC Bellamy,' I said briskly. 'Can you tell me who you are and what you're doing?'

The muscle-man glanced at me. I noted his heavy-set eyebrows and overly tanned skin, not to mention the strong waft of aftershave that he'd applied far too liberally. In turn, he gave me a similarly disparaging look. I knew my petite body and grubby clothes didn't exactly proclaim authority but I couldn't do anything about the former and the latter was because I'd been running around London and climbing up giant observation wheels.

'Detective Inspector Collier,' he grunted finally in a strong London accent. 'As I believe DSI Barnes has already communicated to you and your … team, I'm taking over this crime scene. We'll dust it for prints, question the witnesses and find the perps who thought they could bring my city to a standstill.'

I raised an eyebrow. His city? 'The thieves wore gloves,' I said. Yes, it was important to check for prints but at this stage it wasn't a priority. 'And we've taken witness statements already.'

'My team has skills and expertise that someone like you won't yet have acquired, DC Bellamy. It's not a criticism, I merely want to ensure that things are done properly. Time is of the essence and it's imperative that we move quickly to find these lads. We have a better chance of finding and arresting them in the first twenty-four hours after the crime.'

I was perfectly aware of that; I wouldn't, however, have described a gang who'd murdered eight people in cold blood as *lads*. 'Where are you taking Pralk?'

His brow creased. 'Who?'

I pointed behind me. He was being taken out of the building and he looked none too happy about it. 'Mosburn Pralk,' I said. 'The bank manager.'

'You mean the goblin with the weird skin?'

'I mean the bank manager.'

Collier gave me a long look. 'Are you questioning my authority, detective?'

What? 'No. I'm asking where you're taking a supernatural person. I'm sure you're aware that the law states that supe law is separate to human law. Your usual tactics don't apply here.'

He regarded me coolly. 'We've had two terrorist incidents to deal with today – three, if you include the bank robbery. Those incidents involved humans, which means that I have free rein to take the investigation where it needs to go. I'm not going to pussyfoot around a damned goblin. It's perfectly likely that this was an inside job. And he is a goblin, after all.'

I didn't move a muscle. Whether Collier was right about the inside job theory or not, his methods were totally wrong. 'Are you racially profiling a crime victim, DI Collier?'

'Don't be moronic.' He turned away, dismissing me.

'Those two incidents you've mentioned were not terrorist related. They were diversions to get the supe leaders away from here so the robbery could be carried out without them interfering.'

'I'll be judge of that,' Collier growled. He looked over his shoulder at me. 'I've been a detective for twenty years. You've barely managed twenty days.'

Three months, more like. Not that it would make much difference to Collier. In terms of longevity he had a point, but my knowledge about supes and supe law was better than his. I'd not been sitting on my arse since I came to Supe Squad.

'I'm assigning you to questioning the local businesses in the vicinity,' Collier continued. 'We need to know what they saw. As a member of Supe Squad, the people around here will be more inclined to talk to you. I expect you to canvass the whole street.'

He walked away, leaving me staring after him. I hadn't even had the chance to argue that my skills could be put to better use. From across the room, I saw Lukas watching me, his eyes narrowed, then he put his hands in his pockets and headed for the door.

He was halted in his tracks by two uniformed police officers. 'We need you to stay here, sir.'

'You have no reason to hold me here,' he said.

'We need you to remain for questioning.'

'Questioning?' Lukas's face darkened. 'Am I a suspect now? I've already spoken at length to DC Bellamy. I wasn't here when the robbery took place. I arrived afterwards.'

I saw both officers blanch, but they held their ground. They probably thought that DI Collier was scarier than Lukas. They had a lot to learn.

'We understand you're a vampire,' one of them said, 'but that doesn't mean you're above the law.'

'Actually it does,' Lukas snapped. 'Human law doesn't apply to my kind.'

'It does here.'

I was starting to get the feeling that this wouldn't end well. DI Collier was definitely not the right detective to lead this investigation, and things could get very ugly very quickly. Lukas already despised the police and the human authorities, and right now I couldn't blame him, but that didn't mean I could simply stand back.

I marched over. 'Lord Horvath.' I inclined my head with far more respect than I normally showed him. The two policemen stepped back. I pretended not to notice. 'Thank you very much for your cooperation earlier. Can I suggest that you do as these officers request and stay until they've completed their work? It would be very much appreciated.'

Lukas's black eyes glittered. He wasn't stupid and he knew I'd intervened to ensure that all the police officers were aware of his identity. He knew I was trying to avoid matters degenerating – but that didn't mean he was happy about it.

'One hour,' he bit out. 'No longer.'

I breathed out. That was more than I'd hoped for. 'Thank you.'

The nearest policeman looked as if he were about to start arguing but his colleague nudged him hard in the ribs. 'I didn't realise you were Lord Horvath,' he said with considerably more politeness than before.

'Few people do,' Lukas muttered. He glared at me, as if all this were my fault. I tried to offer a reassuring smile and headed for the door.

From the sound of the raised voices behind me, DI Collier had cornered Lady Sullivan and was demanding that she sit down. The best thing I could do was leave before she turned furry and snapped his hand off. I almost hoped she would.

I nodded to the policewoman at the door and flashed my warrant card, then I slid out my phone and beckoned to Fred across the street. Clearly he'd been sent out here on the same duty as I had. While he finished up with the blank-faced hairdresser he was talking to outside her shop, I jabbed in the number I needed.

DSI Barnes answered immediately. 'I've been waiting for this,' she said drily.

'I can understand that you want CID involved,' I said. 'This investigation is too big for me to handle on my own. But the guy you've sent is a wanker. He's going to cause more problems than he'll ever solve. He's also overstepping the boundaries of supe law.'

'Detective Inspector Collier is a highly decorated police officer,' Lucinda Barnes told me, 'with considerable experience.' She paused. 'But yes. He's also a wanker. It wasn't me who assigned him to this investigation. That decision has come from higher up. It's political. The top brass want to be transparent and to prove to everyone that a bloody crime of this magnitude is being taken seriously.'

'There will be bloodier crimes of greater magnitude if he

doesn't stop treating every supe he meets like they're Jack the Ripper.'

Barnes sighed heavily. 'I'll contact him and have a word. Have you got anywhere yet? Have you found anything that might help catch the bastards who are responsible for this?'

'Not yet, but I'm making some inroads.' I smiled at Fred as he joined me. 'I'd do better if Supe Squad had free rein to pursue my line of investigation, rather than being forced by Collier into grunt work.'

'I can arrange for that. In fact, it makes sense for Supe Squad to run a tandem investigation. It'll keep CID off the supes' back and create less hassle in the immediate future.'

Praise be. At least DSI Barnes was smart enough to see how the likes of Collier could mess things up royally for future supe–human relations. 'I appreciate that.'

'It will put more pressure on you,' she warned.

That was the least of my worries. 'Not a problem.'

She was silent for a moment. 'What were they after?' she said finally. 'What did the perps actually steal?'

'Oh no!' I said suddenly. 'I have to go! There's an argument breaking out across the street.' I hung up the phone.

Fred looked vaguely amused. 'You're not going to be able to pull off that sort of answer for long.'

'All the more reason to solve this crime before the day is out so we can avoid answering at all,' I responded

'What *was* stolen then?'

'I'll tell you on the way to the morgue,' I said. 'But you can't tell anyone else, on pain of death.'

'My lips are sealed.' He glanced at me. 'We're going to ignore Collier's instructions then?'

'We're Supe Squad. We've got far better things to do.'

He raised his hand for a high five. I shrugged and returned it. 'All for one.'

Fred grinned. 'And one for all.'

I'D CALLED AHEAD SO that Dr Laura Hawes, the pathologist at Fitzwilliam Manor Hospital, was already waiting for us at the morgue's entrance. She beamed happily when we approached. 'Detective Constable Bellamy! This has to be the first time I've seen you walk in here on your own two legs instead of being wheeled in on a gurney!'

'It does make a change to be here because of someone else's death,' I said drily

She replaced her smile with a grimace. 'Yes. Supes are having quite a day of it today. I've been following the news. Even before this dreadful robbery, you were busy.'

'And then some. I know it's early and you haven't had long to examine the bodies, but I was hoping you'd have some initial insights that might propel the investigation forward.'

Laura gave me a business-like bob of her head. 'I don't know how useful my insights will be, but follow me and I'll show you what I have so far.'

Great. I'd known I could count on her to have something to share. I glanced at Fred. He was already looking green around the gills at the thought of going inside. 'Can you stay out here where there's better phone reception and contact Liza?' I asked, taking pity on him. 'She'll have to share what she finds on the CCTV footage with DI Collier and his team. She'll appreciate a heads up, and it would be good to know if she's found anything useful.'

Fred's relief was palpable. 'Yes. I'll do that.'

Laura gave him an amused look then led me through to the morgue. Dean, the young bloke who manned the reception desk, looked up from his computer and gave me a friendly wave. 'Coming here,' I remarked, smiling at him, 'is beginning to feel like I'm coming home.'

'Are you any further forward with investigating your own … issues?' Laura asked.

I sucked my bottom lip. 'Not really. I told you last time we spoke that the book I'd come across suggested I'm a phoenix. I visited my uncle this morning to ask if my parents left anything behind that can shed any light. And Lukas has been looking into what a phoenix is as well.'

Laura appeared immediately interested. 'How do you feel about that? He's the Lord of all vampires. He must have an ulterior motive for helping you out.'

I considered my answer for a moment before replying honestly. 'I don't know how I feel about it. On the one hand, it's great to have someone on my side. On the other hand, I've no idea if I can trust him. I feel like I'm one of his pet projects and he's toying with me for his own ends. The clash between his status and my job isn't going to disappear.'

'Have you been round to his house for dinner yet?' Laura asked, pushing open the door to the first examination room.

'No. I'm still avoiding it.' I met her eyes. 'I'm afraid of what might happen if I do.'

'Live a little,' she advised. 'It's only dinner. And if it leads to more, embrace it. I wouldn't say no to his attentions. You can keep your professional life separate, you know you can.' She squeezed my arm. 'But we both know it's not his status as vampire Lord that you're afraid of, it's the thought of losing your heart. It's perfectly understandable, given what your boyfriend did to you. But if you hide away forever because of his actions then he wins. Lord Horvath is not Jeremy.'

No, he definitely was not. I gave a weak smile. 'What if Lukas is only interested in me because he thinks I'm playing hard to get?'

She shrugged. 'Then have some fun with him and move on. What's the big deal?'

Laura was probably right. I had too many hang ups. I sighed and looked at the nearest gurney. The first body was covered in a white sheet. 'Who's this?' I asked.

'Margaret Wick. Fifty-two years old. Human, of course. The bodies of the supes who were killed have already been transferred to their own facilities, so we only have the two dead humans.' Laura consulted her notes. 'She was killed outside the bank. From what I can tell from the angle she was hit, she was unlucky and it was a stray bullet.' She lifted up the sheet and indicated the hole on the side of her ribcage. 'There's no exit wound so I haven't retrieved the bullet yet, but—' her voice darkened '—have a look at this.' She indicated the ring around the bullet wound.

I peered more closely. 'Is that a burn mark?' I asked doubtfully.

'Of sorts. I'll need to test it to be sure, but you usually see this pattern on bullet holes when a particular metal has been used.'

'Let me guess,' I said grimly. 'Silver.'

Laura nodded. 'It's not easy to cast silver bullets. I don't see them very often, even on the odd occasion that a supe is brought here by accident. They also tend to be designed to remain inside the body. The longer a silver bullet stays inside a wolf's system, the greater the likelihood of fatal damage.'

I folded my arms and stared at the dark ring. The bank robbers had come prepared – and not just to steal. They'd been prepared to kill from the outset.

'What about the other body?' I asked. 'I believe the other human was killed inside the bank.'

Laura moved to the second gurney. 'He had no wallet on him and no money or identification. I estimate that he's in his early twenties. And there's this.' She lifted up the sheet to reveal the crude tattoo on his arm. I squinted. The word

Adam was etched into a barbed wire heart next to the word Jane. Hello, Adam.

'He was shot point blank in the face,' Laura said without a trace of emotion.

I recoiled. 'In the face?'

'It doesn't appear to have been an accident. His nose and most of his right cheekbone have been obliterated. He would have died instantly.'

She lifted the sheet and revealed the rest of his body. I held my breath and took a quick look, then hastily glanced away again.

'Preliminary findings suggest he's one hundred percent human.'

'Silver bullet?'

'The damage to his face is too severe for me to tell at the moment but I should be able to confirm it by the morning. As soon as I know, I'll contact you.'

'Okay.' The more information we could get on the ammunition the better. Silver bullets were so rare that we might be able to trace these ones back to their maker. If we were lucky.

I took a deep breath. 'Thank you, Laura.'

'You're welcome.' She dropped the sheet over Adam's shattered face. 'It's rare that we have killings on this scale. It's rarer still that supes are involved. I hope you catch these pricks.'

'Yeah,' I said. 'So do I.'

CHAPTER EIGHT

I JOINED FRED IN THE MORGUE WAITING ROOM. Unfortunately for both of us, I caught the end of his conversation with Dean. 'It's just that I feel like she still wants me, but because I'm a policeman she can't be with me.'

'It's a modern-day Romeo and Juliet, man,' Dean agreed.

Let's certainly hope not. I eyed Fred warily and wondered whether I should broach the subject of Scarlett. I suspected it was a chat that wouldn't go down well, unless I suggested that he position himself underneath her balcony and serenade her with love songs and red roses. Truthfully, I was hardly the best person to advise anyone on their love life. It was a topic best left alone.

'Hey,' I said, interrupting the pair of them.

Fred straightened up and instantly looked guilty.

Dean gave me a lazy smile. 'Hey.'

'Did you get hold of Liza?' I asked.

Fred nodded. 'She's preparing a report based on the CCTV. The first guy, the human, appears to have been shot in the face deliberately, but the others were only killed when one of the wolves tried to get in on the action. Then it was a free for all.'

Hmm. 'Any luck in tracking their vehicle?'

'None. They knew what they were doing. They'd planned their route and escaped through streets that aren't monitored by CCTV cameras. All we know is that they turned left when they drove off. After that,' he shrugged helplessly, 'they vanished into thin air.'

That was not good news. I grimaced.

'Where to now, boss?' Fred asked.

We couldn't locate the robbers, and DI Collier was in charge of the crime scene. I felt certain that the key task was to focus on the stolen items. The trouble was I had no idea where the gang were planning to offload the stuff. Who on earth would want to buy two separate and distinctly different copies of a lost Shakespeare play? Or a bunch of Fabergé eggs? And werewolf hair clippings?

'The office,' I said finally. 'Perhaps if we can come up with a list of pawn shops where some of the stolen goods can be sold we'll get somewhere.' It felt like we were clutching at straws but I had to try something.

'Okay.'

We said goodbye to Dean and walked to the hospital car park where Tallulah was waiting. We didn't get very far; less than twenty metres from the main doors, a red car with tinted windows pulled up and blocked our path. Initially, I thought nothing of it – until the passenger window rolled down and a hand beckoned me. 'Detective. Can I have a word?'

I hadn't recognised the car but I certainly recognised the voice. I stiffened and glanced at Fred. 'Go and get Tallulah,' I said quietly. 'I'll meet you back here.'

'Are you sure?'

I nodded and walked towards the red car. The door opened and I got inside.

To say that Devereau Webb didn't look fit and healthy was the understatement of the year. He was pale and sweating, and there was a rigidity to his body that didn't bode well. I angled myself away from him and looked him up and down. Surely this couldn't be the result of one werewolf bite? 'Mr Webb,' I said, by way of greeting. 'I hear you've been wolf-baiting.'

For a moment he looked surprised, then he smiled slightly and relaxed. 'A misunderstanding, that's all.'

'A misunderstanding?' My tone was both disbelieving and accusatory.

Webb didn't react. 'You can't blame me, DC Bellamy. The werewolves could have helped my niece but they chose not to. Any antagonism on my part is understandable. Rest assured, however, that I will be avoiding any further bites.' He smiled again.

Webb's niece was a whirlwind with plaits called Alice. He had approached the werewolf clans with a hefty bribe in return for turning her into a wolf so she could have a chance to beat her leukaemia. All four alphas had reluctantly turned him down because it was *verboten* to transform anyone under the age of eighteen. They had effectively sentenced her to death. I'd passed over the last remnants of the gruesome potion that Edward Nappey had concocted using wolf bones and vampire blood. Whether it would work was a long shot, but apparently it had done the trick.

'It wasn't the wolves' fault that they couldn't help Alice,' I reminded Webb gently. 'Their hands were tied.'

'I appreciate that, but we're not always rational when it comes to caring for our families. I can't help hating them for not helping her, even though I know they had no choice. We all have our failings.' He offered a self-deprecating shrug. 'In any case, that's not why I wish to talk to you. I'm here on another matter.'

Part of me hoped that this was where he'd confess to the shootings and the robbery so I could arrest him and go home. 'You've sought me out here,' I said. 'It must be serious.'

Webb inclined his head. 'One could say so.' His eyes were feverish and unfocused but a hint of determination remained in the set of his jaw. 'I'd like to thank you for what you did for Alice. We had confirmation a couple of weeks ago that her cancer is fully in remission. The docs don't understand how or why,' his voice was quiet, 'but I do.'

I swallowed. 'I'm glad that she's better,' I said honestly. 'But if you're looking for more of the ... medicine, I told you already. The treatment can never be repeated.'

Webb waved a hand dismissively. 'I'm not here for that. I understand the rules, and I understand what a big deal it was for you to give me what you did.' He paused. 'I found the book.'

I started. Webb smiled faintly. 'You mentioned its title in passing. I located a copy in the Carlyle Library.'

Shit. I'd told the library to lock down the spare copies of *Infernal Enchantments* and keep them away from prying eyes. Devereau Webb shouldn't have been able to get hold of it. The man was proving to be a menace in more ways than one.

'You can't blame me, detective,' he said. 'I had to know what I was giving Alice.'

'What do you want, Mr Webb?'

'To say thank you,' he replied simply. 'And to show my appreciation. I have a feeling that in the future I'll benefit from having you as a friend.'

Devereau Webb was a criminal and I sincerely doubted we'd ever be friends, even though part of me couldn't help liking the man. I couldn't shake the suspicion that he was up to something – and whatever it was, I wouldn't like it.

'In that case,' I told him, 'you're welcome.' As I moved to open the car door, his hand shot out and gripped my arm. He might have been sick but he was still surprisingly strong.

'Wait,' he instructed. He reached into a bag by his feet and drew out a small bottle. 'I want to give you this.'

I stared at it. There was liquid sloshing around inside it; it looked like water but, somehow, I knew that couldn't be further from the truth.

'I've been following the news,' he said. 'Things aren't going well for you today. I think this might help.'

I slowly raised my eyes to his. 'What is it?'

'Something that will help you in your fight against crime. It won't harm you. I promise you that. But it could open up a whole world of wonders.'

No way was I going to swallow some mysterious liquid given to me by Devereau Webb. 'Thank you,' I began, 'but—'

'The recipe is from the book. I've taken it myself and it's perfectly safe.'

'You look like you're half dead,' I said baldly. 'If you've followed some recipe from that damned book and now you're dying, you only have yourself to blame. I'm not about to follow suit, no matter what you say.'

He chuckled. 'I'm not dying. The symptoms of my current … illness are unrelated. Technically. Things will look very different for me tomorrow. And they will look different for you too, if you drink this. It will change everything.' Then he added enigmatically, 'And nothing.'

'Mr Webb—'

'Take it.' He pressed the bottle into my hands. 'It's my way of saying thank you for what you did for Alice. You saved her life. It's my turn to repay the favour.'

I gazed at the bottle. It looked innocuous enough but I wouldn't drink it. However, sometimes the path of least resistance is the best route to take. I pocketed it. 'Thank you,' I said.

Devereau Webb smiled. 'See you around, detective.'

'WHAT WAS ALL THAT ABOUT?' Fred asked when I joined him in Tallulah and we were driving towards the Supe Squad office.

'Beats me,' I said. 'I think it was some sort of bizarre show of power.' As soon as I said the words, I knew I was wrong. Webb had been earnest, and his gratitude for what I'd done for his niece had been sincere. I didn't believe he was trying to poison me – but I still had no idea what he was really about, either.

'This is a helluva strange day,' Fred muttered.

I sighed. 'Yeah.'

Just then my phone rang. I glanced at the caller ID and frowned. 'Hi, Molly.'

'Ems.' Her voice was warm. 'I'm sorry I didn't get the chance to say hello properly earlier. Collier runs a tight ship. He would've been pissed if I'd wandered over for a chat.'

'Mmm. I had enough of a talk with the man to get his measure,' I said. 'Are things okay with you? It can't be easy working for him. He seems quite … stuck in his ways.'

'He's an old-school kind of guy and he doesn't like admitting when he's wrong. There are worse than DI Collier – and there are better. He has a high opinion of himself and gets away with murder because last year he arrested the man who shot that finance guy, Timothy Barratt. It was in all the papers.'

I grunted in response. I remembered that incident. The shooter had almost got away but DI Collier's dogged diligence had brought him to justice in the nick of time. No doubt Collier would be riding on that success for many years to come.

I could almost hear Molly shrug. 'It is what it is. Collier's in charge. We can't all work for ourselves like you do.'

I had to admit that I enjoyed the freedom that working at Supe Squad granted me, even if some days it felt like I was picking my way through a magical minefield.

'Anyway,' Molly said, 'I'll get to the point. I'm calling because I know Collier won't, and I figured you'd want to know. I'd prefer it if he didn't find out that you heard it from me.'

Wariness flooded my system. 'Go on.'

'We think we've found the getaway car. A burnt-out florist's van has been located in an old tunnel to the east of Lisson Grove.' She gave me the coordinates.

I exhaled. 'I appreciate this, Molly,' I said.

'I thought you might. I'll expect several drinks in return at a future date.'

'Done,' I said. I hung up and glanced at Fred. 'Change of plan.'

CHAPTER NINE

THE TUNNEL, WHICH TURNED OUT TO BE AN OLD VICTORIAN-built electrical distribution structure that had been out of use for decades, was located to the edge of Ealing in west London.

We parked as close as we could, not far from the flashing lights of numerous police cars and a cluster of white-suited forensic technicians. I hopped out of Tallulah and strode forward with Fred in my wake. I could already see DI Collier striding around and barking out orders. I hoped he wasn't planning to kick up a fuss about my presence.

The police officer manning the cordon recognised me and ushered us through without any hassle. That was a positive start. I looked around, taking in the scene. In terms of suitable places to dump a vehicle in the middle of a city, this was about as good as it got – it was all but concealed from the nearby road. Certainly anyone in a passing car would be unlikely to notice anything unless they craned their necks or stopped at the side of the road and got out. And, given the busy traffic, it was unlikely to have much pedestrian footfall. There were also no cameras to be seen anywhere nearby.

I glanced at the old graffiti tag adorning the side of the tunnel. It was faded and several of the letters were covered in creeping moss. There wasn't even much litter. This spot was not visited often. I checked the ground, where several technicians were taking photos. Two sets of tyre tracks; the van had been driven in here, set alight, and then another vehicle had driven out. Wherever the robbers were now, they were long gone from here.

I walked to the shell of the van just inside the open tunnel. A few wisps of smoke were still rising from its twisted metal carcass. Collier gave me a black look from the other side of the burnt-out vehicle. 'How did you get here?' he asked.

'I drove.'

'That's not what I meant,' he snapped.

I sighed. 'We're both on the same side here.'

'If that were true, you wouldn't have gone behind my back and tattled to Barnes. You might think you're something special because you have vampires and werewolves hanging off your every word, but I can assure you that in the real world it's only results that receive praise.'

'In that case,' I returned, 'tell me what you've got and let's work on achieving those results.' I tried to stare him down. He stared back, then his mouth twisted and he yielded to the inevitable.

'They must have driven straight here after the robbery,' he said, begrudging every word. 'The fire was called in by a passenger on the top floor of a double-decker bus who spotted the smoke. It took the fire service almost an hour to get here. It wasn't a priority, given the location and obvious lack of casualties. By the time they arrived, the worst of the damage had already been done.'

'What about the weapons?' Fred asked. 'They had a whole arsenal with them at the bank. Throwing them into the back of the van and leaving them to burn along with the other evidence would have been the smart move. Is there any indication that they left the guns here?'

It was a clever question. Unfortunately, Collier shook his head. 'There's no sign of any guns. Either they dumped them somewhere else or they took them when they left.'

I pursed my lips. Quite often the easiest way to trace criminals was by tracking their guns. Most denizens of the underworld understood this and would quickly get rid of weapons by dumping them in the Thames, where the river's wash and silt would erase their existence, or by burying them in the ground. A fire like the one that had destroyed the van would have done the trick just as effectively. It was possible that the gang hadn't considered leaving the guns here, or that they'd been afraid the fire wouldn't be hot enough to destroy enough of them.

There was another possibility: the robbers might not be finished with their plans and they might have more violent deeds to undertake. That worrying thought nibbled at the edges of my brain but I wouldn't give voice to it yet, not until I was more sure of Collier.

'What about the van?' I asked. 'Has anything been uncovered about where it came from?'

'It was reported stolen late last night,' another police officer offered helpfully. Collier sent her a dirty look. He still didn't want to volunteer too much information.

'Where from?' I asked.

This time, the policewoman kept her mouth shut.

'The East End,' Collier said shortly.

'Where in the East End?'

'That's not relevant. We've checked and there's no way of telling who stole it. It's a dead end.'

I'd have liked to have checked that for myself but it wasn't a priority; I'd have to trust the older detective about this at least. Just because he was a grumpy bastard who hated my involvement didn't mean that he was incompetent.

'There's no doubt in my mind,' Collier declared, 'that this is an inside job. Someone from the bank – or one of the customers – is responsible for this mess. For all we know, the wolves and the bloodsuckers could be working together.'

I folded my arms. 'And what would be their motive? Let's not forget that there are dead supes at the scene.'

His lip curled. 'From what I hear, they've always had a disregard for life even when it comes to their own kind. But it was probably the vampires working on their own. That Horvath fellow was very obstructive when my officers spoke to him earlier, and he refused to stay long enough for me to talk to him. It can't be a coincidence that there were no dead bloodsuckers at the bank. And let's not forget it was a vampire clambering up the side of the London Eye earlier today.'

'No, it wasn't,' I said patiently. 'A pair of fake fangs was found at the bottom of the wheel. Best guess is that it was another student who'd been fooled into acting like those idiots dressed up as werewolves on the bus.'

'Only a vampire could climb that thing,' Collier said dismissively. 'The goblin – Pralk, is it? – he doesn't seem to know anything. We let Horvath go but we need to get him back for questioning. I've spoken to my superiors and they've agreed that we can hold him for forty-eight hours before we charge him.' At my look, he laughed coldly. 'You can protest his innocence all you want and quote supe law, but humans were killed during this robbery. That means I can have him. I'll get the fanged bastard to talk.'

'If you rush in gung-ho and haul the vampire Lord in for interrogation,' I said, 'there will be consequences. The supes don't like police interference, and the relationship between us and them is delicate. Supe Squad have been working hard to improve matters. The wrong move could set that relationship back by years.'

'I don't give a fuck about your relationship with the supes. Our job isn't to be mates with criminals.'

I tried hard to keep my temper. 'Supes aren't criminals. They're people like you and me.'

'We all know that isn't true.' He glowered at me. His true colours were on display. Detective Inspector Collier was the worst kind of person. Deep down, he believed that supes didn't deserve to exist and they should all be locked up. I'd thought that sort of attitude had gone out with the Dark Ages but, alas, I regularly encountered people who thought that way. It was wholly irrational – and downright dangerous.

'How would the bank robbers have known which safety deposit boxes to target?' Collier enquired.

'I don't know.'

'I'm told that silver bullets were used. I'm sure you can confirm that sort of ammunition is lethal to werewolves in particular. Is Lord Horvath aiming to incite war against the clans?'

'I very much doubt it. He was a victim of this crime as much as the wolves, even if no vampires were killed.'

'Then why are he and the other supposed crime victims refusing to tell me what was stolen? Why are *you* refusing to tell me?'

I winced. 'I made a deal with them…'

Collier rolled his eyes. 'Whatever. Isn't it convenient that Horvath and all the supe leaders have alibis for the time of robbery? That they were called away to deal with other matters just before the guns opened fire?'

'It was obviously a diversion to get them out of the way.'

'It wasn't obviously anything,' he snapped. 'You are blind to their faults, DC Bellamy.'

Something else that wasn't true. 'Look,' I said, trying to stay calm and keep control of the situation, 'I'm not suggesting you shouldn't question Lord Horvath and the other supe leaders again. I'm just saying that there are smarter ways to go about it than treating them like criminals. I'm the Supe Squad detective. Let me approach Horvath and the others. I'll request that they come to the Supe Squad office and—'

'No. We don't want to give them any warning. We have a better chance of getting real answers if they don't know we're coming after them. We'll catch the bastards unaware.'

I'd seen the way the vamp community acted around Lukas. As far as they were concerned, he was akin to a god. If Collier went in all guns blazing and treated him like a criminal, there could well be rioting in the streets of Soho. Even if that didn't happen, the vamps would close their doors on us. As much as Lukas was keen on dinner with me – and goodness knew what else – his number-one priority would always be his own vampires.

I gazed helplessly at Collier, wondering what I could say that would get him to back off slightly. Then I suddenly realised why he was acting in such a bull-headed fashion. This was all my fault.

'DI Collier,' I said carefully, walking round the burnt-out van so I could draw him to the side. It wouldn't be a good idea for the other officers on the scene to hear what I was about to say. 'I realise that you're pissed off that DSI Barnes told you to stop treating the supes like terrorists and that you feel undermined. I know that you're trying to maintain your order and authority, but you should put your feelings to one side for now and think rationally about this. Your question about the safety deposit boxes was a good one. We should focus on who might have known which boxes belonged to the supes and the bank, and who might have got hold of that information. I don't think this was an inside job. Put your prejudices to the side. Let's work together.'

He looked at me incredulously. 'Are you trying to manage me? *Me?*' He shook his head in disbelief. 'You've got delusions of grandeur, girl.' He jabbed a finger at me. 'If you warn Lord Freak that we're coming for him, I'll have you arrested for obstructing the course of justice.' He stalked away, yelling out commands at anyone who'd listen to him.

Fred sidled up to me. 'This isn't good,' he murmured.

I rubbed the back of my neck. 'No,' I said. 'I've handled it all wrong.'

'It's not your fault,' Fred said. 'He's afraid of supes and what they represent and his fear is manifesting like this.' He waved at Collier's departing back. 'He knew Tony,' he said, referring to my now-dead predecessor. 'I've been trying to place him and it suddenly clicked. DI Collier is the reason Tony ended up at Supe Squad. Tony clocked him after he spouted off about something. Collier got away with it because he kept his hands to himself and Tony got sent to Supe Squad as punishment. It was years ago and long before my time, but Liza told me about it.'

'So DI Collier has even more reason to despise Supe Squad.' I ran a hand through my hair. I couldn't investigate the robbery and deal with that idiot at the same time.

'What are we going to do?' Fred asked.

'I've been explicitly ordered not to warn Lukas in advance,' I said thoughtfully. 'There's no actual evidence against him. Collier is simply making a show of his authority.' I looked at Fred. 'Right?'

He nodded. 'Right. He probably won't question Lord Horvath himself. He'll leave him to stew in a cell while he gets on with the rest of the investigation.' He sighed. 'And the entire vampire population will despise us for the rest of time. Is what Collier's doing even legal, considering supe law?'

'It's murky when human casualties are involved.' I straightened my shoulders and started marching out of the tunnel. Fred trotted to keep up with me. 'We can't warn Lukas. Speaking to DSI Barnes again and asking her to intervene will only inflame Collier further. If we ask Lukas to help with other details of the investigation, we might have a way out. As long as he's out of Collier's path and sticking with Supe Squad, nobody can complain.'

'DI Collier will.'

'Then let's get to Lukas before Collier does, and before Collier finds out about what we're doing.'

Fred was wide-eyed. 'We could get into a lot of trouble for this.'

'You're welcome to stay out of it. You don't have to put your neck on the line.'

'Are you kidding me? I'm with you all the way, boss.' He rubbed his hands together. 'This will be fun.' He nudged me. 'And I love that you're running to rescue big bad Lord Horvath like he's a damsel in distress.'

'I'm no knight in shining armour.'

Fred winked. 'Lukas Horvath won't see it that way.'

CHAPTER TEN

WE ARRIVED OUTSIDE LUKAS'S GRAND HOME NOT LONG AFTER ten o'clock at night. Now that it was summer, it didn't get dark until late. I often didn't realise the time until the sky pooled into a blanket of indigo marred only by the odd passing aeroplane. I'd been afraid of the dark for a while after my boyfriend slit my throat in the graveyard at St Erbin's church. I had jumped at shadows and felt a tightening in my stomach whenever the sun started to set. These days, however, it was comforting. I'd come a long way.

I hopped out of Tallulah and gazed up at the grey, granite building. I'd yet to cross the threshold, despite Lukas's attempts to invite me round for dinner. I couldn't help wondering what his taste in décor was like. I thought about the ruffled shirt he'd been wearing. Decadent, probably. And with lots of frills.

Fred hung back, waiting for me to do the honours. I sucked in a long breath and glanced round. Collier wasn't here yet. There was still time. I stepped up to the perfectly varnished door, painted ostentatiously in a glossy blood-red colour, and knocked.

It wasn't Lukas who answered. Instead I found myself faced with a young vampire whose face I didn't recognise. When he saw me, he blanched. 'Lord Horvath is not home,' he said, his eyes shifting from left to right nervously.

'I need to find him immediately. Where is he?'

The young vamp scratched his head. 'Uh… I'm not sure.'

'Has he gone to Heart?' I asked, referring to the nightclub that Lukas ran.

'Maybe,' the vamp said hesitantly.

That was a no, then. I frowned, vaguely irritated – then a cold chill descended through my body. Suddenly I knew exactly why Lukas wasn't in. Bastards. I should have acted on my earlier instincts. 'The bank robbers have been in touch, haven't they? He's gone to meet them.'

Alarm lit his expression. 'What? No!'

I ground my teeth. Damnit. I glanced at the vampire again. This might work. I licked my lips and raised my chin, summoning all the power I had within me. I'd achieved similar results with weaker werewolves but I'd never tried it on a vampire before. 'Tell me,' I intoned, the thrum of compulsion ringing through every word, 'where Lord Horvath has gone.'

Strain contorted the vampire's face. He clamped a hand over his mouth and gave me a panicked look, stepping back as if to get away. He shook his head violently from side to side, desperately trying not to speak.

'Tell me,' I repeated.

'Westminster Bridge,' he blurted out. Relief at yielding to my command flooded his eyes, followed by guilt. 'Shit,' he muttered.

I paid him no attention. I was already running to Tallulah.

'What?' Fred asked. 'What is it?'

We jumped into the car. I'd already started the engine and was driving off before I'd clipped on my seatbelt. 'Why does anyone rob a bank?' I asked, performing an illegal U-turn in the middle of the road.

'For money,' Fred said. 'Obviously.'

'Except,' I changed gears and accelerated, 'these bank robbers didn't take money. They didn't waste time trying to access the Talismanic Bank's vaults, or bother with the small amounts of cash available from the tellers. They went for the big guns. They've got a whole bunch of items that are priceless to the werewolves and the vampires, but which will be difficult to offload to others. What's the best way to make money out of what they've got?'

Fred hissed through his teeth. 'Selling them back to the people they stole them from.'

'Exactly. I'd bet my eye teeth that's exactly what's going down now on Westminster Bridge.' I tossed my phone into Fred's lap. 'Call Lord Horvath. Get him to wait until we get there.'

He did as I asked. 'He's not picking up. I think his phone is turned off.'

My hands tightened on the steering wheel. Fuck.

'Lord Horvath doesn't strike me as the kind of person to happily hand over a wad of cash in return for his belongings and then skip away,' Fred mused.

'No,' I said grimly, 'he does not. The robbers must be prepared for that. They must have some sort of setup that will keep them safe while they get the money they want.' I gave Fred a dark look. 'But *we* have to be prepared for a bloodbath that might be about to occur smack-bang in the centre of London.'

Fred adjusted his seatbelt. 'Drive faster, boss.'

LONDON, like New York, Tokyo, Berlin and a whole host of other metropolises across the world, was supposed to be a city that didn't sleep. At this hour, however, there was scant traffic on the streets and Westminster Bridge was all but empty. Empty, apart from the two cars in the middle of the bridge, both of which were at a standstill. They were facing in opposite directions and on opposite sides of the road. I recognised the first one as belonging to Lukas. The second was a beaten-up Volvo. Shivers of deep foreboding ran down my spine.

I urged Tallulah forward, deciding to drive directly to where the action was. Before I could, two vamps appeared out of nowhere, flew through the air and landed directly in my path. I slammed on the brakes and unrolled the window. 'Get out of the way!'

'The bridge is closed,' the nearest vampire said. 'Find an alternative route.'

'You know who I am,' I said flatly. 'And I am ordering you to step aside.'

'We can't do that, ma'am.'

'Uh oh,' Fred murmured under his breath. 'He ma'amed you. We're in serious trouble now.'

I gave him an exasperated glare and stepped out of the car. I looked from one vampire to the other. Neither of them moved an inch. With slow, deliberate movements, I reached into Tallulah and drew out my crossbow. Both vampires remained where they were but I definitely saw the younger one flinch.

'Step aside.' Once again I allowed my voice to fill with the power of command.

The first vampire's face spasmed with rage but his feet were already moving. I was on a roll; stress must have been enhancing my ability to compel. I glanced at the crossbow then back at the cars. The driver's door on Lukas's vehicle was opening and, as I watched, Lukas got out. Then the front passenger door to the Volvo opened and a masked figure emerged. I gritted my teeth. Damn it.

I leapt inside Tallulah. 'Get out and stay here, Fred,' I instructed. 'Don't let anyone else through.'

He nodded and quickly left the car. I changed gears and drove forward slowly, one hand on the steering wheel and one hand on the crossbow. Assuming the robbers were human, I wasn't allowed to use it against them – the law forbade it. But that didn't mean that I wouldn't fire off a bolt if I had to. I had to be ready for anything.

As I approached, another figure stepped out of the Volvo. This one was holding a gun. With casual insouciance, he – or perhaps she, it was difficult to tell – raised the muzzle in my direction.

I kept driving, stopping only when Tallulah's bonnet was metres away from the boot of Lukas's sleek black vehicle. He watched me with a hooded gaze as I turned off the engine and climbed out to join the party. Neither the masked figure opposite him nor the one with the gun reacted. I glanced inside the cars. There appeared to be a third person sitting in the driver's seat of the Volvo. All three members of the gang were here.

'Hi, guys!' I trilled. 'How's it going?'

'D'Artagnan,' Lukas bit out, no doubt using my nickname to hide my police identity from the bank robbers. 'This is not a good time.'

A garbled, accentless, male voice came from behind the mask of the person holding the gun. 'Listen to the bloodsucker. Get into that car and leave.'

'I don't think I'm going to do that.' I lifted my chin and stared at the masks. They were made of moulded plastic and covered the whole of both robbers' faces. Even their eyes were shielded from view; neither of them was displaying so much as a millimetre of skin. Black, white, Asian, young, old – I couldn't begin to tell. These bastards were taking no chances with their real identities. 'You are under arrest.'

Lukas glared at me.

The other masked figure, whose body shape indicated she was female, laughed. '*You're* a police officer? Give me a break.' She had a strong Cockney accent; this had to be the woman identified during the robbery. She shook her head, laughed and waved at her colleague. 'If she comes any closer, shoot her.'

'This is between me and them, D'Artagnan,' Lukas said quietly. 'It's best if you don't get involved.'

'They're human and they're criminals,' I said, without taking my eyes off the disguised pair. 'That means they're mine to deal with. Not to mention that I'm already involved.'

'If she interrupts again,' the woman said to Lukas, 'we're gone. You'll never see or hear from us again – and you'll never get your belongings back. Give us the money and we'll give you the location of the boxes. It's as simple as that.'

There was a small beep. I stiffened before realising it was a watch or some kind of timer. The bastards were organised and weren't going to hang around for long.

Her next words confirmed it. 'Sixty seconds,' she said. 'Then we walk.' Her head turned to me. 'And if we don't get away, he never gets his stuff. Neither do the werewolves. We have safeguards in place.'

I quickly weighed up my options. Although Fred was at the end of the bridge, to all intents and purposes I was on my own. I could bring down one of these bastards, but I wouldn't manage all three of them. Especially as it seemed that Lukas was going ahead with the exchange.

My police training didn't extend to this sort of scenario. It wasn't that I was afraid of getting shot – even if they killed me,

I'd wake up again in twelve hours. But I would lose a lot of ground in the intervening time. The best thing I could do was to hold back and do what I could to identify these fuckers after they'd gone. I could track the Volvo, or wait until they tried the same trick with the werewolves and I was better prepared. Right now, the robbers held all the cards. But just because I was about to lose the battle didn't mean the war was over. Far from it.

Lukas reached into his car and slid out a briefcase. 'Very well,' he murmured, with a black-eyed look of warning in my direction.

I gritted my teeth but stayed where I was. Despite my decision not to act, it was beyond frustrating not to do anything when a crime was taking place. I was supposed to stop events like this from happening, not stand by idly and watch them like a damned lemming.

The briefcase looked innocuous enough. It was aluminium with simple catches on the top. Lukas handed it over to the woman who tested its weight, then placed it on top of the bonnet of his car and opened it. Unable to help myself, I leaned forward.

There was nothing there. The briefcase was empty.

'What the fuck is going on here?' the woman snarled. I stared at her. All of a sudden, her broad Cockney accent had slipped. Russian: there was no doubt in my mind.

Lukas smiled, baring his fangs. 'Did you really think that I'd allow you to blackmail me in this fashion?' he asked softly. 'Did you really think I'd hand over five million pounds in cash and walk away? I'm Lord Horvath, the most powerful vampire in this country.' His black eyes glittered. 'And I don't negotiate with the likes of you.'

For one long second neither of the masked figures reacted, then the woman raised her head. 'You'll never see those safety deposit boxes again.'

Lukas shrugged. 'So be it.' He clicked his fingers – and all hell broke loose.

From either side of the bridge, where they must have been hanging out of sight, several vampires swarmed over. The male robber swung his gun towards Lukas and prepared to fire. I lifted my crossbow. I'd shoot him in the damned leg if I had to. I didn't have to bother, however; with lightning speed, Lukas sprang forward, spinning his body until he was behind the man. He yanked up the mask just enough to reveal an expanse of white throat then he sank his teeth in it.

The woman didn't utter a sound, she simply ran for her car. I tossed the crossbow to the side and ran after her. I was fast – but the vampires were faster. They brought her down in seconds.

Lukas pulled his bloodstained mouth away from the man's neck. 'Don't hurt her,' he ordered. 'We want to have a chat first.'

The vamps nodded and hauled the woman to her feet. Scarlett stalked forward and peeled away the woman's mask and I stared at her furious face. Blonde, younger than I'd thought, perhaps in her mid-twenties. She had a long scar across her cheek and angular features. She didn't look like someone I'd want to encounter on a dark night.

Lukas wiped his mouth with the back of his hand and glanced at me. 'I'm sorry, Emma. I didn't want you to have to see that.'

'I know you drink blood, Lukas,' I said, although I averted my eyes. 'That's hardly news.'

'Yes.' He nodded. 'But the reality of it can be … unpleasant.' He was still holding onto the man, who was groaning.

Lukas pulled off the man's mask and gazed into his face. The robber was swarthy, with a curling moustache that seemed too pantomime villain-esque to be real. His eyes were unfocused, but he managed to hawk up a ball of phlegm that he intended to spit in Lukas's direction. He didn't get very far; Lukas thumped him hard on the back of his head and he went down like a sack of bricks. Lukas sniffed with grim satisfaction.

'Was this wise?' I asked

'Anything is better than being held to ransom by these fuckers.'

'You will regret it!' the woman hissed. 'You shouldn't have done this. In fact, you will discover that…'

We never got to hear the end of her sentence. Without any warning, there was a loud crack and her head exploded. Blood and bone and brain matter sprayed out in all directions. Then there was another crack and the body of the fallen moustachioed man jerked violently.

The vampires scattered, desperate to seek cover. I threw myself flat onto the ground. Shit. Shit. A third crack and the sound of breaking glass. A masked body slumped out of the robbers' car on the opposite side of the road. A fourth pop. Where were the shots coming from? Who had done this?

My heart thumped as adrenaline coursed through my veins. Fear tingled across my skin. I raised my head to look around – and that was when I saw Lukas. He was flat on his back, his head at an unnatural angle.

I crawled over to him, ignoring the shattered glass. 'Lukas!' I grabbed his arm and shook it. 'Lukas!'

His head flopped towards me. There was no light in his eyes – and there was a gaping bloody hole in the centre of his forehead. My breath shuddered in my lungs and the air around me seemed to still. I fumbled for his neck, desperate to feel his pulse even though I already knew the truth and my efforts were wasted.

Lukas Horvath was dead.

CHAPTER ELEVEN

NOBODY MOVED FOR A LONG TIME. I COULD HEAR SIRENS approaching us from a distance, but even when the armed police arrived they would proceed with great caution. An active yet invisible sniper was not someone to underestimate.

My whole body felt numb. I kept expecting Lukas to sit up and grin at me. He didn't. I reached for his hand and held it, though I wasn't sure why. Perhaps for comfort. Perhaps because I knew it wouldn't be long before his skin turned cold and I wanted to feel the searing heat of his touch one last time. Strangely, there were no tears pricking at my eyes. I couldn't feel much of anything at all.

After several long moments, I carefully unwrapped my fingers from Lukas's hand and stood up. I waited for a shot, for the onrush of sudden pain and the familiar blackness of death. There was nothing.

I swivelled round and scanned the area. 'Where did the shots come from?' I asked. It sounded as if my voice was coming from a long way away.

Scarlett got to her feet, her expression as dazed as mine must have been. 'I … I don't know,' she said. She shook her head. Her blonde hair was mussed and her red lipstick smeared like a bloody wound across her cheek.

I heard a shout and saw Fred running towards us at full pelt from the other side of the bridge. His recklessness shook me out of my stupor and I waved at him, angrily, gesturing that he should stay back. He was making a perfect target of himself. But there were no further shots; the sniper had done his work and had probably already gone.

As Scarlett let out a cry and sank to her knees beside Lukas's corpse, my eyes narrowed. We were a stone's throw from Parliament. Even at this hour, you'd have to have a death wish to shoot a gun anywhere near here.

'Who chose this location?' I demanded, urgency colouring my every word. Scarlett only moaned in response.

The other vamps were getting to their feet, anguish etched on every face as they stared at their dead Lord. One of them tilted back his head and started to howl. A split second later the others joined in. The keening sound rent the air with far more force and emotion than I'd ever heard from the werewolves, even during the full moon.

I shivered then repeated my question. 'Who chose this location? You or the robbers?'

This time Scarlett heard me. 'They did,' she whispered. She stroked Lukas's face. 'They chose it. They told us when and told us where.'

I nodded stiffly. So they'd been in control. The sniper must have already been in position before Lukas got here. I wondered if the shooter was with the gang or was someone entirely different, before deciding it didn't matter.

The robbers had been prepared for everything to go to hell from the very beginning. The Russian woman and her fake Cockney accent, and the swarthy man with her, had been collateral damage. Was killing Lukas the objective from the start? I frowned and discarded the idea. A sniper could have shot him at any time on any day. The craziness that had led up to here, from the London Eye idiocy to Tower Bridge to the robbery itself, was unnecessary. The sniper was merely a contingency plan in case Lukas decided not to play by the robbers' rules.

Those bastards. Those fucking, murdering bastards. Sudden pure rage rippled through me but I tried to shake it off. It wouldn't help me now.

Fred was panting when he finally reached us. 'Behind us,' he gasped. 'The shots were fired from behind us.' He waved a hand in the general direction.

I frowned. There were few places where a sniper could conceal themselves – but there was a hotel. I squinted. There, high up on one of the top floors, was an open window. A curtain flapped in the light breeze.

I stared at it. And then I started running.

By the time I reached the end of the bridge and swung right towards the hotel's entrance, half a dozen police cars had arrived. Collier stepped out from one of them. 'The hotel,' I spat. 'There was a sniper in the hotel.'

Collier gazed at me for a long moment, his expression inscrutable. I rolled my eyes; there wasn't time for his obtuse attitude. I spun round and continued moving forward. We couldn't allow that sniper to escape. Fortunately Collier seemed to have come to the same conclusion. I heard him bark orders and send several officers after me.

I slammed through the glass front doors. The night receptionist, who was reading a book, jerked in surprise and looked up. 'Can I help you?'

'Police! Nobody comes in or out!'

Her mouth dropped open. I ignored her astonishment

and ran for the lift, burst inside and jabbed the button for the top floor.

'Wait!' the receptionist shouted.

The doors slid closed, swallowing her voice.

I leaned against the mirrored wall and closed my eyes. Lukas … Oh God. *Lukas.* Then the lift jolted slightly and the doors opened again.

I opened my eyes and stepped out.

This wasn't a huge hotel. There were only twenty-odd rooms on the entire floor and I could discount half of them immediately as they faced in the wrong direction. The room with the open window had been about halfway along the building.

I reached where I thought the sniper's room would be. 824. I traced the numbers with the tip of my index finger, then I stepped back and used all my strength to kick open the door. The more I did this, the easier it became; one or two more deaths and the strength imbued to me as a result would mean no door could hold me back. Because when I died, I came back. When I died, I grew more powerful.

Vampire or not, when Lukas died he just died.

I swallowed my thoughts and entered the room. I'd stupidly left my crossbow on the bridge but it didn't matter. I'd use my bare hands to kill anyone who was in here.

The room was empty. The wind continued to tug at the white curtain, making it billow into the night air. I checked the bathroom then strode forward, examining the floor. There was a single spent bullet casing near the window but no other sign of any sniper.

I stepped forward and gazed at the dramatic scene below. Several ambulances had joined the police cars and a helicopter was buzzing overhead. Paramedics, police, even a fire crew were all present.

'I knew that only fuck-ups got sent to Supe Squad,'

sneered a voice from behind me. 'But I didn't realise until now how much of a fuck-up you actually are.'

I turned slowly, my eyes meeting those of DI Collier.

'Still,' he continued, 'I suppose you've done me a favour. My hands are clean as far as this entire mess is concerned. You didn't inform me about what was going on, and you made it official by speaking to Barnes behind my back. Not only that,' he added with a sly smile, 'but you got Lord Horvath killed. He's dead because of you. You stood by and let the Lord of all vampires get shot. One less vampire in the world can only be a good thing. Well done, detective. If you weren't about to be fired, I'd be putting you forward for a commendation.'

I didn't think, I simply reached for the small vase on the small table next to me and flung it in Collier's direction. It smashed into the side of his head. He howled in pain and a trickle of blood oozed down his temple.

'You bitch.' His voice was low and controlled. 'You crazy, psycho bitch.'

'Get out,' I said. 'Get out of here.' I reached for another object. Collier's face twisted into a snarl and he backed out of the room.

I gazed after him until I was sure he wasn't returning then I turned to the window, my eyes searching for Lukas's prone body. One of the vampires was shoving away a paramedic. Several others were lifting Lukas up, preparing to take him home.

I watched for a moment or two, heaviness descending on my entire soul. My eyes filled with tears and I choked back a sob. He wasn't supposed to die. There should have been more time. *We* should have had more time. He was right that I'd avoided his calls and found excuses not to join him for dinner. I hadn't been sure that I could meld his stature as Lord of all London vampires with my job as the only detective in Supe Squad. I hadn't been sure that I could trust him, and I was still nervous about forming any kind of relationship after what Jeremy had done to me. I'd stalled because I was scared – and now I'd never know what might have been because I'd been a coward. Lukas was lost to me forever.

I put my hands in my pockets and searched for a tissue. Instead, my fingers curled around a small glass bottle. I drew it out and frowned. At first, I couldn't remember for the life of me what it was, then I remembered that Devereau Webb had given it to me. What had he said? That it was something which would help me in my fight against crime? He'd also said it'd work wonders. As if.

I shook the bottle, watching as the clear contents sloshed against the sides, then I shrugged and pulled out the stopper. I sniffed it; whatever it was, it smelled earthy and clean.

Without another sensible thought in my head, I raised it to my mouth and swallowed the contents. As I dropped the bottle, my eyes caught the digital display on the alarm clock beside the bed. 11.59pm. How did it get to be so late?

I rubbed my eyes and was about to head for the door when I spotted the smoke. It was a mere wisp at first, uncurling seemingly from nowhere and rising up from the floor around me. My brow creased. Had the sniper also taken the time to set a fire to ease his escape? I blinked and looked again. More smoke. It wasn't simply rising from beneath me – now it was swirling into a cloud and wrapping around my body with its tight grey tendrils.

I started to choke. I flapped my arms to wave it away but it enveloped me. It was everywhere. What was going on? What the hell was happening? What…?

THERE WAS a loud crackle and bright light. My body was jerked forward suddenly and I heard the sound of crunching metal. I blinked in confusion, just in time to see the front door of a taxi in front of me open and a burly man step out. He marched towards me, glancing first at the rear end of his vehicle before glaring at me. 'Look at what you've done! Look at it!'

I stared at him open-mouthed. Huh? Blinking rapidly, I shook myself. I was in Tallulah. On a bridge. There was another crackle. My police radio. I frowned at it. Ignoring the taxi driver who was gesticulating furiously, I slowly picked up the radio.

'DC Bellamy, this is Dispatch. Please acknowledge.'

I scratched my head, dull pain aching in the centre of my chest. Lukas. Oh, Lukas.

The taxi driver knocked loudly on my window, demanding I roll it down, and the radio continued to demand my attention. I fumbled, finally pressing the button on the side of it to answer. 'This is … DC Bellamy,' I replied.

'What is your current location? Your presence is required at the London Eye.'

I passed a hand in front of my eyes. 'I don't understand,' I whispered.

'There's a suicidal vampire at the London Eye,' the radio operator said with a trace of impatience. 'How quickly can you get there?'

'Uh…' What? My mouth felt painfully dry. I licked my lips. 'Ten minutes?'

'Good. I'll inform the officers on the scene.' The radio clicked off.

I stared at it and dropped it. Then I got out of the car.

'What the fuck is your problem, lady?' the taxi driver bellowed in my face.

'I'm sorry.'

'You will pay for that! This was your fault!'

I nodded slightly and, as if in slow motion, reached for my wallet. I drew out a card and handed it to him. He looked at it. 'You're with the police? I've been hit by a damned copper?' He blew air out through pursed lips. 'That's fucking rich!'

'I have to go,' I said. I could feel the cool breeze on my skin and goose bumps rising across my arms. It felt real. *This* felt real.

I cleared my throat and met the taxi driver's angry eyes. 'I can be reached on this number. I'll pay for the damage. And compensation. I admit full liability.'

'You're bloody well right you will. It was your fault! And you're not going anywhere yet. I want this in writing.'

'Call my office,' I said. 'They'll sort you out.' I got into Tallulah. 'I really am sorry.'

'Wait! Where do you think you're going?'

I mouthed sorry at him again and started Tallulah's engine, then swerved round his taxi as he jumped out of the way. A moment later, I was heading towards the London Eye.

'What's going on, Tallulah?' I muttered. 'I don't understand what's happening.' I'd blacked out – or I was suffering from memory loss. Or something. My brain felt unusually foggy and dim and a pulsating pain was throbbing behind my eyes.

I drove to the London Eye on auto-pilot, parked badly and walked towards it as if I were in some kind of dream. There was a collection of people hanging around and a police cordon keeping back the gawkers. I frowned at the uniformed officer standing at the front. He looked familiar; he looked *very* familiar.

'You need to keep back, ma'am,' he instructed. 'It isn't safe here.'

105

I continued to stare at him as my jaw worked uselessly. I fumbled for my warrant card and held it up.

He peered at it. 'My apologies, DC Bellamy. They're waiting for you below.'

All I managed was a nod. I ducked under the police tape and walked towards the foot of the Eye. Hannigan, wearing the same tailored suit as last time, was flapping his arms and yelling. 'You have to get that idiot down!' he shouted. 'There are already news crews here. This is not the sort of publicity we need right now!'

I stopped and looked at him, then I rubbed my eyes and looked again. My gaze drifted to the man standing beside him and my stomach dropped. No. It couldn't be. I started walking again. With my gaze trained on him, I took slow deliberate steps. I was dreaming; I had to be.

I only stopped again when I was near enough to reach out with one finger and gently poke Lukas's chest. I ignored the ostentatious frills on his shirt and the gaping astonishment from both Hannigan and Paige.

Rather than looking surprised, Lukas merely appeared curious. He raised his own finger and, with such a light touch that I barely felt it, poked me back. 'D'Artagnan,' he said softly. 'You look pale. Are you alright?'

I didn't answer. Instead I reached up with shaking fingers and ran my hands through his jet-black hair, which was far softer than I'd imagined. There was no wound. No blood. He appeared perfectly fine.

'Emma?' Lukas sounded more concerned now. 'What's wrong?'

I pulled back a fraction and looked into his eyes. 'You're alive,' I breathed.

'He's a vampire,' Hannigan muttered. 'He's undead. Not alive.'

'That's a ridiculous fallacy,' I said, still staring at Lukas.

'Why did you think I wouldn't be?' Lukas asked, ignoring Hannigan.

I shook my head. Words failed me – everything failed me. I did the only thing that I could do, the only thing that seemed right; I pushed myself up onto my tiptoes, coiled my arms round Lukas's neck and kissed him.

Initially, he didn't respond then his hands reached for my waist and pulled me against his hard body. His tongue pressed into my mouth, hot and insistent. I moaned, unable to help myself. He was breathing. He was alive. I needed this moment to last forever.

There was a loud cough. 'What exactly is going on here?' Hannigan yelled, anger vibrating through his words. 'What do you think you're doing?'

Lukas broke the kiss and stepped away. He looked surprisingly flushed and his black eyes raked my face. 'Emma,' he murmured. 'I was about to ask you why you'd been avoiding my calls but all of a sudden I no longer seem to care.'

'What about the vampire on top of my wheel?' Hannigan screamed. 'What are you going to do about him?'

'What day is it?' I asked Lukas, disregarding the irate manager's complaints.

'Tuesday.'

'What date?'

'June 22nd.' He hesitated. 'Emma...'

Hannigan exploded. 'The fucking vampire!'

I shook myself and glanced at him. Paige was at Hannigan's side, staring at me with a mixture of envy and delight. I managed to give her a brief smile.

'That's not a vampire,' I said. Then I froze and stared at my watch. 'The bank,' I whispered. 'I have to get to the bank.'

'What's going on, Emma?' Lukas asked.

'Nothing!' I was already stepping away. 'Stay here. You can deal with this yourself.'

He ran a hand through his hair. 'Where are you going? I don't understand.'

I didn't understand either. 'I'll see you later.' I turned away. 'I have to go.'

'Emma!'

I didn't answer. I was already running back to Tallulah.

CHAPTER TWELVE

Tallulah's engine didn't start immediately; the collision with the taxi had done her more damage than my confused brain had realised. Her bonnet was crumpled and both headlights had been taken out. I'd worry about that later.

I crossed my fingers and tried her engine again. 'Please, baby,' I prayed aloud. 'Don't let me down.'

She spluttered and choked but her engine juddered into life. A second later, I was careening through the busy city streets. By my reckoning, I had fifty-eight minutes before the robbery began and I had to get there before the bank robbers started shooting. The Talismanic Bank wasn't that far and I could make it with time to spare but I didn't want to take any chances – not when lives were at risk.

With one hand on the steering wheel, I slid my phone out of my pocket and used a voice command to locate the bank's number. By the time I reached the first set of traffic lights, their phone was already ringing.

'Good afternoon,' trilled a chirpy voice. 'You've reached the Talismanic Bank. How may we assist you today?'

I cleared my throat. 'This is Detective Constable Bellamy with Supernatural Squad. I need to speak to Mosburn Pralk immediately.'

There was a brief pause. Now the voice on the other end of the phone sounded more uncertain. 'Mr Pralk is busy at the moment. I can ask him to call you back within the next hour or two.'

'This is an urgent matter. I have to talk to him immediately.'

'I understand, detective, but—'

I interrupted. 'Listen.' My voice was harsh and raw. 'Lives are in danger. If you don't connect me to Pralk in the next ten seconds, I will initiate a charge of obstruction.' That would be difficult, given that I didn't know who I was talking to, but I had to say something to get through to Pralk.

The response was stiff but promising. 'I'll see what I can do.'

Tallulah's engine rumbled ominously as I changed gear. Lunchtime traffic was a bitch and unfortunately she wasn't equipped with a portable police siren, so there was little I could do to encourage the cars in front of me to get out of the way. I gripped the steering wheel as I calculated the fastest route. If I turned left up ahead, I'd avoid the inevitable snarl up at the next crossroads. I flicked on my indicator just as I heard Pralk's deep voice.

'DC Bellamy.' He sounded cold. 'Why are you threatening my staff?'

'Because I had to get through to you,' I answered shortly. 'In less than an hour, an armed gang will storm your bank. They're prepared to shoot anyone who gets in their way. Their target is the safety deposit boxes. You need to shut the building down now and get everyone to safety.'

There was a beat of strained silence before he spoke again. 'How do you know all this?'

Good question. 'I received a tip-off,' I said. 'I have every reason to believe it's genuine. You need to act now. I'm on my way to you, but it'll be at least fifteen minutes before I arrive. Shut down the bank.'

Fortunately the goblin bank manager was made of stern stuff. 'Understood. I'm hanging up now and will do as you ask.'

I breathed out. 'Thank you.' I turned left and tossed the phone onto the passenger seat. I'd barely made the turn when Tallulah spluttered. A dark spiral of smoke belched out from her crumpled bonnet. A split second later she stopped completely, coming to a dead halt in the middle of the road.

Shit. I slammed my hand on the steering wheel. Shit. Shit. I tried to re-start the engine but the only response was another plume of smoke. I leapt out without lifting the hand-brake and pushed her awkwardly to the side of the street. It was hardly expert parking but at least other vehicles could pass.

I paused to grab the phone and pick up my crossbow from the back seat, and then I began to run.

My newly enhanced phoenix skills meant that I was fast on my feet but I knew that I couldn't possibly be fast enough. I wove in and out of the pedestrians and the traffic, ignoring the cars that beeped at me in annoyance and the people who scowled. I almost got entangled with a family carrying a bunch of colourful helium-filled balloons who rounded a corner unexpectedly, and I was nearly knocked over by a Lycra-clad cyclist who'd definitely chosen the wrong place for speed training.

Despite the near collisions, I didn't give up. My feet pounded the ground and the wind whipped at my hair as I continued to sprint. A shred of tattered hope clung to my heart. Lukas had returned from the dead; the robbery hadn't yet happened; there was *always* hope.

Then my phone rang again.

I debated ignoring it but eventually I answered, although I didn't stop running. I couldn't afford to lose any more time.

'Emma.' It was Detective Superintendent Lucinda Barnes. 'What in bejesus' name is going on? Why am I watching the lunchtime news and seeing reports of a damned vampire climbing the London Eye?'

'It's not a vampire,' I said. My heart rate was rising. I swerved round yet another group of idling pedestrians and continued sprinting.

'What? How do you know that? From what I can see, he looks like a vampire.' She paused. 'Is Lord Horvath there? That man probably planned this. He probably wanted to remind the world of just how powerful the vampires are. I'm surprised he didn't arrange for a group to abseil down Big Ben at the same time.'

'DSI Barnes,' I began, 'this isn't a good time. I'm no longer at the Eye. I need to get to the Talismanic Bank. In fact, if you can send back-up there too—'

Like the worst possible case of déjà vu, I heard voices jabbering at DSI Barnes. I couldn't make out the words but I knew what they were saying.

'What?' she snapped. '*What?*'

'DSI Barnes,' I repeated. 'There's an incident about to happen at the Talismanic Bank. You need to send as many officers there as possible.'

'I don't understand what you're talking about. Besides, that bank is the supes' concern. There's a problem elsewhere that I need you to deal with. You have to get to Tower Bridge as fast as you can.'

She wasn't listening to me. It occurred to me how smart

the bank robbers had been. They'd chosen the places for their diversions to create maximum impact. Nobody wanted to see supposed supernatural crimes occurring in some of the busiest, most well-known spots in London. Unfortunately, no matter what I said to the contrary, Barnes would be no exception. Her immediate priority would always be protecting the city and its reputation.

'There are three werewolves there who've hijacked an open-top bus,' Barnes continued. 'I'll send someone to the Talismanic Bank when I get the chance. In the meantime, you need to get to Tower Bridge. Now.'

She hung up before I had the chance to say anything else. I cursed loudly. There was no point in heading to Tower Bridge; the bank was my focus now. I'd explain it to Barnes later, if I ever got the chance.

I turned right onto the main road that led to the bank. I was starting to feel breathless but it was a reaction born more from adrenaline than any physical reaction to my sustained sprint. At least from here it was a straight route all the way to Grosvenor Road and the bank – and there was a chance I'd catch a glimpse of the gang on their way either to or from the heist.

I kept my eyes peeled for a florist's van, just in case, and that was why I spotted the small boy dressed in denim dungarees and the woman by his side who was checking her phone in a distracted fashion. When the football he was hugging slipped from his arms and bounced across the road, I shouted in panic. But I was too late. He ran forward at the exact moment as a car appeared.

The accident; there had been an accident that had blocked this very road. That's why it had taken me so long to get to the Talismanic Bank the first time. Right now, I was witnessing that accident in real time.

While I watched helplessly from too far away, the car

clipped the boy's body. There was no way the driver could have stopped in time. The child was thrown up into the air, spinning helplessly as his mother let out a bloodcurdling scream when she registered what was happening.

I forced myself forward but I was already pushing myself to the limits of my physical capability. By the time I reached them, the car had already screeched to a halt and the boy was lying face down in the middle of the road. He wasn't moving.

I skidded to a stop and whipped out my phone, dialled 999 and breathlessly called for help. The mother was still screaming as she knelt at her son's side, her fingers clawing at his body. People from every direction were rushing over to try and help. But the boy's neck was at an unnatural angle and his body looked lifeless. With sinking horror, I knew any efforts to resuscitate him would be too late.

I was numb from head to toe. Towards the end of the road, the ball was still dribbling along the gutter. I knew there was nothing I could do, and that more horror that I might be able to stop might be happening at this very moment less than half a mile away. With a heavy, reluctant heart I ripped myself from the scene. That boy was dead. Oh God. That poor little boy was dead. I blinked back tears and started running again.

BY THE TIME I ARRIVED, panting, at the imposing façade of the Talismanic Bank, the crowd on the pavement told me that I'd arrived too late. Again. It was becoming the story of my life. I didn't need anyone to tell me that the bank robbers had been and gone.

The only silver lining was that Pralk had taken me at my word. Steel shutters had been dropped in front of the bank's doors and the robbers hadn't been able to get in. That meant that seven, maybe eight, people who should have been dead were still alive and well.

I pushed my way through the shocked onlookers. Right in front of the bank's steps, lying on his back, was a single corpse. It was a man wearing a black hooded top and black jogging trousers. He'd been shot in the face, causing most of his face to be obliterated. Blood was smeared on the pavement around his body.

I stared, wishing for a moment that I was anywhere else but here, then I pulled myself together and grabbed the disposable gloves I always carried. I knelt down, and fumbled with his hooded top. It took some effort but I managed to roll up the sleeve enough to reveal the tattoo on his arm: a barbed-wire heart, Adam, Jane. Huh. This was the same human who'd ended up with a bullet in his face inside the bank yesterday. Or today. Or whenever it had been.

I looked around, searching the expressions of the witnesses. 'Did anyone see what happened?'

For a moment nobody spoke then an elderly woman shuffled forward. She must have been in her eighties. She was wearing a brightly coloured, tent-like, pink dress that smothered her diminutive body. Her eyes were such a striking cornflower blue that I knew immediately that she was a pixie. I wondered if she was related to the pixie who'd been killed inside the bank the first time around.

'There was a van.' She spoke with a London accent. 'A small white van. It was driving along the road down that way,' she pointed behind her, 'when it sped up without warning. I was sure it would hit some poor pedestrian. Then that young man ran up from the same direction – he looked as if he was heading for the bank. The van stopped suddenly, the window rolled down and someone shot him. I didn't see what happened next. I was hiding. Everyone was.' Her head dropped sadly. 'But that poor boy didn't make it. One minute he was sprinting and the next…'

'Thank you,' I said quietly. 'I'll need you to make a statement later.'

'I can do that. My name is Esmeralda Strom and I live right over there.' She pointed to a black door not far down the other side of the street. She clicked her tongue. 'It's because of the bank, isn't it? It's a wonderful institution that does a lot for our community. What is society coming to when people are gunned down outside it in broad daylight?'

What indeed?

I stood up as my phone started to ring. I answered it distractedly, most of my focus still on the unfortunate Adam. It was DSI Barnes yet again. She didn't bother with any niceties.

'Would you like to explain what on earth is going on, DC Bellamy?' she snapped. 'I'm told that you abandoned the scene at the London Eye without lifting a finger to help, and that you ignored my order to go to Tower Bridge. PC Hackert is there. He can't deal with this sort of incident on his own. And what is this I'm hearing about a murder in front of the Talismanic Bank? You told me about the bank but you mentioned it before anything happened there. You need to explain yourself, Bellamy! Where are you?'

'I'm in front of the bank now.' I gestured at the gawking onlookers to move back. 'What's happening on Tower Bridge is a hoax.'

'What?' she barked. 'How can you possibly know that?'

'I can't explain right now.' I glanced up and down the street. I didn't know where the gang was but I knew where they were going. I hissed through my teeth. I needed a vehicle.

'You're on your own,' Barnes said. 'I suppose it's understandable that you're out of your depth.'

'I'm not out of my depth,' I lied.

'Whether that's true or not, other police officers are on their way to join you. It was fortunate I took you at your word earlier and arranged for CID to send a squad to the bank.'

'That's no longer necessary. I have everything under control. Please don't…'

'It's out of my hands. CID is heading your way now.'

'Let me guess,' I said through gritted teeth. 'A team headed by DI Collier.'

'How did you know that?'

Annoyed, I shook my head. 'Whatever,' I said. 'I'm leaving the scene. I think I know where the gang that's orchestrated this is heading.'

'*What*? DC Bellamy, I need you to—'

I hung up. It wasn't fair on DSI Barnes, and I knew I'd cop hell for it later on. but I wasn't in a position to give her any answers. And I had to get to that disused tunnel.

'I need a car,' I called to the crowd. 'Which one of you has something I can borrow?'

The elderly pixie shook her head and there was a discontented muttering from the other watchers. An angry-looking werewolf with a yellow zeta tag on his arm pushed forward. 'You're going to leave? There's a dead body lying in the middle of the street and you're going to steal one of our cars and walk away as if nothing's happened?'

Why was it that I always ended up with the werewolves with attitude?

'CID are on their way,' I said calmly. 'I think I know where the perps are heading. I need to get there before they do to have any chance of catching them.'

'What? How do you know that?'

I didn't bother answering, I simply gave up on the argument and stepped into the middle of the road. A small red

Smart car approached, stopped and the white-haired lady behind the wheel blinked at me. I flashed my warrant card. Her wide, frightened eyes drifted down to the crossbow I was still holding loosely in my right hand and she rolled down her window. 'What's going on? Is that a dead body? What's happening here?'

'I'm with Supe Squad, ma'am,' I said politely. 'I am commandeering this vehicle.'

Her mouth dropped open. 'What? You can't do that!'

'I certainly can. *Posse comitatus*. Power of the county. I am legally entitled to make use of any help or equipment required.'

She continued to stare at me.

'Get out of the car,' I ordered.

Shakily, she obliged. I took her place and checked the petrol gauge. The tank was full. Perfect. 'Your vehicle will be returned to you later,' I said. 'Thank you for your service to your country.'

While both the woman and the crowd stared at me in astonishment, I drove away.

As I GOT close to the old electrical tunnel, I kept my eyes peeled for any signs of smoke. My foot was pressed to the accelerator but the little Smart car was no Ferrari – it wasn't even as zippy as Tallulah – but it was better than nothing.

I overtook a slow-moving lorry with great difficulty and debated what to do if I reached the gang before they swapped vehicles and made their escape. They were armed to the teeth; supernatural prowess or not, I had no chance against them. And I already knew how determined they were to avoid arrest. The best I could do was to follow them to their destination and call in the cavalry. This time they wouldn't have the chance to set up snipers beforehand.

I smiled grimly. I still wasn't sure how this strange repeat had occurred, but I'd make the most of it. I'd foiled the robbery; now it was time to bring the perpetrators to justice.

It seemed like an age before I saw the turn off for the tunnel. There was no evidence of a burning van and I allowed myself a tiny fist pump; I'd made it in time. All I had to do was find somewhere to stop where I had a clear view of the action, then I could identify what kind of vehicle the gang had moved to and I'd have them.

Spotting a layby, I indicated hastily and pulled in. I got out and turned, shielding my eyes from the sun's glare. There: from this vantage point, I could just make out the scene below me, less than a hundred feet away. There was the tunnel and there was the florist's van. There was also a battered old family saloon – and a group of angry-looking people standing between the two vehicles and yelling at each other. There were three of them: one blonde woman; one dark-haired, heavily-built man, and one sandy-haired bloke with glasses. Gotcha.

I heard a loud toot. A moment later a car pulled into the layby behind me and a man about my age got out. 'Hi there!' He raised his hand in friendly greeting. 'Are you having car trouble? Let me help you.'

Fuck off. I forced a smile. 'I'm not having trouble, I'm absolutely fine. You can continue on your way.'

He grinned at me. 'Feminism in the twenty-first century,' he declared with a dramatic click of his tongue. 'There's no shame in asking for help, you know. You can't be expected to do everything on your own. Be grateful that I stopped. It's not every day that you get a knight in shining armour coming to your rescue. What is it? A flat tyre?' He stepped in front of me, blocking my view of the gang.

'Get out of my way,' I hissed. I tried to move to the side so I could continue to watch but he moved into my path.

'Well,' he huffed, 'if you don't want my help…'

'I don't.'

He threw up his arms, clearly annoyed at the vagaries of women, and walked to his own car. Praise be. 'Screw you!' he called over his shoulder. 'I was only trying to help!'

I waved at him then glanced back at the gang. The woman had a phone to her ear and was gesticulating with sharp, frantic movements. Who the hell was she talking to? I glanced to the right. Oh no. The other two had stopped arguing, opened the rear door of the florist's van and were hauling out a struggling woman. I focused on her face and my stomach dropped as I recognised her face. The last time I'd seen her, she'd been on a slab in Laura's morgue. It was Margaret Wick, the unfortunate woman who'd been hit by a stray bullet from inside the bank. Her luck obviously hadn't improved; this time she'd been taken hostage.

It was no doubt a move born out of panic rather than planning when the van had stopped in the middle of the street. Once they'd discovered the bank was shuttered against attack and they'd killed Adam, at least one of their number had freaked and assumed someone had tipped off the police. They'd grabbed Margaret Wick as insurance against what might happen next. The elderly pixie who'd witnessed the shooting hadn't mentioned anything like this.

I watched the scene, panic shooting through my veins. My plan to hold back then follow the gang to their hideout flew out of the window. The last thing they'd want right now was a human hostage, so her life was being measured in seconds. I couldn't stand by while they shot Margaret Wick in the head.

I moved like lightning. As the would-be Good Samaritan

finally started his engine and drove away, still glaring at me, I leapt to the Smart car and grabbed the crossbow.

I spun around, checked it was ready and took aim. Thanks to the lessons I'd received from Kennedy, I was far more adept with it than I'd been a few months earlier but that didn't mean I was an expert marksman. I'd have to be careful. I couldn't use the crossbow against anyone who wasn't supernatural – that was against the law – and this gang appeared to be human. But a woman's life was in real danger so I had to do something. I focused on my breathing. In. Out. In. Out. In. Then I pressed the trigger.

The silver-tipped bolt flew out, zipping through the air. I released my breath when it hit its intended target and embedded itself in the concrete exterior wall of the tunnel, right in the centre of the faded graffiti.

The gang scattered, dropping Margaret. Two ran for the family saloon and dived inside. I could already hear its engine starting. The other figure darted behind the florist's van. I flicked my gaze to the hapless Margaret Wick, who wasn't totally witless – she was scrambling away, one shoe on and one shoe off. She ran for the tunnel's entrance without once looking back. Good move, I decided. She was safely out of the way. That meant...

Something slammed into my shoulder. I was thrown backwards against the side of the Smart car while the shot echoed and sharp pain flooded my body. I'd erred by taking my eyes off the gang to check on Margaret. It had only been a moment – but it was enough.

I staggered up and looked over again, tears of agony blurring my vision. I glimpsed the figure emerging from behind the van and strutting towards the saloon car. The hip sway made it clear that she was female. She glanced towards me and I knew that, if I could have seen beyond her mask, I'd have seen her smile. It had taken her seconds to work out that I was alone. She got into the front passenger seat and I heard the engine start.

A lorry swept past me, its horn blaring. I lost my footing and stumbled yet again. With a great effort, I clawed my way to the driver's seat of the Smart car and fell in. Wiping my eyes, I straightened up. The saloon was already pulling out of the exit and joining the road in front of me. I swallowed and started the engine. I was in no fit shape to drive but I couldn't stay here. I had to try to follow them.

I revved the little car as hard as I could and took off. The saloon was already fifty metres in front of me. I tried to change lanes, almost hitting another car in the process, and cursed. My left arm was all but useless; changing gears and steering at the same time was almost impossible. I gritted my teeth and fought through the pain. Come on, Emma. Bloody come on.

Even in the best of circumstances, I'd have never managed it. No matter how hard I pushed the little Smart car's engine, it wouldn't do what I needed it to do. In less than a minute, the saloon had vanished. I had no number plate and no way of catching them up.

The gang had gone. And I'd failed again.

CHAPTER THIRTEEN

I CALLED FRED FROM THE SIDE OF THE ROAD AS BLOOD continued to leak from the wound in my shoulder. I'd bound it as best as I could, somehow managing to peel off my T-shirt and wrap it round the bullet hole but that was doing little to stave off the bleeding. My bra was already soaked red. Any normal person would have done the sensible thing, called an ambulance and gone to the nearest hospital. Alas, I wasn't normal.

'Boss!' Fred said, his words coming in a rush. 'I've been trying to reach you. So has Liza. I'm at Tower Bridge but I heard something went down at the Talismanic Bank. Where are you? What's going on?'

It took a great effort to get the words out. 'You need to put out an all-points bulletin,' I said. 'Family saloon car. Volvo. Three people inside, armed and dangerous.'

He sucked in a breath. 'Number plate?'

'I don't know. It was last seen heading north on the Westway towards Wormwood Scrubs. Dark blue. There's also a woman hiding in an old tunnel.' I gasped out the details about Margaret Wick.

'I'll get someone there now.' He paused. 'You don't sound very well. Are you alright?'

Another wave of pain assailed me. 'I'll be fine,' I muttered. One way or another. 'Don't worry about me.'

'What the hell kind of craziness is going on today? I've never seen anything like this shit.'

He took the words right out of my mouth. 'Yeah,' I said. 'Be careful out there, Fred. These people don't care who they kill.' I hung up; I had to go while I still had some shreds of consciousness. It was high time I got some answers.

I PULLED up in front of Devereau Webb's tower block and slumped against the steering wheel. I'd done most of the journey in a daze. I'd been as careful as I could to avoid any bumps or potholes that might cause more damage to my bleeding bullet wound, and taken care not to get close to any other road users and endanger them. The driver's seat was now sticky with blood. It wasn't a good sign. I needed to speak to Webb before I blacked out completely. I heaved myself out of the car and staggered to the tower block's main entrance.

For the first time in what seemed like days, I was in luck. As I pressed a bloody thumb on the button to call the lift, it arrived and a familiar face blinked at me. Gaz. One of Devereau Webb's men. 'Jesus,' he exclaimed. 'What the fuck's happened to you?'

I waved at him weakly. 'Webb,' I croaked. 'I need to speak to him.'

'The boss is sick,' he began. He looked at me again. 'But I think you're sicker.' He stepped forward, hooked my arm over his shoulders, and hauled me awkwardly into the lift. 'Come on then, detective.' He pressed the button for the fourteenth floor. 'Do I get a medal or summat for helping a police officer?'

I gave him a long, tired look. Gaz was as much a criminal as his boss but I supposed I should be grateful he wasn't dangling me out of a window for daring to return here.

It seemed to take an eternity for the lift to reach the right floor. I focused on breathing. Breathing was good. Oxygen was my friend. What worried me was that I wasn't in much pain – the left half of my body felt numb.

When the lift doors finally opened, Gaz almost had to drag me down the corridor. I left a bloody trail behind me. 'You know we're going to bill you for that,' he said cheerfully.

He knocked loudly on the door of flat 1412. Devereau Webb owned pretty much the entire building and moved through various properties as he saw fit. It was just as well Gaz had found me because I'd never have found Webb without him.

The door opened and the freckled face of a young girl peered out. The last time I'd seen her, she'd been pale and scrawny as leukaemia ravaged her body. Now her cheeks were glowing with healthy chubbiness and her smile was bright. Until she saw me.

'Why did you bring that pig here?' Alice asked, frowning. Then she brightened. 'She's bleeding. Did you hurt her?'

'Don't be ridiculous,' Gaz replied.

The girl shrugged but I didn't miss her worried look. She was more concerned about my well being than she was letting on. It was enough to warm the cockles of a tired, wounded police detective's heart.

'Boss,' Gaz called. 'We've got a bit of a situation here!'

Alice stepped to the side and Gaz hauled me in. I glanced round, blinking blearily before my gaze settled on Devereau Webb who was slumped on the sofa. He didn't look much healthier than I felt.

Gaz deposited me on a chair as Webb sat up. He was shirtless and I counted three wounds on his body. They looked like bite marks and I felt a deep chill run through me.

'DC Bellamy.' Webb raised an eyebrow. 'You're bleeding all over my furniture.'

'Should I fetch the doc?' Gaz enquired.

Devereau Webb looked me over. 'I think that would be a good idea.' He turned to Alice. 'This would be a good time for you to go home to your mum.'

She jumped onto the sofa beside him and stared at me with unabashed curiosity. 'I want to stay.'

'Alice.' His tone brooked no argument. 'Go.'

Alice wrinkled her nose and huffed loudly, but she did as she was told.

'Yara will come and look after you,' Webb said to me when she'd gone. 'We call her the doc, although she's not allowed to perform any deeds of derring medical do in this country legally. She was a surgeon in Syria. In this country, the most she can be is a cleaner.' His mouth turned down in disgust. 'We offered her an alternative that was more suited to her skills and she was only too pleased to take it. It's a shame our government wasn't more willing to do the same but,' he gave a half smile, 'their loss is our gain.'

This wasn't the time to get into a political discussion. I tried to sit up straight. 'What did you give me?'

'Pardon?'

'What did you give me? What did I drink?'

Webb's brow creased in confusion, then he threw back his head and laughed. 'I gave you the potion? And you drank it?' He chortled.

I failed to see what was so funny. 'Webb…'

He continued to grin. 'Presumably I didn't tell you what it could do.'

'No.'

'And presumably you were having a very bad day. I've been watching the news. Your day is still not going well.' He'd muted the television but I could see flickering images of the London Eye, Tower Bridge and the Talismanic Bank. I spotted DI Collier on the scene in front of the bank, barking out orders at some poor underling. I hoped it wasn't Molly. I turned my gaze away.

'I was considering coming to find you,' he said, still grinning broadly. 'But it appears I already did.'

A sudden wave of dizziness overtook. Damn it. I couldn't let myself pass out – I had to get answers. 'What was it? What was in that bottle?'

Devereau Webb settled back against the cushions. 'Forgive me if you've heard any of this before because I don't know what I've already told you. Or why you decided to drink what I gave you.' He linked his hands together behind his head, stretching the muscles across his chest. He was in surprisingly good shape. 'After what you did for Alice, I went in search of the book you mentioned.'

I nodded. '*Infernal Enchantments*. That part you told me.'

'Well,' he said, 'when I got hold of a copy from the Carlyle Library, I went through it.' He shook his head. 'There's some weird shit inside that book, dangerous too. You ought to be more careful, detective. Anyone could get hold of a book like that and do some bad stuff with it.'

I gritted my teeth and Webb smirked at my expression.

'I'm not normally beholden to others,' he told me. 'Under any other circumstances, I wouldn't have gone to the werewolves for help with Alice. It hurt me to ask for their assistance. It hurt me even more when they denied it. It was not a sensation I enjoyed so I decided to take matters into my own hands. When I found the Carpe Diem recipe, I knew it was exactly what I needed.'

'Carpe Diem?'

'It means seize the day.'

'I know what it means,' I snapped. 'What's in it? What does it do?'

He shrugged. 'It's mostly herbs. It's certainly not as gruesome as the potion you gave me to help Alice.'

'And?' I glowered.

'And when you drink it, your timeline is … altered. You get a repeat of the same twelve-hour period. After that, your life is yours to do with as you will.'

'I don't understand.'

'Neither do I really.' He leaned forward. 'How many times?'

'Huh?'

'How many times have you had a repeat?'

'Once.' I stared at him hard. Did that mean there was more to come?

'Then,' Webb said easily, 'you've got two more to go. The same twelve hours will repeat a further two times. That's two more chances to solve whatever this,' he gestured at my blood-covered body, 'is about. You'll remember every episode. And you'll still have that bullet wound. The day might reset, but your body won't.'

If I'd not already been experiencing it, I wouldn't have believed it was possible. 'What about everyone else?' I asked, struggling to understand what Webb was telling me and to think past the increasing pain in my shoulder. 'What do they experience?'

He pursed his lips. 'I've questioned everyone closely. As far as they're concerned, they only remember the last twelve hours that you experience, nothing else. Maybe there are parallel universes where versions of themselves continue in the original timelines. I have no idea.' He smiled disarmingly. 'I'm no quantum physicist. I don't know how it works, I only know that it does work.'

My mouth felt dry and a throbbing in my skull was getting worse. 'So it's Groundhog Day. What you've given me is a damned Groundhog Day.'

'Essentially.' Webb looked very pleased with himself.

'And you did this? You took the ... Carpe Diem potion and had the same thing happen.'

He nodded. 'I did. I survived. And I achieved what I wanted to.'

I looked at the marks on his body. I couldn't deal with Devereau Webb's subterfuge on top of everything else. 'What have you done with the book?' I whispered. 'Where is it now?'

His answer seemed to come from a long way off. 'I burned it. And I made no copies. What you're experiencing is a power that nobody should be allowed to experience. After this, there will be no more of what you took.'

'Then why do it at all? And why give it to me?'

'I owed you, DC Bellamy. Consider my debt to you paid.'

'But...'

The door to the flat opened and Gaz reappeared with a small woman in tow. 'Doc's here,' he announced.

I grimaced. I didn't want a doctor. I swung my head to Webb. Black clouds were edging around my vision. I frowned and tried to shake them off. 'But...' I tried again. 'But...'

It was no good. Darkness was overtaking me. Before I succumbed, a single image spun through my head over and over again of the small boy in dungarees as he lay motionless in the middle of a London street.

CHAPTER FOURTEEN

This time, the sunlight streaming in through Tallulah's windows was almost blinding. My radio crackled. In the nick of time, I pressed down hard on the brake pedal. Tallulah's bonnet nudged forward, gently kissing the rear of the taxi in front of me.

While the burly taxi driver flung open his door and stormed out to check the damage, my fingers went to my shoulder to examine the spot where the bullet had entered. My T-shirt was clean and undamaged, although the gunshot wound was definitely still there. It was tender to my touch and, although it appeared much less serious than it had been the day before, it ached painfully.

Devereau Webb had been right: not everything was wiped clean when the day reset itself. It also explained his own collection of wounds – and it suggested that Dr Yara had worked on me at Webb's flat while I was unconscious. I definitely hadn't died, and I must have received a good few blood transfusions.

The taxi driver rapped hard on the window. 'You ought to

be more careful!' he yelled. 'You could have done some real damage!'

Yeah, yeah. I raised a hand in apology as the radio crackled again. I checked the clock. I didn't have long. I crossed my fingers and prayed that Devereau Webb had been telling the whole truth and I still had another repeat after this one. A moment later I pulled out, almost hitting the fuming taxi driver, and sped off towards the London Eye.

This time I took more care with my parking. Rather than simply slide Tallulah into the first available space closest to the Eye, I performed a U-turn and found a spot on the opposite side of the road. It took more time than I wanted to waste but it would be worth it. Once I left this scene, I wanted to be sure that I could get to the Talismanic Bank before the gang arrived. Even coming to the London Eye was a risk but, given the little information I'd managed to glean so far, it felt like a risk worth taking.

I waited for a break in the traffic then crossed the road to the police cordon. I could already see the black-clad figure clambering up the London Eye. I hoped I was right about this.

Sliding out my warrant card, I waved it at the police officer. The same police officer. He nodded and gestured me through. I jogged down to the bottom of the wheel where Paige, Mr Hannigan and Lukas were having their argument.

'You have to get that idiot down!' Hannigan shouted. 'There are news crews here already. This isn't the sort of publicity we need right now!'

'Are you suggesting, Mr Hannigan,' Lukas enquired, 'that the pages of tomorrow's newspapers are more important than a person's life? Perhaps we should hope for a gust of wind to knock the poor fellow off his perch? Then you can clean up the bloodied mess of brains and splattered internal organs while the tourists get back on board for their selfies.'

'I'm Detective Constable Emma Bellamy,' I stepped between the pair of them. 'I'm with Supe Squad. I'm assuming full control for this situation. Nobody needs to worry, everything will be resolved shortly.'

Lukas seemed surprised by my calm confidence. 'Unless it's resolved with that vampire being brought down safely, I think there's every need to worry.'

'Agreed,' Hannigan growled.

Paige plucked at her sleeves, flicking nervy glances at Lukas when she thought he wasn't looking. I simply smiled serenely. The more I saw of Lukas in that daft shirt, the more I enjoyed the sight. Especially when he was still breathing.

'How are you, Emma?' he was watching me carefully. 'You've been avoiding my calls.'

'We'll discuss it later. I'll explain about the kiss, too.'

His inky black eyebrows shot up to his head. 'Kiss? What kiss?'

Oops. I'd momentarily forgotten myself there. I felt my cheeks redden and I coughed. Now I was acting like Paige. 'Uh, never mind,' I muttered. I stepped back and looked up. 'I'm going to climb up and encourage the … vampire down.'

'You're going to do *what*?' Lukas snapped.

Hannigan looked relieved. 'Good,' he said. 'Anything to bring that freak down.'

I nodded, strode over to the steel structure and placed one foot on it. My shoulder was hurting a lot more now. I hoped I wouldn't have to clamber very high because I doubted I'd reach the heights I had before.

'Emma,' Lukas said, 'what the fuck do you think you're doing?'

'I've told you before, I prefer it when you call me D'Artagnan.' I glanced at him. 'I'll have a wee chat with your vamp and do what I can to persuade him to climb down to solid ground.'

'Don't be an idiot. You might fall.'

I paused. 'Hmm,' I said. 'Okay. Do you have a head for heights? Do you think *you* could climb up?'

He looked at me suspiciously. I didn't normally back down from a challenge so quickly and Lukas knew it. 'What's going on, Emma?'

'You're going to climb up a famous London landmark to retrieve a vampire who seems to have a death wish.' I smiled. 'I'll wait down here. Just in case.'

'In case of what? Are you planning to catch him if he jumps?'

I gave a fake laugh and started climbing. Lukas watched me for a moment, aware that something odd was going on. He'd never begin to guess what, however.

'Very well,' he muttered as he reached up. I marvelled at how easy he made it look, not to mention the way his muscles strained and the ruffles on his daft shirt flapped in the breeze. He wouldn't look out of place striding across moors in a gothic novel. I gazed up at him fondly, then I realised what I was doing. Experiencing Lukas's death had clearly erased my desire to maintain a distance from the vampire Lord.

'He's amazing,' Paige breathed. 'I've never been this close to a vampire before. He's so handsome. And strong.'

Mmm-hmm. I couldn't blame her for her reaction when I felt the same. I smiled tightly.

'How long will this take?' Hannigan barked. He wasn't eyeing up Lukas's athletic build or tight muscles; his only concerns were revenue and reputation.

I glanced at my watch. 'About thirteen minutes,' I said, 'give or take.' I turned on my heel and walked towards the cordon. I'd take the long way round.

I ignored the strange looks from the other police officers. Assuming nothing sent him off course, I knew exactly where the fake vampire was planning to go. When Lukas got high enough, the 'vamp' would climb down, jump the security barrier and run away. I would stop that from happening.

I followed the path to the other side of the security barrier until I was at the exact spot where the black-clad, rubber-fanged bloke had escaped the first time. The Thames glittered in the sunlight; pleasure boats and tourist vessels chugging past. I angled my head upwards. Lukas had reached the glass pod with the gaping family inside. I crossed my fingers tightly and slid out my phone. There was more that I had to do.

'Fred,' I said, the second he answered, 'I need you to listen very carefully. In about fifteen minutes' time, you'll be called to an incident on Tower Bridge. Three werewolves are about to hijack a bus there.'

'*What?*'

'They're not werewolves,' I said, 'and you need to ignore the call.'

'*What?*'

'Instead,' I continued, not responding to his shocked disbelief, 'you must get to the Talismanic Bank. A trio of bank robbers is planning to storm it, shoot a bunch of people and steal the contents of several safety deposit boxes.'

'*Whaaaat?*'

I kept my eyes trained upwards. There. I breathed out. The would-be jumper was coming down. I had to be ready.

'Get everyone out of the bank,' I ordered.

'I'll speak to the manager. I'll get the bank shut down and—'

'No,' I said. 'That won't work. I want to catch the bastards during the robbery. Just get everyone to safety and clear the street. Get back-up from DSI Barnes, if you can.'

'You know I trust you, boss. But the manager of the Talismanic Bank is never going to shut down the entire building on my say-so.'

I nodded, my gaze continuing to track the black-clad figure. Lukas was doing a good job of reversing and catching him up – but I knew it wouldn't be good enough.

'Tell the manager, Mosburn Pralk, that the contents of the bank's own deposit box are in danger, and that he wouldn't want the names of every supe with an account advertised to the world.'

'I don't understand.'

'You don't have to,' I said briskly. 'Just tell him and he'll do what you say. Then get out of there. The robbers are armed and very dangerous.'

'Boss…'

I didn't have time for a discussion. The fake vampire had stopped about fifteen metres from the ground and was preparing to jump. I ended the call and got ready.

'Left!' Lukas yelled from above, his voice indistinct. 'Go left!'

The dangling figure pushed away from the wheel and jumped. My view of his landing was obscured by the barrier between us, but I didn't need to see it to know he'd nailed it.

I heard shouts and the sound of feet pounding on the tarmac, then fingers appeared above me and curled over the top of the barrier. In one smooth movement, the hooded bloke leapt over. He noticed me a second too late. My hand snapped forward and caught his arm. I wrenched it back and forced him face down onto the ground.

'You're nicked,' I said with satisfaction. I took a plastic cuff from my pocket and looped it round his wrists before yanking him to his feet and spinning him round to face me.

I looked him up and down, then pulled up his sleeve as far it would go. I couldn't see the whole tattoo but I could see enough. I knew exactly who this was. Alive, and with his facial features intact, he was younger than I'd expected. His face still displayed the last vestiges of adolescent acne.

'It might not feel like it right now but today's your lucky day, Adam,' I said.

His expression, which had been one of pure hatred, turned to blank astonishment. 'How do you know my name?'

I answered his question with a smile, then marched him up the path towards Tallulah. We didn't get very far before a group of police officers ran up.

'You got him!'

I nodded. 'I'm taking him away for questioning. Clear up the mess here and get the wheel moving again so those people in the pods can get down to solid ground.' I continued moving, my grip on Adam's arm tight and unyielding. There wasn't a lot of time to spare and I couldn't waste the precious seconds I had in unnecessary discussions.

Lukas appeared a moment later. He looked at Adam and his black eyes narrowed. 'You're no vampire,' he said angrily. His hands curled into fists.

'No,' I said cheerfully. I kept moving, dragging Adam with me. 'He's not.'

'Emma.' Lukas's voice was terse. 'Will you stop for a moment, please?'

'There's no time. We have to get going.'

'Get going where?'

I didn't answer. Lukas put out a hand to stop me. When he touched my shoulder, I winced involuntarily and he froze. He raised his fingers and sniffed them. 'I smell blood,' he said darkly. 'Your blood.'

I shook him off, reached the pavement and quickly looked both ways before crossing over to Tallulah.

'Goddamnit, Emma!' Lukas exploded. 'What's the rush? What's going on?'

I opened the driver's door, pulled back the seat and threw

Adam into the back. 'There's no room in here!' he protested. 'And is that a fucking crossbow? What is this shit? This is against my human rights!'

'He has a point,' Lukas said. 'An old Mini Cooper is hardly effective prisoner transport. There are plenty of police cars around. Use one of those, or let me get my car.'

'There's no time.' I climbed in and fastened my seatbelt. I glanced at Lukas. 'Are you coming or not?'

He offered me a black-eyed glare before walking round and getting into the passenger seat. Tallulah was already moving before he closed the door. 'Emma…!'

I accelerated as I checked the clock and estimated our arrival time. The gang were due to enter the bank at 1.34pm. There wasn't long to go. I accelerated harder. As I did so, my phone rang.

'Are you going to answer that?' Lukas enquired through gritted teeth.

'It's only Barnes,' I said, swerving left and then right. I kept my eyes on the road but I could still feel his glare.

'What,' he bit out in a voice that was seething with anger, 'the fuck is going on?'

'Buckle up,' I said. 'And I'll tell you.'

CHAPTER FIFTEEN

I GAVE HIM THE CONDENSED VERSION. AFTER I'D FINISHED, Lukas folded his arms and glowered. 'You have a bullet wound in your shoulder and you're speeding through the streets of London? You need to get to a hospital.'

Adam piped up from the back seat. 'That's what you get from that story? That she's been shot in the shoulder? How about the fact that she's telling us she's re-lived the same day three times? Or that I'm supposedly in collusion with a gang of bank robbers? I've never heard anything so fucking stupid.'

'You might want to keep your voice down back there,' I said. 'The reason I know your name is from the tattoo on your arm. The one that I saw both times after you were shot in the face. What's happened to Jane? Does she know you're doing this?'

'You're a lying bitch. Have you been bugging the shop? Is that what this is?'

Lukas opened his mouth but I shook my head in warning. I waited, hoping Adam would reveal more. When he didn't, I shrugged and glanced at Lukas. 'You have a safety deposit

138

box filled with information about me. At some point we're going to have words about that.'

Lukas was silent for a moment. 'What about the kiss?' he asked finally, his voice tight with tension.

'Pardon?'

'Earlier you said something about a kiss.'

I concentrated harder on the road ahead. 'That was yesterday, the second time I went through this. After you died, I was just happy to see you. That's all.' I sneaked a look in his direction. He wasn't smiling but I was certain I saw the glitter of satisfaction in his eyes.

'This is bullshit,' Adam declared.

We zipped past the people carrying a bunch of brightly coloured helium balloons and chattering eagerly to each other. I turned onto the main road then I slammed on the brakes. 'Wait here,' I muttered.

I unclipped my seatbelt, jumped out and ran across the road. The mother, whose screams from yesterday still echoed through my head, was running an exasperated hand through her hair. 'Look,' she said into her phone, 'I'm here with Alfie and we're on our way to the park. I can't stand here all day talking to you. I need that money back. I've got bills to pay.'

I sent her a sympathetic glance as I knelt down so I was face to face with little Alfie. He blinked up at me with blue eyes that perfectly matched the denim of his dungarees. His mum looked at me warily as I smiled at her. A moment later, I snatched the ball out of Alfie's hands and strode away with it. He began to bawl while his mum yelled after me. 'What do you think you're doing? That's my son's! You stole my son's football!'

I ignored her and got into Tallulah, throwing the ball into the back where it landed next to Adam. Up and down the street, people were staring at us.

'And you think I'm a criminal,' Adam muttered. 'That nutter just robbed a kid's toy.'

I'd omitted the small boy from my brief explanation earlier. I shrugged and got Tallulah moving again. Lukas sent me a curious frown but remained silent. I knew that his lack of censure meant he'd believed every word I'd told him. It was surprising how much that pleased me.

With eight minutes to spare, we pulled into the street where the Talismanic Bank was located. I spotted Fred ushering a few people away; they didn't look very happy about it, but at least they were doing as they were told. When he caught sight of us, his expression transformed with relief.

I parked beside him, jumped out and snagged the crossbow. I was going to need it. 'Good work,' I said. I pointed to the back seat. 'That's Adam. I don't know his last name but he's under arrest. Charge him and take him to Supe Squad.'

'We don't have proper facilities to hold detainees,' Fred protested.

I shook my head. 'That doesn't matter right now.'

'What's he under arrest for?'

I shrugged. 'Impersonating a vampire.'

Fred blinked. 'Is that illegal?'

Not in the slightest. I tossed him the car keys and chose not to answer. 'Is the bank clear?'

'Yes – but Mr Pralk is very upset.'

'He'll get over it.'

I ran toward the imposing building. Lukas ran with me. 'I can get my people here,' he began.

'No.'

'Emma…'

'These people are prepared to kill. There's not enough time to create adequate protection. I've thought about this over and over, Lukas. I could have called in an armed response unit but the result would be a bloodbath, even if

140

they got here in time. Besides,' I added in a harder voice, 'if Devereau Webb is right, I've got one more shot at this day.'

'And what happens if you die?' Lukas asked, as we reached the bank's steps. 'Do you still resurrect? Does the day still reset?'

'I don't know,' I replied grimly. I glanced at him. 'But I'm not planning on dying.'

'You'd better not,' he growled.

I paused, meeting his eyes. 'You're in more danger of that than I am,' I said quietly.

'If it means I get a kiss, that's a risk I'm willing to take.'

I frowned – and then we entered the bank where Mosburn Pralk was waiting.

Unlike the first time we'd met, the thin golden-skinned goblin looked angry rather than upset. 'This is completely unorthodox,' he hissed. 'Supe Squad or not, I fail to see how the police can demand that we get rid of all our customers! And how the hell do you know what's inside our safety deposit box in our own bank?' His voice rose with every word. A vein was bulging at the side of his head; it was hard not to stare at it.

'In little more than five minutes' time,' I said calmly, 'three armed robbers will enter this building. They're prepared to kill anyone who gets in their way, inside or outside the bank. Their target is the safety deposit box room. They're planning to steal the box that belongs to the bank, the three boxes used by Lord Horvath,' I nodded at Lukas, 'the two boxes belonging to Lady Sullivan and the two belonging to Lord Fairfax, Lord McGuigan's single box and also Lady Carr's.'

My knowledge of the number of safety deposit boxes each supe leader owned caused Pralk to hesitate, though not for long. 'How do you know all this?' he asked, with the sort of faint sneer that only a goblin could pull off. This was a different man to the one I'd met the first time around. He was defensive and rather annoyed, but that was better than the terrified, grieving and horror-struck version.

'Let's just say I had a tip off.' To suggest anything else would lead to more questions than I could answer.

'You can trust DC Bellamy,' Lukas interjected. 'I give you my word that she is speaking the truth. This is a very serious matter.'

Pralk's green eyes fixed on him. 'Far be it for me to argue with Lord Horvath,' he muttered. 'Very well. How are you going to manage this situation?'

'There are no customers left in the building?' I asked.

'None.'

'And your employees?'

'I've sent them all out, too. We have a muster point in the park down the road. They're waiting there.'

I nodded. 'Make sure they stay there and don't come back.' I looked round. 'How do you operate the external shutters?'

'There's a button behind the first teller's chair.'

'Okay. How long do they take to close?'

Lukas looked at me sharply. 'You're planning to get the robbers inside and trap them here?'

'Yep.'

'Is that wise if they're carrying guns?'

'It is if you make damned sure you don't get shot again.'

Lukas jerked his thumb at my shoulder. 'Speak for yourself.'

Pralk started. I glanced down and saw a dark patch on my T-shirt. I wasn't losing a lot of blood, but there was enough for me to know that I wouldn't be wearing this T-shirt again.

I brushed off Lukas's concern. 'I'll get it bandaged later.' I raised my eyebrows at Pralk. 'So? How long do the shutters take to close?'

He swallowed. He finally seemed to be taking matters

seriously. 'They're designed to be used in an emergency. From the moment the button is pressed until the shutters are sealed is less than four seconds.'

I could work with that. 'Thank you.' I checked my watch. Three minutes to go. I nodded at the doors. 'Go and join your staff in the park. Lord Horvath and I will manage on our own.'

Mosburn Pralk drew back his shoulders and his eyes took on a steely glint. He hadn't risen to the lofty position of manager of the Talismanic Bank for nothing. 'I most certainly will not,' he said stiffly. 'This is my bank and I'm not leaving.'

'You can trust us. It's in your best interests to go.'

He glared at me and I sighed. There wasn't enough time to argue. 'Very well.' I glanced round, checking the layout. 'I'll head behind that pillar. Lukas, you can take up position on the opposite side. Mr Pralk, if you take the bank teller's chair behind the glass screen then you can control the shutters. The glass there isn't bullet proof, so you'll have to be careful.'

He stared. 'How do you know the glass isn't bullet proof?'

I didn't waste time or breath in answering. 'Make sure you wait until all three robbers are well inside before you close the shutters. We don't want them escaping onto the street. My colleague evacuated most of the pedestrians but he's gone now. The last thing we need is for any innocent passers-by to be caught in the crossfire. Or,' I added, thinking of Margaret Wick, 'taken hostage.'

Lukas looked at me grimly. 'These guys are serious.'

'Yeah,' I said. My mouth flattened. 'They are.'

CHAPTER SIXTEEN

I PRESSED MY SPINE AGAINST THE COOL MARBLE PILLAR AND double-checked my crossbow. It was loaded and ready, though with any luck I wouldn't have to use it. The gang would quickly realise that we'd trapped them. According to what Liza had seen on the CCTV footage from the first time the robbery took place, they'd only started shooting when Toffee, the Fairfax beta who'd been waiting in line, had decided to play hero and attack. If we could avoid anything similar happening, they might surrender. Might. It was unlikely, but I was still optimistic.

My biggest concern was Lukas. He'd already been killed once because of these bastards. I wasn't sure I could cope with watching him die a second time.

I felt his eyes on me and glanced over. He flashed me a grin then blew me a kiss. I blinked and pulled back, feeling myself blush. Don't be so stupid, Emma, I told myself. *Carpe diem*. I sucked in a breath, returned his look and blew him a kiss in return. His grin broadened. From the bank teller's chair, Mosburn Pralk frowned.

I glanced at my watch. 1.33pm. I estimated that the gang

were now seconds away. My heart thudded against my chest, my adrenaline firing on all cylinders. I shifted my weight onto the balls of my feet. Any second now. Any … second…

'Hello? Is anyone there?'

I spun round, jumping out from behind the pillar with my crossbow raised. 'Police!' I yelled. Then I recognised the man: he was one of the McGuigan werewolves. The last time I'd seen him, he'd been lying by the exit on this very floor and he'd been *very* dead. Fuck.

'Get out,' I hissed.

The wolf stared at me. 'Huh?'

'Get. Out. Of. Here.' I tried to use my innate power to compel him to leave but I was too tense. My words echoed emptily around the hall and he didn't budge an inch.

'I've got to deposit a cheque,' he said with a tiny pout. 'You can't make me leave. I've got every right—'

Lukas stepped out from behind his pillar. 'Leave. Turn round and go outside now.' This time, the wolf paled and did as he was told. 'See?' Lukas offered me an arch grin. 'Sometimes I have my uses.'

I managed a tight smile and waved him back to his hiding place. The gang would appear at any moment. In the next ten seconds or so all hell would break loose. I waited, poised and ready.

Nothing happened.

From behind the glass screen, Pralk looked at me pointedly, as if demanding to know what was going on. I avoided his eyes and checked my watch again: 1.34pm. It was time – so where were they?

I waited. More seconds ticked by and it was 1.35pm. What the hell was going on? I shook my head. What had changed?

A moment later, I had a chilling thought. The collision that had resulted in little Alfie's death had caused a traffic jam. Anyone heading for this area would have been delayed. But I'd prevented the accident – and that meant that not only was Alfie alive but the roads were clear. The bank robbers would have arrived earlier than 1.34pm – except there was no sign of them. It wasn't that they were late; it was because they weren't coming.

'I don't understand,' I whispered. 'I don't understand why they haven't come.'

Lukas looked concerned. Pralk merely glowered. 'They're not here, detective.'

I ground my teeth. 'I know.'

'My staff and customers have been thrown out, you have made dire warnings of death and larceny, and yet nobody is here. Nothing has happened.' He flashed his green eyes at Lukas. 'Lord Horvath, you told me I could trust this woman. I'm beginning to feel like this is nothing more than a very sick joke. Your supposed tip off…'

I pushed myself away from the pillar. 'Tip off,' I breathed. Goddamnit. Either someone outside had been keeping watch or it was indeed an inside job and one of the bank employees had contacted the robbers. Someone had seen Fred clear the street and speak to Pralk. Maybe they'd watched Lukas and me enter the bank's front doors. It was the only thing that made sense. My tongue darted out to wet my dry lips. I'd screwed everything up. *Fuck*.

'Emma?' Lukas asked.

I cleared my throat and thought aloud. 'The first time they came into the bank at 1.34pm. Everyone, including Adam, was killed inside this building. The only other death was Margaret Wick, and she was killed by a stray bullet.'

Pralk stared at me. Lukas waited.

'The second time,' I continued, 'the van came down this street at high speed.' I paused. 'At high bloody speed.' I passed a hand over my eyes. 'They already knew the bank had been shuttered and they weren't planning to stop. But when they saw Adam run up, they took the time to stop driving and shoot him. That's when they must have grabbed Margaret Wick. Three robbers here, three on Westminster Bridge – but there was also that damned sniper. Where was the sniper when the robbery was taking place the first time around?'

'What in the name of all that is holy are you talking about?' Pralk asked.

I didn't answer, I simply turned on my heel and ran for the door.

The street outside was bathed in sunshine. It bounced off the nearby windows and the few trees dotted along the pavement threw dappled shade on the ground below. There was nobody nearby. I squinted, searching desperately for anything or anyone that looked out of place. I spotted a woman walking towards me, a distant expression on her face. Margaret Wick, alive and well. I exhaled loudly and moved so she could pass. She smiled vaguely at me in thanks and continued on her way.

'You think someone is out here watching us right now?'

Lukas's voice made me jump. I nodded and continued to scan the street as I curled my hands into fists. I couldn't see anything suspicious. They could be long gone by now. I had no way of knowing. 'I'm not making this up, Lukas. The robbery happened. You were killed.'

His voice was quiet. 'I believe you.'

I pressed my palms into my temples. I could jump in Tallulah and head back to the old disused tunnel and try to catch the gang there, but that hadn't exactly worked the first time around. Anyway, I suspected that if they did swap cars on this occasion I'd already be too late. They'd been warned off.

There was only one thing – or rather one man – that I

had now that I hadn't had before. 'I have to get to Supe Squad and speak to Adam,' I said.

'The fake vampire.' There was a curl of distaste in Lukas's voice.

'The one and only.'

'Then let's go.' He smiled at me. 'The day's not over yet. And if Devereau Webb is telling the truth, you still have one more chance after today.'

I set my mouth into a thin line. He was right. Detective Constable Emma Bellamy, D'Artagnan to some of her friends, was not defeated yet. Not by a long shot.

MAX, the liveried bellman at the hotel next to the Supe Squad building whose duties normally involved opening the door for guests and welcoming them in, as well as arranging for transportation and sorting out luggage, gave me a friendly wave. 'It's busy at your place today.'

'Busy is one word for it. Are you well?'

'Always.' He tipped his hat. 'Keep those streets safe, detective.'

I grinned. Max glanced at Lukas, obviously recognised him and inclined his head respectfully. He was considerably nicer than his night-time counterpart. Lukas passed a few pleasantries while I opened the Supe Squad door, the familiar smell of verbena and wolfsbane tickling my nostrils.

We'd barely moved halfway down the corridor when Fred appeared from the office, his anxious expression smoothing into relief when he saw us. 'There you are,' he said, suddenly smiling. 'What the hell has been happening? Was something going down at the Talismanic Bank?'

I grimaced. 'Not exactly. It's a long story.'

Liza appeared behind Fred. Unlike him, she wasn't smiling. 'The phone has been ringing off the hook! First there was that idiot at the London Eye, then a bunch of idiots dressed up as werewolves at Tower Bridge. I've had DSI Barnes screaming at me to find you. She says you're not answering your phone.' She put her hands on her hips and glared. 'And what is Lord Horvath doing here?'

Lukas smiled at her. 'Good to see you again, Liza.'

She sniffed imperiously. 'I suppose you're both going to want a coffee. I'm telling you now that I don't have any biscuits. Or cake. There's definitely no cake.'

'Coffee would be great,' I said. 'Thank you.'

She sniffed again and whirled away. Fred shrugged amiably. 'I put that Adam guy into Interview Room 1.' He pointed at the closed door. 'He's not very happy. He kept talking about making a formal complaint about police brutality and unfair arrest. I checked up, you know. It's not illegal to impersonate a vampire.'

'No,' I agreed. 'But he did trespass on private property and climb up the London Eye while pretending to be a vamp. We need to focus on the vamp part before CID or Barnes or whoever start asking questions and take him away from us.' My voice hardened. 'I have to speak to him before that happens.'

We walked into the office. Liza had flicked on the kettle. She straightened up hastily from the fridge and turned to face us. It looked to me as if she'd been shoving in a chocolate cake. I suppressed a smile.

'Okay,' I said. 'I understand you both have a lot of questions. I've already explained to Lord Horvath what's happened.' I swallowed. 'I don't have a lot of time to go into details but essentially I took a strange potion from Devereau Webb and drank it. This is the third time I've experienced this same twelve-hour period. At midnight tonight, my day will re-set itself and I'll experience it again for one final time.'

I paused to allow both Fred and Liza to absorb my words then I continued. 'A gang of bank robbers set up the events at the London Eye and Tower Bridge so that they could pull off a heist at the Talismanic Bank. For whatever reason, during this episode that we're experiencing now they've not attacked the bank. Someone probably tipped them off that we were inside waiting for them. I need to find out who the gang is so that I can stop them when they try again. Got that?'

Liza and Fred stared at me. The kettle whistled and Lukas ambled over, reaching behind Liza to switch it off. 'I'll make the coffee, shall I?' he said to no one in particular.

Fred cleared his throat. 'You're living the same day over and over again,' he said.

'Yep.'

'Like…' His voice trailed off and he struggled to find the words.

'Like Groundhog Day,' I supplied helpfully.

He swallowed. 'And this happened because of some concoction you got from Devereau Webb?'

'Yep.'

'Can I get some?'

I blinked. 'Pardon?'

His expression was suddenly animated. 'Imagine the possibilities! If I could re-live the same day then I could go after Scarlett. I could try different ways of getting her to go out with me again.'

I glanced at Lukas. To his credit, he appeared not to be listening. Given that I was fairly certain he had ordered Scarlett to stop toying with Fred and to stay away from him, that was a good thing.

'That ship has sailed,' Liza said. 'Forget her.' She looked at me. 'Can I get some?'

'Uh…'

'I only need it to work once. Choose the right day and have knowledge of the national lottery numbers and,' she waved her arms, 'I'll never have to work here with you people ever again.'

This time all three of us looked at her. She caught our look and shrugged. 'Hey,' she said, 'don't take it personally. Besides, I promise I'll cut you all in.'

I shook my head in amusement. It was a measure of what life was like in Supe Squad that neither of them questioned the veracity of what I'd told them. They didn't even ask for proof. Then again, they also knew that I could die and come back to life again. I supposed re-living the same day over and over was mundane compared to repeatedly cheating death.

'I don't know what was in the potion,' I said. 'Webb told me he's destroyed the copy of *Infernal Enchantment* that gave him the recipe. Once all this is over, I'll make damned sure that nobody else ever gets their hands on that bloody book. It's too dangerous.' I was glad that I had these chances to stop the robbers and keep Lukas alive, but I was well aware that the opportunity to replay events to my personal satisfaction could cause chaos. I'd reap the benefits now – but I was going to destroy every copy of that damned book and remove the temptation of attempting to replicate this bizarre scenario ever again.

'Our focus,' I said, getting back to the matter in hand, 'needs to be tracking down the robbers so that I can stop them and bring them into custody when the day resets again.' I turned to Liza. 'They use a florist's van to get to and from the bank, then they swap it for an old blue Volvo. I don't have number plates for either vehicle but I know the florist's van was taken from the East End so—'

Liza interrupted. 'I'll search recent reports of any stolen vans in that area and then locate CCTV to see if I can find any Volvos nearby. We might get lucky.'

'Thank you. Fred, you and I will question our London Eye gymnast.'

'What's his involvement?'

'I'm not quite sure yet, but he's already ended up being shot in the face twice. That can't be a coincidence. The costumed wolves at Tower Bridge were drama students. I suspect that Adam is something different.' I bared my teeth; I could play predator when the need arose. 'We'll soon find out.'

Lukas raised an eyebrow. 'What shall I do?'

I looked at him innocently. 'You're making coffee.'

Fred and Liza jerked in horror but Lukas merely laughed. 'That I am.'

I grinned. 'You can go home, Lord Horvath. We've got this.'

'And if I choose to stay?'

I met his eyes. 'That's your prerogative.'

'Then perhaps I'll hang around.' He dug a phone out of his pocket. 'I'll use the time to track down various contacts. Someone might know who these bastards are.'

My grin softened into something else. He gazed back at me, tiny crow's feet crinkling the corners of his eyes. I had to fight the temptation to walk over and brush them with a feather-light kiss.

'I wish I knew what you were thinking,' Lukas murmured.

I licked my lips. 'I…'

Liza coughed loudly. 'Save the drooling over each other for later, will you?'

Fred stifled a laugh.

Pulling back my shoulders, I pretended that I was completely unflustered. 'There is no drooling. Come on, Fred. Let's see what our fake vampire has to say for himself.'

CHAPTER SEVENTEEN

FRED AND I SAT DOWN OPPOSITE ADAM. HE WAS SLUMPED IN his chair with an expression that wavered between seething rage and overwhelming boredom. 'You've been holding me here for hours!' he said indignantly.

Hardly. 'And you'll be held for years if I have anything to say about it,' I snarled.

Fred sent me a worried look before addressing our prisoner. 'Would you like anything to drink? You've got water, but I can fetch you a tea or coffee if you'd prefer.'

Adam's gaze shifted slightly. 'The water's fine.'

'Ice?' I asked. 'A little paper umbrella at the side? A slice of lemon, maybe?'

'Boss...' Fred murmured.

I ignored him. Adam glared.

'I know PC Hackert took your fingerprints when he brought you in,' I said. 'We're running them through the system – we'll find out who you really are soon enough. So why don't you tell us your full name now?'

Adam didn't answer. He had perfected the art of the

sullen pout and it made him look younger than he really was, more like an angst-ridden teenager than a grown man.

Fred leaned forward. 'It'll be easier on you later if you cooperate with us now,' he said gently.

The seconds ticked by. 'Jones,' he muttered finally. 'My name is Adam Jones.'

'Explain to us, Mr Jones,' I said, 'what you were doing at the London Eye today.'

He sneered at me defiantly. 'I was climbing it.'

'Why?'

His nostrils flared. He was starting to hate me. That was good. 'It was there,' he said, taunting me.

I leaned forward until I was nose to nose with him. 'Cut the cutesy act. We know you weren't planning to jump off the Eye and kill yourself, and we know you were passing yourself off as a vampire. Do you want to be a supe, Adam? Is that what this is about? Do you really think that the vamps would want someone like you in their ranks?'

'I don't want to be a fucking bloodsucker,' he spat.

'Then why pretend to be one?'

He looked away. 'I ain't saying nothing.'

I huffed and got to my feet. 'This is a waste of time. I'm going to see if my coffee is ready.' I pushed back my chair and stalked out of the room. The door closed behind me. As Lukas handed me a steaming mug, I pressed my ear against it so I could listen in. It would have been a lot easier if we'd had a two-way mirror but instead I had to eavesdrop the old-fashioned way.

'Being bad cop doesn't suit you,' Lukas murmured.

I made a face at him. I'd not particularly enjoyed it but it suited Fred even less. I pressed a finger to my lips and strained to hear what was going on.

'Sorry,' Fred said. 'She's under a lot of pressure.'

'She's a bitch.'

Fred didn't disagree. 'It's impressive, what you did. I wasn't at the Eye but I saw it on television afterwards. You climbed up really high and you did it without a net. Are you a gymnast?'

'Free runner,' Adam Jones answered.

Fred gave a low whistle. 'Impressive. Is that why the gang got you involved? Because of your free-running skills?'

'It's one of the reasons.'

Fred waited, stretching out the silence to encourage Jones to fill it. It worked.

'They didn't respect what I could do. They thought it was easy, but that shit is a lot harder than it looks.'

'I'll bet.'

I nodded approvingly. Fred had injected just the right note of admiration into his voice.

'With skills like yours,' he continued, 'you must be a real asset to that team, whether they realise it or not.'

'They don't realise it. They were trying to keep me out of the way. I wasn't supposed to know what they were doing but I overheard them when they were talking about it. They tried to shut me out but I wasn't having any of it. I ain't stupid.'

'No,' Fred said. 'I don't believe you are.' There was a pause. 'I'm not supposed to tell you this,' he said carefully, 'but DC Bellamy told me there's a chance you'll be charged with terrorism.'

'*What?*' Adam Jones's voice grew louder. 'That's not fair! I didn't threaten anyone! I didn't hurt anyone!'

'We've been bugging the shop for some time,' Fred said, taking what little Jones had already revealed to us and using it against him in a deft lie. 'It's how we already knew your first name. In fact, we know more than you think – and it's not good. We know they were planning to kill you, Adam.'

There were several beats of silence before Adam spoke

again. 'She said in the car that she'd been shot. She said that she'd taken some magic potion and kept re-living the same day over and over again.'

'She only said that because she thought you were gullible enough to believe it. DC Bellamy was trying to get you to talk. She didn't realise how smart you really are.'

'I knew it!' he burst out. 'I knew all that was a lie!'

'Desperate times call for desperate measures. I don't want you to become collateral damage, Adam. None of this was your fault. All you did was go for a climb.'

'Exactly! I'm not a terrorist! I'm not a bad person! I just wanted to make some fucking money.'

'I can't blame you for that,' Fred soothed. 'But the London Eye is a big tourist landmark. Between you and the students who pretended to be werewolves on Tower Bridge, half of London was brought to a standstill. People are jumpy these days. I think the charges might stick.'

'No way, man. No way. I want a lawyer. Get me a solicitor now. I'm not saying anything else.'

'If that's what you want,' Fred said calmly, 'that can certainly be arranged. Either way, if you tell us the whole truth about what really happened, we can find a way to make the charges disappear. I bet that if you tell DC Bellamy everything you know, she'll let you walk.'

'Really?'

'Really. You're not the priority here, Adam. It's the bastards who put you up to this and who don't respect what you're capable of who are the *real* criminals.'

'You're right. They're the ones who should be locked up.' There was another pause. 'Alright. Go get her. I'll tell her everything now.'

'Are you sure? Because I can get you that lawyer first. There are some good duty solicitors who I can contact.'

'No.' Offering him the choice had made up his mind. 'Get the bitch in here. I'll tell her everything.'

'Very well.'

I heard Fred's chair scrape against the floor and I pulled back from the door. A moment later he came out and we moved down the corridor so we were out of earshot before he spoke.

'You were right,' he said. 'It worked. I didn't think it would be that easy.'

'Deep down Adam Jones is nothing more than a scared boy who knows that he's in way over his head. I reckon there's a part of him that always suspected the gang were going to kill him. He *wants* to talk.'

Lukas watched me. 'If he tells you everything, will you let him go?'

I shrugged. 'I don't see why not. He's going to do it all over again soon and,' I added, not without a trace of sympathy, 'he's proved very easy to manipulate. That gang used him and then shot him. He deserves a break.' I pondered the matter some more. 'Let's wait and see what he has to tell us first.'

I drained the rest of my coffee, handed the cup to Lukas and strode into the interview room. 'So, Mr Jones,' I said in a more friendly tone, 'I hear you want to make a deal.'

He folded his arms and glowered. 'I ain't a terrorist.'

'Well, that remains to be seen.'

'If I tell you what I know, will you let me go?'

I stayed calm. 'Again, that depends on what you have to say.' His eyes narrowed and I could tell he was preparing to clam up again. 'However,' I conceded, 'if I can be sure that you didn't intend to hurt anyone—'

'I didn't!'

'—then,' I continued as if he hadn't spoken, 'I'll make sure you're not charged with any serious crimes and your name is kept out of any proceedings relating to the gang that you seem to be mixed up with.'

He watched me for a moment or two. 'Fine,' he said, relenting.

I wanted to tell him that he should have held out for a solicitor. I also wanted to tell him that unless an agreement was put into writing, it wasn't worth a jot. At this moment, however, it would be pointless. This day was going to re-set itself and soon none of these events would even exist.

I sat down. 'Then proceed.'

'They approached me,' Adam said. 'It was all their idea. At first all they told me was that they wanted me to climb up the London Eye and draw as much attention as possible. I was to wear a pair of fake fangs and make everyone think I was a vampire. They said it was a stunt to prove that humans are as strong and capable as vampires. That's all. They were supposed to pay me two grand – one grand up front before and one grand afterwards.'

'Okay.' I nodded. 'And who are they? What were their names?'

'I don't know.'

I sighed. 'Adam.'

He threw up his hands. 'I'm not lying! They didn't tell me their names. They said it was safer that way. There were four of them…'

'Four?' I asked sharply.

He bobbed his head. 'Yeah. Two women, two men.'

'What did they look like?'

'If you've been watching the shop, you must know all this already,' he huffed.

'It's my job to cross the Ts and dot the Is,' I said. 'I want to hear it from your lips. What do they look like?'

He cast his gaze upwards. 'One man has dark hair and a big moustache, kinda like Tom Selleck, you know? The other guy is smaller, light-brown hair. He is pretty weedy and wears glasses. I think of him as the professor. He seems to know a lot of stuff.' He was describing the man who'd been shot in the car on Tower Bridge.

'And the women?' I asked.

'Some blonde chick. Sounds like she's walked off the set of *EastEnders*.'

That would be the Russian with the fake Cockney accent.

'And,' Adam said, 'there's an old bird.'

I sat up straight. 'Old bird?'

'Yeah.' He sniffed. 'An old woman.'

'What does she look like?'

'I dunno. She looks old. Wrinkly.'

I sighed again. 'You're not giving me a lot to go on here.'

'I'm doing my best,' he whined. He raised his shoulders helplessly. 'I think she had blue eyes?'

'Is that a question or are you telling me that she had blue eyes?'

He dropped his head. 'Uh, I dunno. I'm not sure.'

I gritted my teeth. 'Tell me about the shop.'

'I wasn't supposed to know about it.' His features suddenly took on a sly cast. 'But I followed them back to it without them realising. I should have guessed what they were up to when I saw that they worked out of a locksmith's crib.'

I held my breath. 'Uh huh. And this is the locksmith's on...'

'Chase Road,' he said with a trace of impatience, 'not far from Acton Cemetery.'

Not all that far from Wormwood Scrubs; in fact, it was less than a mile from the disused electricity tunnel where the gang had switched vehicles. Suddenly it felt like everything was sliding into place. I did my best to keep the satisfaction off my face. 'Go on.'

Adam sighed loudly. 'They didn't want me to know what they were really up to because they knew that, if I did, I'd ask for more money. I sneaked into the locksmith's from a back entrance and heard it all. They were planning to rip off the vamps and the wolves.'

I leaned forward. 'So you confronted them?'

'Hell, no. I'm not stupid. They might have found someone else to take my place. It was all in the timing, see.'

Adam Jones was on a roll. He was ridiculously proud of the plan he'd come up with and, rather than stay quiet, he wanted us to know how smart he'd been.

'I altered their schedule slightly so I could get in on the action,' he continued. 'They wanted me to start climbing the Eye at one o'clock but I did it at noon instead.' He gave a satisfied smile. 'I knew that would give me enough time to get to the Talismanic Bank afterwards. I had a bike nearby, all ready to go. If I managed to get there at the same time as they were robbing the bank, they'd have to cut me in to keep me quiet. It would have worked,' he added, 'if you hadn't nabbed me.'

Not as well as he thought it would. His appearance during the robbery led to the gang shooting him dead so that there were no loose ends to worry about. Adam had rolled the dice and lost. Three times.

'Let's backtrack,' I said briskly. 'Where and when did the gang approach you the first time around?'

Adam's self-congratulatory expression transformed into a scowl. Perhaps he was upset that I wasn't admiring his tactical genius. 'Last week,' he began. 'I was…'

He was interrupted by the sound of the Supe Squad front door thudding open and several loud shouts echoing down the corridor. I frowned. 'Hold that thought,' I muttered to him. Then I went to see what the noise was about.

DSI Barnes, wearing an immaculate grey suit and a

severe expression that matched it perfectly, was standing outside the interview room. She wasn't alone; there were several uniformed officers with her and, I noted unhappily, the familiar hard features of DI Collier. This time there was no sign of my friend, Molly. That was probably a good thing because I doubted the next few minutes would be pretty.

'Detective Constable Bellamy,' Barnes said coolly. 'I've been trying to reach you for some time.'

'I've been busy.' I folded my arms defensively across my chest. 'I was planning to call you as soon as I'd finished interviewing my suspect.' I was lying, of course, but DSI Barnes didn't need to know that.

She tapped her foot. 'I'm sure you were. Unfortunately, the events today have proved serious enough for responsibility for the investigation to be referred to CID. We don't believe it's a coincidence that there was an incident at the London Eye shortly before we had to deal with a stand-off at Tower Bridge.' She looked at me sternly. 'Your presence at the bridge was requested but you were out of contact.'

'From what I understand,' I said carefully, 'the hijacking at Tower Bridge was not a supe matter, despite appearances to the contrary.'

Her brows snapped together. 'How do you know that? We only discovered it for ourselves in the last fifteen minutes.'

Ah… I had no answer to that, no answer that she would believe. I shuffled awkwardly, painfully aware of Collier's suspicious glower. As far as he was concerned we'd not yet met, but he already seemed to mistrust me.

'Detective Superintendent Barnes!' Lukas called, appearing from the office in the nick of time. Fred and Liza shuffled in behind him. 'How lovely to see you again.'

DSI Barnes gazed at him then flicked her eyes at me. 'What is Lord Horvath doing here?'

'He was helping out with the suspect from the London Eye incident,' I said, suddenly on surer ground.

'And is that suspect a vampire?'

'No,' I replied. 'The suspect is called Adam Jones and...'

'If Mr Jones is not a vampire, DC Bellamy,' Collier interrupted, 'then he's not Supe Squad's concern.'

I dropped my arms. 'Okay. I understand why you would think that, but actually Adam Jones is part of another ongoing Supe Squad investigation.'

'What investigation is that?'

This time I had no reason to lie. 'A suspected bank robbery that's being planned for the Talismanic Bank.'

Even Collier looked shocked at that. 'A bank robbery? That's even more reason for this Jones fellow to be transferred into our custody. Supe Squad hasn't got the resources to deal with a crime of such magnitude.'

As DSI Barnes looked at me something flickered in her face. 'The Talismanic Bank is a supernatural institution,' she said mildly. 'Any crime relating to it is a matter for Supernatural Squad. It's part of DC Bellamy's remit.'

I breathed out. I might have pissed her off by ignoring her calls but she was still on my side – at least in public.

'Yes.' I forced a smile. 'I appreciate your offer of help, DI Collier, but we have this covered. Mr Jones and I have come to a mutually beneficial agreement already. He's talking. That's all you need to know at this point.'

Collier didn't look at me. His attention was wholly on Barnes. 'Is that man over there actually Lord Horvath?' he enquired.

'I am,' Lukas said.

'He is,' I replied.

Collier ignored us both. Slowly Barnes nodded, which seemed to satisfy the grizzly bastard.

'Surely then, DSI Barnes,' Collier said, 'you realise that

your detective is jeopardising any future legal proceedings against the suspect by having a vampire Lord in the building at the same time as an official interview.'

'He's not a vampire Lord,' I snapped. 'He's *the* vampire Lord.'

'Just so,' Collier replied. He raised an eyebrow. 'I suggest that we take custody of Mr Jones to avoid any conflict of interest. We'll pass over any details he reveals about this supposed bank robbery, but he is human and he committed a human crime. He shouldn't be here. He certainly shouldn't be here at the same time as Lord Horvath!'

Barnes outranked Collier so she could refuse his request. Unfortunately, she believed that he was right. I could see it written all over her face. Even I knew that Supe Squad was on shaky legal ground.

'Very well,' she muttered. I opened my mouth to object. 'But DC Bellamy will accompany you and will be included in any further questioning.'

'That's not necessary,' Collier said.

Barnes glowered at him. 'It is necessary because I say that it's necessary.' She turned to me. 'If there is an assault planned on the Talismanic Bank, you'll require back up. You can't possibly deal with it on your own.'

'I can assure you,' Lukas said, his voice cold, 'that DC Bellamy has the vampires' full backing.'

'That doesn't matter. This isn't your call,' Collier growled.

I gritted my teeth. I could stand here and argue until I was blue in the face but I doubted it would make any difference. And just because I disliked Collier and he was a prejudicial bastard didn't mean that he wasn't good at his job. Perhaps he could offer me some insights into tracking down the gang.

'I look forward to learning from DI Collier,' I said. I pushed open the interview room door. 'Mr Jones is here.'

Collier nodded at two of the uniformed police officers. They walked into the interview room and prepared to hand-cuff Adam.

'Hey!' he protested. 'What's going on?' He looked at me. 'What about our deal?'

The officers ignored him, cuffed his hands and hauled him to his feet before leading him out. 'This is bullshit,' he muttered.

'Don't worry, Mr Jones,' DSI Barnes said. 'You are simply being transferred to CID for further questioning. We'll arrange for your legal representation to meet us there, if you like.'

Adam was propelled down the hallway and out of the front door. Suddenly he turned his head and looked at me. 'Wait,' he said slowly. 'How did you know where to wait for me? When I climbed over that barrier to get away from the London Eye, you were in exactly the right spot to catch me. You'd never have caught me otherwise. Back in the car, when you said that shit about the magic potion stuff, was that true?'

I didn't get the chance to come up with an answer. There was a loud pop and a cloud of dust appeared from the side of the doorframe. Then there was another pop and a perfect 'oh' of surprise lit Adam's face. A split second later he collapsed, blood blossoming from the wound in his skull.

I stared at him, momentarily frozen into inaction. Oh shit. It was starting all over again.

CHAPTER EIGHTEEN

THE TWO POLICE OFFICERS WHO HAD BEEN HOLDING ADAM sprang into the Supe Squad hallway, slamming the door shut and leaving his body sprawled on the pavement beyond.

'Shots fired!' Collier barked into his radio. 'Shots fired at Supernatural Squad. One victim so far. Armed response immediately requested at this address.' He grabbed hold of my arm and yanked me back from the door. I shook him off and strode towards it, my heart hammering in my chest.

'Back! Get back!' Barnes shouted.

I ignored the yelled commands and placed my hand on the doorknob. I knew without looking that Lukas was directly behind me.

'I think we can assume,' he said darkly, 'that whoever killed Adam Jones a few seconds ago is the same bastard who killed me. He's also probably the same guy who warned off the gang from the bank.'

'Actually,' I replied, 'I don't think it's a guy at all.'

'Detective Constable Bellamy!' Barnes roared. 'Get away from there!'

'Don't worry,' I called. I opened the door an inch.

'Emma!' she yelled again. 'Fucking get back here!'

I turned and met her eyes. 'It's fine,' I said calmly.

'Whether you are resurrected or not, you need to stay back! The last thing we need is for you to hang around on a morgue slab for twelve hours!'

Collier stared at her. 'What are you talking about? Resurrection?'

I waved a hand. 'The shooter's already got their target,' I said flatly. 'Adam Jones is dead. He won't be talking to anyone any more.'

'You don't know that's who they were after!' Barnes protested.

I felt a leaden weight settle across my shoulders. 'Yeah, I do,' I whispered. Then I raised my voice. 'If I'm going to catch whoever fired those shots, I have to go now. Trust me on this.' I glanced at Lukas. 'Stay here. Please.'

'I can't do that, Emma. You said it yourself – they wanted Adam and they got him. They're already hotfooting it out of here.'

I gave him a grim look. 'Fine,' I muttered. 'But if you die again, I'll bloody kill you.'

He dipped his head suddenly, surprising me as his lips brushed against mine. 'Noted,' he said. He pointed at the door. 'Let's go.'

I wrenched open the door. I knew that Collier's radioed request would bring half of the Metropolitan Police Force here at top speed – but I also knew that they might not be quick enough to catch the sniper. I had to act fast and smart.

The shot had cleared the street of people. Apart from a single pigeon flapping overhead in search of some tasty snacks, there wasn't a flutter of movement. I stepped past Adam's body, avoiding the blood splatter. Collier and Barnes were still jabbering at me from inside the building but I paid no attention. I could already hear the wail of sirens several streets away.

Lukas knelt down next to Adam. 'As far as I can tell from the wound, the shot came from a high angle.'

That made sense; a passer-by opening fire from the pavement would be too risky. I looked up at the buildings across the road. The terraced row of shops, residential properties and small hotels stretched for more than a hundred metres. I couldn't see anything beyond stacked chimneys and sloping roofs but I was certain the shooter was somewhere up there.

'The rooftops.' I swung my head. But to the left? Or the right?

The glass door to the hotel next to Supe Squad opened and a head popped out. Max was pale and shaking. My heart lurched. 'Are you alright?' I asked. 'Were you hit?'

He shook his head. 'I'm fine.' He pointed up to the right. 'But before that poor guy fell, I saw something over there. Somebody was on that roof, I'm sure of it. They were right above the chemist's.'

Lukas and I were running before he'd even finished his sentence.

Blue lights were already flashing at either end of the street. Lukas sprinted for the first building, scrambling up its smooth brick façade like some kind of spider. I didn't stop to watch his progress but pelted along the pavement, heading for the scaffolding that had been erected outside the flats twenty metres away. Without pausing, I leapt and swung my body up, forgetting about the wound that was only just starting to heal. My shoulder screamed in agony. I lost my grip and dropped back to the pavement. When I tried again, it was only through sheer willpower that I clung on and managed to climb. Move, Emma, I ordered myself. Bloody move.

Up to the first storey, then the second storey and the

third. Five seconds later, I was on the roof. Lukas whipped past me, roof tiles scattering in his wake. I scanned around and saw a flash of something – or rather someone – disappearing from the ledge at the far end. Damn it. The sniper was already heading down to the ground again.

I cursed and sped back down the scaffolding. At least going down was less painful than going up. My feet landed squarely on the ground and exhaled my breath in a loud whoosh. Then I started sprinting again.

'This way!' I yelled at the first of the armed police who were already getting out of their cars. I pointed to where I thought the sniper had vanished. I didn't wait to see whether they responded to my shout, I simply thundered past them.

The scenery around me blurred as I ran faster than ever but my efforts were in vain. When I finally rounded the corner, there was no sign of anyone except Lukas, who had already abandoned his own pointless sprint across the rooftops.

I cursed aloud and joined him. 'This is bullshit.' My words were barely audible even to my own ears. I raised my voice. 'This is bullshit!' The shout bounced uselessly off the walls and buildings around us.

From down the road, someone stuck their head out of a window and yelled back, 'Shut up!'

I opened my mouth to shout again, then I remembered who I was and what I was supposed to be doing. I subsided, my body sagging in response to my own ineffectiveness.

Lukas turned to me, his black eyes roving across my face and body. 'You need to get some rest, D'Artagnan.'

'Adam Jones was just shot dead on the steps of the Supe Squad headquarters. I can't rest.'

He reached under my chin and gently tilted it up. 'This is the third time you've experienced this day. You're tired and wrung out, not to mention bleeding from that damned bullet wound again.'

I met his eyes. 'Until this day is over – and I mean *properly* over – I can't rest.' I set my jaw.

'You're far too stubborn for your own good.'

I shrugged, then immediately regretted the impulse when more pain shot through my shoulder.

'Let's get you back to Supe Squad and bandaged up properly,' Lukas said. 'Whoever shot your Adam Jones is already in the wind.' The street was now a sea of blue flashing lights. 'You're not alone, Emma.'

I sighed. Then I let him take me back to the scene of Adam Jones's latest death.

NONE of us were used to this many people hovering around Supe Squad. Liza took up position in the corner of the office, her arms folded and her face expressionless, watching the comings and goings without comment. Fred gazed at everyone like an eager puppy; he was still young enough to find the action exciting rather than depressing. For my part, I kept out of the way and allowed Lukas to tend my shoulder with the Supe Squad first-aid kit.

'You should go to a hospital,' he muttered. 'But I've already told you that and I know you won't go.'

'You could lick me,' I suggested. Vampire saliva contained special healing properties. It was a quirk that allowed them to pierce human skin and drink blood without fearing that their victim, willing or otherwise, would bleed to death.

'I would love to lick you,' he said, his voice low enough for my ears only. 'Very slowly.' His fingers brushed my lips. 'From here all the way down to here.' His hands moved to my hips. 'But perhaps I'll save that for later.'

I sucked in a breath and stared at him.

'Is it because I died?' he asked suddenly. 'Is that why you seem to have changed your mind about me? Until today, you seemed determined to avoid me at all costs.' His face was inscrutable. 'I'm not looking for a sympathy fuck, Emma. I want far more from you than that.'

'I...'

'Emma!' Molly appeared in the doorway. She bounded towards me with her arms outstretched as if to offer me a tight hug. 'Are you alright? I couldn't believe it when I heard the news. How would someone dare to attack a police station in broad daylight?'

Lukas was already moving away. She glanced at him quickly, then did a double take. 'Wait,' she said slowly. 'Are you...'

'This is my ... friend,' I told her. 'Lukas. He's a vampire.'

Her mouth dropped open. 'I know who you are,' she breathed. 'You're Lord Horvath.'

He offered her a lazy smile. 'Please,' he said, 'call me Lukas. Any friend of Emma's is a friend of mine.'

Molly all but melted into a puddle right before my eyes. 'I'm Molly.' She blinked at him. 'It's lovely to meet you.'

'There is someone at the door for you, Lord Horvath,' another police officer interrupted. 'Scarlett somebody?'

Fred straightened up, his gaze darting to the window. Lukas nodded and glanced at me. 'I'll be right back.'

I swallowed and managed a smile, then grabbed my T-shirt and hastily pulled it over my head. I wasn't particularly modest but I wasn't going to wander the office in my bra when so many people were around.

'Oh my God, Ems.' Molly stared at me. 'I didn't realise he was so ... magnetic. Are you and he having a thing? When I walked in here, he was completely absorbed in you.'

I coughed. I was not having this conversation right now.

'And,' she added, 'you were completely absorbed in him.' She grinned at me. 'Does he have any single friends?'

I didn't have to answer because DI Collier marched into the room and cleared his throat. For the first time I was glad to see him; normally he had a way of sucking the life out of everyone around him.

'Listen up all,' he intoned. 'DSI Barnes has left in order to brief the Prime Minister about today's events. In her absence, I'm assuming full authority and any questions should be directed to me. Nobody is to say a word to the press. There will be a statement later on today – any journos that complain can be told to wait until then. For now, all orders run through me. I'm sure I don't need to emphasise that this is an incredibly serious situation. We have an active shooter on the loose. Initial indications seem to suggest that he was hiding on the rooftops opposite this building until he had a clear line of sight to his target. The weapon appears to have been a high-calibre rifle with a silencer attached.'

There was a murmur amongst the assembled police officers. I heard more than one person whisper 'execution'. I swallowed. They were right; that's exactly what it had been.

Collier held his hand up for silence. 'We can't be sure whether he was aiming for us, or for the suspect in custody who was being transferred to headquarters. We have to assume, however, that the shooter still poses a very real risk to the public and that he or she is linked in some way to the events this morning at Tower Bridge and the London Eye. I know you'll agree that terrorism has no place in our city.'

My hand shot up into the air. Collier ignored it.

'All main railway and bus terminals in and out of London are being monitored. The police presence at Gatwick, Heathrow and London City Airports has been increased.'

I waved my hand several times and hopped up and down, just in case he was short sighted.

'Given the nature of all three incidents today,' he continued without blinking, as if he were some kind of damned lizard, 'we have to assume that supernatural beings are involved. The shooter knew the area well enough to know where Adam Jones was going to be taken. Also he or she was able to find an unobtrusive spot to fire shots from. That means that the shooter is probably supernatural.'

I noted that several police officers stiffened.

'Under normal circumstances,' Collier intoned, 'the law states that we can't arrest supes and that their own justice prevails.' His mouth turned down, indicating exactly what he thought of that particular quirk. 'However, given the real threat to human life, all bets are off. We have full permission to treat every supernatural creature, be they vampire, werewolf or Frankenstein himself, as we would any other criminal.'

I understood what he meant and why he'd said it, but his choice of words made it clear that he believed every supe was a criminal simply because of the power that ran through their blood. I stopped trying to be polite and interrupted him. This was *my* office, not his.

'Frankenstein was human,' I said. 'He created the monster who, I should point out, had far more humanity and intelligence than his human creator. But that's beside the point. This cannot be an excuse for open season on supes. First of all, it's the supe community that's being targeted. Secondly, I have good reason to believe that we're looking for humans. And finally, this is not about terrorism. It's about money.'

Collier stared at me then cleared his throat. 'For those of you who don't know,' he said, 'this is Detective Constable Bellamy. She's been working here at Supe Squad since she qualified a mere three months ago.' He smiled nastily. 'And I think we all know what assignment to Supe Squad means.'

There were several intakes of breath from around the

room. Some of the police officers nodded, others looked embarrassed at his sneering tone. Molly put a warning hand on my arm.

'I don't know what you're talking about,' I said loudly, making sure that every pair of ears in the room heard me. I wouldn't allow Collier to get away with suggesting that I was a lesser detective because I was in Supe Squad, or that Supe Squad was only for losers. Or that my lack of experience suggested I was talking out of my arse. I wasn't going to pretend I had all the answers – but I knew more than most of the people in this room. 'Other than it means that I have a far greater knowledge of supes than anyone else here.'

Liza coughed.

'Apart from my two Supe Squad colleagues, that is,' I added, with a nod towards her and Fred.

Collier did his best to stare me down. When that didn't work, he elected for a different approach. 'Excellent. If anyone has any questions relating to supes and their specific abilities, you can direct them to DC Bellamy. In the meantime, we will canvass this entire area street by street. I want doors knocked, pavements pounded and every damned shed and outbuilding searched. Perimeters have been set up. Soho and Lisson Grove are closed off. No supe is to leave the area unless they've been searched, checked and identified.' He paused. 'Whether he was in handcuffs or not, Adam Jones was a young man struck down in his prime. He is a victim. It's up to us to find his killer.'

He gestured at a prim-looking officer standing at the door clutching a clipboard. 'DC Smith will assign you specific streets to search. You are to remain in groups of no less than three at all times. Let's find this bastard and prevent any other innocent humans from getting killed.' Collier turned away and marched out of the room.

Fred sidled up to me. 'Why is he in charge? He didn't

listen to anything that you said. Why can't we have Barnes? She outranks him by a long way.'

'She's not an operational officer any more,' Liza said grimly. 'And when the T word was mentioned, any decisions about what happens next would have been taken out of her hands.'

Molly looked at us. 'I know he's a wanker,' she said quietly, 'but it does appear that we're looking for a supe here. All the evidence points that way.'

I opened my mouth to speak, but before I could my attention was dragged away by a flicker of movement outside the window. Fuck. Lukas and Scarlett were being confronted by two stony-faced police officers. One of them reached for Scarlett and she bared her fangs in response.

My stomach dropped as I darted out of the room, pushing my way through the uniformed officers and assembled detectives and ignoring PC Clipboard. Seconds later I was out on the street, almost throwing myself between the police, who already had their hands on their Tasers, and the two vampires.

'Enough!' I roared with such force that I surprised myself. 'These two are not involved!'

'We need to clear them first,' the nearest policeman said.

'I've already cleared them.'

'DI Collier said...'

I ground my teeth. 'I said I've already cleared them.' I glared, daring them to challenge me. Fortunately for all of us, they decided to back off.

'This is ridiculous,' Scarlett huffed. 'We're being treated like criminals.' She jerked her head at the Supe Squad door. 'It's hardly the vampires' fault that your police security is so lacking. Even the werewolves have better systems. At least they have guards outside their buildings, and now that Fairfax has installed metal detectors at his entrances the others will follow suit.' Her mouth pursed in disgust. 'Anyone can be gunned down here in broad daylight. So much for the skills and security at Supe Squad.' She rolled her eyes.

I knew her anger wasn't really directed at me but I felt it all the same. The failure to protect Adam Jones from yet another bullet was mine.

'Scarlett,' Lukas murmured, 'go back to the car, please.'

Her bottom lip curled then she stomped off, her stilettoes beating a furious staccato on the tarmacked road.

'And you wonder why I have such a mistrust of the authorities, D'Artagnan.' Lukas's expression was calm but I sensed a seething rage beneath his smooth features. 'It's just as well that you have another chance at this day. If the human police continue in this manner, there'll be a lot of blood shed before long. My contacts in the government are refusing to take my calls.' His black eyes met mine. 'This is not going to end well.'

I wished he wasn't right. 'You need to get back to Soho,' I said. 'Get your people inside, and make sure they don't do anything to inflame matters further. Contact the clans and tell them to do the same.'

'We're not the criminals here.'

'I know,' I said quietly. 'But assuming I do get another reset, I'll need every spare minute to find out about the gang that's created this mess. That's the only way we can avoid this sort of situation tomorrow. I don't want to waste time dealing with confrontations between you and police.' I reached for his hand and squeezed it. 'I need you to trust that I've got this. I need you to trust *me*.'

'If you were anyone else,' he began. He ran a hand through his hair and sighed. 'Very well. Where will you go?'

'There are two clear lines of investigation – the bank and the locksmith's where Adam Jones followed the gang.' I checked my watch. 'There's less than seven hours to go for me to cover both. The bank will be closing soon so I'll head there first.'

'Fine. I'll meet you later.' His thumb gently stroked the side of my hand. 'Don't get shot.'

I shivered from the heat of his touch. 'Ditto.'

CHAPTER NINETEEN

MOSBURN PRALK'S BODY LANGUAGE WAS STIFF AND unyielding. 'From what I understand,' he said, 'you should be breaking down doors and looking for someone with a gun instead of bothering me again. Despite your assertions, the real trouble today has been on your doorstep, detective. Not mine.'

I needed Pralk on my side. 'It's all related. Please believe me, Mr Pralk, your bank is in very real danger. I'm trying to avert a catastrophe and it'll be far easier to save lives, including those of your staff, if you cooperate.'

A crease appeared between his eyebrows, darkening the golden colour of his skin. 'What do you need?'

This was where things could get tricky. The goblin bank manager had already given me a list of his staff, but he'd done so after the bank had been robbed and the floor was littered with corpses. Naturally, I no longer had the list to hand. I had to persuade Pralk to give me another copy and let me interview everyone on it. Regardless of what he might think, someone knew which safety deposit boxes to target and someone had tipped off the bank robbers. The only logical answer was that it was someone who worked in the bank.

I glanced at Fred. 'Can you give us a minute?' He smiled amiably and stepped away. Keeping my voice quiet, I addressed Pralk. 'I didn't want to mention this before because I vowed that I'd keep the information to myself.'

The crease in his brow deepened. 'Go on.'

'The bank uses one of its own deposit boxes to store confidential paperwork. You ought to stop doing that, you know,' I added as an aside. 'The paperwork includes the name of every supe in the country, not just the supes who live legally here in London but those who survive incognito outside the city. We're talking about a thousand or so people.'

The only indication that Pralk was flustered by this information was a tiny fluttering at the base of his throat. 'How do you know all this?' he asked evenly. 'And please, detective, do me the honour of telling me the truth. I don't require further storytelling or prevarication.'

Okay, then. 'Your bank was robbed, Mr Pralk. Eight people were killed and several deposit boxes were stolen, including yours. There was a shoot-out later on Westminster Bridge when the robbers tried to sell the contents of Lord Horvath's box back to him. In the process, he was also killed. I took a potion shortly afterwards which means that I am re-living that same period of twelve hours over and over again. This is my third time. I'm told by the person who gave me the potion that I only have one more repeat left. That's one more chance to stop the robbery and find those responsible.'

I was expecting the pragmatic Pralk to laugh in my face. Instead, however, he folded his arms and uttered two words, 'Carpe diem.'

I started. 'You've heard of it?'

'We have a copy of *Infernal Enchantments*.'

I sucked in a breath. 'You...'

He held up a hand. 'Before you tell me that it's a dangerous book and should be kept under lock and key, I'm already aware of that. And no, I haven't tried to make any of the recipes in it.'

'Does anyone else have access to the book?'

He shook his head. 'Only me. It's held in a secure box in our vault.' He raised his thin eyebrows. 'Do these robbers try to gain access to the vault?'

'They do not. But, Mr Pralk, that book...'

'You don't have to worry about it, detective. It's for my eyes only – and the eyes of whoever succeeds me.' His gaze held steady. 'I read it once. I have no desire to do so again.'

That cursed book. If Pralk had read it, he'd have seen the section about the phoenix and its capabilities. By now, every supe in the city knew that I had the ability to resurrect. Pralk was an intelligent man; he must have put two and two together. On the other hand, he was circumspect and trustworthy – his lack of comment proved it. He went up another notch in my estimation.

'I haven't managed to talk to your staff,' I said. 'But somebody told the robbers which safety deposit boxes to target.'

'And you think it was someone from this bank.' His voice was flat.

'I do,' I said. 'There are hundreds of boxes back there. I can't see any other way that someone would know which ones belonged to the clan alphas, Lord Horvath and yourself, unless they had insider knowledge.'

'There's always a way,' he answered. 'I have total faith in my employees, DC Bellamy. No matter what you might think, goblins are about more than gold skin, green eyes and a penchant for financial matters. We are also trustworthy to a fault.'

I stayed quiet. I couldn't disagree with him – but I had to speak to his staff.

He sighed. 'Very well. I'll get you a list and tell everyone that they have to stay behind to be questioned. Does that meet with your approval?'

It did. 'Thank you. I appreciate your help.'

He didn't look away. 'And I appreciate yours. The Carpe Diem potion has given you an extraordinary gift. Don't waste it.'

All I could do was nod in return.

THERE WERE NINETEEN BANK EMPLOYEES, not including Pralk: three cleaners; five bank tellers; one HR manager; three administrative assistants; three account managers; one assistant bank manager; one janitor; one IT administrator, and one security specialist. There wasn't much time to speak to them all, or to delve into what they did or didn't know. What I did have, thanks to Pralk, were their true names. And that gave me considerable power.

'Rexta Stimms,' I said. 'How long have you worked here?'

'Thirteen years.'

'What does your job entail?'

'I clean.' She shrugged, her fingers twisting nervously in her lap. 'That's it. That's what I do.'

'You clean every part of this bank?'

She nodded. '*Da.*'

'That means you have access to a lot of private information.'

Her golden skin paled and she shrank in her chair. '*Da.*'

'Do you know who owns safety deposit boxes at this bank?'

She swallowed. 'Some. I see the people come. Sometimes I see them leave.'

'Rexta,' my voice thrummed, 'do you know which box Lady Carr owns?'

Her head shook wildly from side to side. '*Nyet!*'

'How about Lord Horvath?'

'*Nyet*! No!'

'Okay. You can go.'

'You're sure?' Fred asked, making a mark on his list.

'I'm sure. Send the next one in.'

I leaned forward. 'David Finti. How long have you worked here?'

'Th–three years.'

'What is your job exactly?'

'I manage the IT system and troubleshoot when there are any issues.'

'Do you know who owns safety deposit boxes at this bank?'

'Ye–yes. I have full access to the bank's information systems.'

'David, do you know which box Lord McGuigan owns?'

'Z523.'

I folded my arms. 'You can remember that information off the top of your head?'

'I'm g–good with numbers. I remember a lot. Not deliberately. It just happens.' His hands were shaking. Mr Finta was fully expecting to be arrested at any moment.

'Have you ever told anyone that number? David Finta, have you revealed to anyone which safety deposit box belongs to Lord McGuigan?'

'No!'

'Are you working with others to steal his box?'

'You're crazy!'

'Answer the question, David.'

He sagged. 'No.'

'You can go.'

Each face was replaced by another. Some were angry and sullen, some were scared, some were eager to cooperate. All of them answered the questions and none of them raised any red flags. Slightly more than two hours later, we were done. I cursed, slumping my shoulders. Nothing. Not a goddamned thing.

'I thought it would take longer than that to get through everyone,' Fred said. 'It'd be pretty handy if that compulsion thing worked on humans.'

'Yeah,' I sighed. 'It doesn't work on every supe. Even with their real names, it's not foolproof. One or more of them might still be lying. And you can't compel someone to do or say something that goes beyond what lies within their own heart. For instance, I couldn't compel you to rob this bank unless a part of you already wanted to do so.'

'Do you think any of them are lying?' Fred asked.

'Do you?' I countered.

His mouth flattened. 'No.'

I pushed back my hair. Exhaustion was gnawing at the edges of my very soul. 'Neither do I. We're at a dead end. But that gang got those box numbers from somewhere.'

'Now what?'

'Now we talk to Pralk again.'

WE FOUND him in the main hall, talking to the security specialist who hadn't been on the premises until recently. 'What would you do,' Pralk asked, 'if someone came through that door right now with a gun and demanded that you open the vault?'

'The vault is on a timer,' the specialist, whose name I remembered as Billo Tritt, said. 'It can't be opened, no matter what happens. Shoot me. Threaten my family. Say what you like. I can't open the vault.'

'And what if this gunman demanded to be taken to the safety deposit boxes?' Pralk questioned. 'What would you do then?'

I cleared my throat. He turned and gestured to Billo Tritt to leave, then looked at me. 'It's not his fault that any of this happened, you know. He's not responsible for the flaws in our security system.' His lanky body hunched over. 'We've relied too much on protection from the more powerful supes and our own reputation for zero tolerance. The board believed that further investment in security wasn't necessary. I didn't argue. If anyone is to blame, it's me.'

It took considerable strength to take full responsibility for a robbery that, to all intents and purposes, hadn't happened. 'You know that you can speak to Tritt and the others as much as you like, and prepare as much as possible,' I said. 'When this happens again, neither you nor they will remember any of it.'

Pralk offered a wan smile. 'It's better than feeling helpless. This is my bank, after all. It's my baby.'

I smiled back. 'I understand.' I paused. 'You've not asked if I've uncovered anything from your staff.'

'I don't have to, DC Bellamy,' he said simply. 'I told you already, I trust them all implicitly.'

'You're a good boss.'

His jaw tightened. 'Not good enough if people get killed on my watch.'

'That's not your fault.'

'The buck stops with me, detective. That's the way it works.' He stared into the distance for a long second then glanced back at me. 'Are you finished here now?'

'There's one more thing.'

'Go on.'

I looked around. 'Do you have a back entrance to this place?'

'There is a door to the rear, yes.'

'Can you show it to me?'

A muscle jerked in his cheek. He knew why I was asking. 'Very well.'

Pralk led me out of the main hallway into the corridor. We passed the safety deposit box room and the expensive paintings. Something niggled at me, a vaporous thought that seemed important but wouldn't quite coalesce.

I frowned and followed him through the building. I noted the way as I glanced into the other rooms, from the small computer server room with its blinking lights and wires, to the staff room with its coffee machine and saggy sofas. Eventually we reached a steel door. Pralk tapped on it with his fingernails; the tinny sound echoed ominously.

'Despite the damning evidence to the contrary,' he told me, 'we do take security seriously. This door is reinforced and self-locking. It can only be opened with a code, which is generated randomly and which changes every three days.' He reached up to a small number pad and tapped several of the buttons. There was a click and the door swung open.

I peered out, noting the few chairs sitting outside in the high-walled courtyard and the utilitarian ashtray. So goblins weren't immune to the addictive allure of nicotine, then. I looked around some more. The steel door appeared to be the only way in or out. This was going to be more complicated than I'd thought.

'There are invisible sensors laid into the top of the wall,' Pralk told me. 'Anything heavier than a pigeon will set them off. When that happens, they immediately sound an alarm inside the bank and we automatically go into shut down.'

I chewed on the inside of my cheek. 'Has that ever happened?'

'Just once. Some kids playing football kicked their ball over here.' He smiled faintly. 'I can only assume it was curiosity on their part. They climbed over, the alarms went off and all hell broke loose.'

I walked into the centre of the courtyard and slowly turned round. 'What's that?' I asked, pointing at the roof beyond the wall and just to the right of the bank itself.

'A doctor's surgery. It's more of a leap from there to here than you'd expect. A wolf could make it and I expect a vampire could too, at a push.' He gave me an assessing look. I pretended not to notice. 'A human would not manage.' He raised his eyebrows expectantly and waited for me to protest that I was human. I didn't bother; both of us knew otherwise.

'Okay.' I turned to the door. There was an identical keypad on the outside of it. 'When is the code due to change?'

'The day after tomorrow.'

'So?'

'Five-oh-two-three-seven-four,' he told me.

I repeated it under my breath a few times then I tried it. There was a satisfying click. 'What happens if someone gets the code wrong and puts in different numbers?'

Pralk twirled a finger above his head. 'Sirens. Lockdown. Hell breaks loose.'

Got it. 'Thank you,' I said.

Pralk watched me. 'Can you do it?' he asked. 'Can you prevent the robbery, stop anyone from dying and find the culprits at the same time?'

'I'll have to,' I answered simply. 'But unless something miraculous occurs to me in the next few hours, there's no other way to do it than through this back door.'

CHAPTER TWENTY

Liza had already called, first to complain about the copious number of mugs of tea she was being ordered to make, the loss of her prized chocolate cake, and the mess that Collier's team were creating in our office, and second to inform me that, despite her best efforts, she hadn't managed to track down any records about who might own the locksmith shop that Adam Jones had mentioned. The best she could come up with was a gentleman whose address was an anonymous PO Box and whose name was Joseph Bloggs. The lack of imagination depressed me, particularly when it appeared that Mr Bloggs' little business had managed to avoid filing a single tax return for the half-dozen years that it had been up and running. Her Majesty's Revenue and Customs had definitely missed a trick.

I sighed and told her to finish up for the day. Collier would manage without her tea-making skills. I also sent Fred home. Another pair of eyes would be useful, but I was wary of what might be waiting at the locksmiths. In the end, I needn't have worried about having someone with me. By the time I pulled Tallulah up in front of the darkened shop,

Lukas was already there. When I stepped out of the car, he stepped out of the shadows. I didn't need to see his expression to know that it was grim.

'How are things going in Soho and Lisson Grove?' I asked. 'Is everyone behaving themselves?'

A beat passed before Lukas answered. 'There have been some … discussions between various supes and various members of the Metropolitan Police.'

I swallowed. 'Loud discussions?'

'Oh yes.'

'Violent?'

'No.' He put his hands in his pockets. 'Even the wolves have been behaving.'

I sensed there was more he wanted to say but he was unwilling to say it. 'Are you alright?'

Initially, I didn't think he was going to answer. His eyes were hooded and his body language suggested deep discomfort. Eventually, however, he licked his lips and displayed the briefest flash of white fangs. 'This is very difficult for me, Emma.' He sighed. 'When it comes to a situation like this, my people look to me. But in reality, I am the vampire Lord of nothing. I'm entirely impotent and at the mercy of whatever the human authorities decide. They're using the suggestion of terrorism as a loophole to do whatever they want. We've put a great deal of work into creating a façade to the public that portrays vampires as frivolous and unthreatening. We follow the laws, although we chafe at them. And still,' he added heavily, 'all it takes is a couple of hours and a few unpleasant incidents for all that to be undone.'

He gazed at me. 'It doesn't help that I know this is nothing more than a test run, and anything that happens today will be undone tomorrow. And the only person who has any chance of controlling it is you.' He took a step closer until our bodies were almost touching. 'You have so much power. You don't realise how much.'

From the look in his eyes, he was no longer talking about either the bank robbery or the police. He took my right hand and stroked my pinkie gently. 'You have the ability to wrap everyone round your little finger. Especially me.'

I tilted my face up to his. 'It terrifies me,' I whispered, truth vibrating through every word.

His response was quiet but laden with meaning. 'I know.'

A car passed by, its headlights illuminating the darkening road. It broke the reverie and Lukas and I moved back like mirror images of each other. I shook myself and turned to the locksmiths. It didn't look like much.

'You're sure this is the place?' Lukas questioned.

'According to Adam Jones it is,' I said. 'He told me that he followed the gang here, sneaked inside and overheard them planning the robbery.'

It wasn't a large place; from here, its interior seemed to be no bigger than that of a tiny corner shop. At one point, the front had been painted a brick-red colour, no doubt to stand out, but it was a long time since it had enjoyed a touch-up. Years of pollution had added layers of grime, the colour had faded and the paint was peeling. The door and windows were protected by an ugly steel mesh to ward off would-be invaders; it seemed to me that it would be the height of irony for anyone to attempt to break into a locksmiths. The name itself wasn't much more inspiring: *AAA Locksmiths*. It might have garnered them top billing in the old *Yellow Pages* but it didn't do much else.

'Have you been here long?'

'About twenty minutes or so,' Lukas said. 'I was considering heading in to investigate on my own, but I didn't think you'd appreciate the effort.' His black eyes glinted. 'I wanted to be a good boy.'

I sent him a sidelong look. 'You've been a very good boy,' I murmured. 'Perhaps I'll reward you later.' And then my cheeks flushed. I coughed to hide my thoughts. I wasn't usually this easily embarrassed.

Lukas winked but fortunately didn't pursue the subject and add to my mortification. 'There's been no sign of life inside,' he informed me. 'No shadows, no lights, no sounds. I'm pretty certain it's empty.'

My stomach tightened. Maybe I'd been wrong to prioritise the bank over the locksmiths. Maybe I should have come here first. If I had, would I have had the chance to confront the gang?

'It's good that they're not here,' Lukas said, reading my mind. 'Arresting them now won't do any good. This is your chance to find out as much about them as possible so your final re-set not only stops them in their tracks but brings them to justice before anyone is killed.'

'Yeah.' The trouble was that there was a huge amount riding on that last re-set. If I didn't get it right, the only person I could blame was myself. 'Come on then,' I said. 'Let's see how good their locks actually are.'

He flashed me a quick grin and we crossed the road. I squinted in through a mesh-covered window, trying to make sense of the shadows. Lukas did the same, before letting out a loud fake gasp. 'Oh my goodness! Detective, I think there's someone in there who's collapsed! We'd better break down the door and check that they're alright.'

I gave him a long look. 'In a few hours' time, these events won't exist – they'll be erased from history. The only person who'll remember them is me. I don't have the slightest qualm about illegally entering this shop.'

Lukas raised an eyebrow. 'You're saying that the end justifies the means?'

Fuck it. 'Yeah,' I said sadly, realising I was crossing a line I might never return from, whether anyone else would remember it or not. 'I guess I am.'

'In that case,' he murmured, 'I'll do the honours.' He stepped sideways to the door, curled his fingers through the mesh and yanked it off with one swift tug. Then he used his elbow to smash the glass and reach inside for the lock. A moment later the door swung open. I'd barely had time to draw a breath.

'Hey presto.' Lukas smiled. 'Although I don't think I'll be hiring these guys myself any time soon.'

I didn't smile back. 'It seems too easy.'

'Sometimes things are easy because they're easy, D'Artagnan.'

'Is that supposed to be a deep, philosophical statement?'

He shrugged and waved his hand dismissively. 'There's no alarm. There's no one inside.' He glanced around the deserted street. 'No one is running towards us with a gun.'

'Maybe it was easy because there's nothing inside to find.'

Lukas stepped across the threshold. 'Then let's find out if that's true.'

I hesitated for a second before following him in. Part of me was expecting to be gunned down or slammed into a headlock by a blonde Russian with a fake Cockney accent, but nothing happened. It really was that easy.

The wall on the right was covered with uncut keys, a range of padlocks and some plastic-wrapped burglar alarms. A single tattered poster pinned to the wall behind the counter demanded, *How Safe Is Your Home? Let AAA Lock-smiths carry out an assessment so YOU can sleep safely at night.* The clipart picture of a cartoonish burglar with a sack over one shoulder and a striped jumper suggested that it had been designed many years earlier. From the evidence on display, AAA Locksmiths was not exactly a thriving business.

Lukas vaulted over the counter and rummaged underneath. 'Dust balls, old receipts and,' he paused to pull out a bag, 'mint humbugs.'

I pulled a face.

'You don't like mint humbugs?'

'They get stuck in my teeth.' I pointed at the flimsy wooden door that led beyond the shop floor. 'Shall we?'

Lukas bowed. I twisted the doorknob and opened the door. The rusty hinges creaked but there was no other sound. Fumbling around, I found a light switch and flicked it on. Several fluorescent strip lights buzzed into life, illuminating some sort of all-purpose back room. The piles of cardboard boxes indicated that it was a store room, but there was also a desk to one side with a dusty computer and a dirty mug with an inch of cold coffee inside it. I pressed the computer's power button, hoping that there might be something useful in its digital history. Lukas, who had followed me in, reached for a wastepaper basket and started rummaging through its contents.

The computer took an age to start up. While I waited, I flicked through the various books and folders stacked on a shelf. Three health and safety manuals, a guide to lock picking, instructions for using a handheld drill, and a dog-eared copy of Stephen King's *Pet Sematary*. I sighed.

'Anything?' I asked Lukas.

He shook his head. 'Not that I can see. It's all just crap.' He balled up a flyer for a local pizza delivery outfit and threw it back into the bin. He stood up and gazed at the beige wall before pointing at small scraps of Blu-tack. 'Something was pinned up here.' He stretched out his arms to measure the width. 'Something larger than a poster or a calendar. A map, maybe.'

I wrinkled my nose. 'Or perhaps blueprints of a certain bank.'

We exchanged glances. The computer finally beeped and

its screen lit up. I turned my attention to it and tapped a few keys. Hope flared in my chest when I saw that it wasn't password protected, but it didn't last long. There were no documents or files, either on the virtual desktop or hidden away in the hard drive. I checked the trash for deleted documents. That was empty, too.

'They've wiped it clean,' I muttered. I brought up the internet and checked the history. It was blank. Forensic IT technicians with specialist knowledge might have more luck but I wouldn't count on it. 'They knew that if they pulled off the robbery, this place would eventually be discovered. They cleared it out and aren't planning to come back. It's a dead end.'

'It certainly seems that way,' Lukas agreed.

I massaged the back of my neck. 'The robbery didn't happen today so they must have gone somewhere, either to run and hide or to re-group for another attempt.' I raised my head and met Lukas's eyes. 'This is the third time I've lived through this – the third fucking time – and I'm no further forward than I was when you were shot dead on Westminster Bridge. I don't know what to do, Lukas. I can stop the robbery from happening, I can stop you being killed but I still can't find these fuckers. I don't even know their names.'

Lukas strode over to me. 'It's not over yet. There's still time.'

I managed a small smile. 'Oh, I'm not giving up. DI Collier thinks I'm a waste of space because I'm in Supe Squad and I have only a few months' experience. I won't allow him to be right. And I certainly won't allow these bastards to escape.'

He grinned. 'If I were them, I'd be very afraid.'

Maybe if I kept telling myself that, it might actually be true. I lifted the copy of *Pet Sematary* from the shelf and held it up. 'Have you ever read this?'

Lukas shook his head. 'Can't say that I have.'

'It's a horror story about a place where dead bodies are buried. Family pets to begin with – the family in the story bury their cat there. The cat comes back, rises from the dead, but it's not the same as it once was. It's changed. It's evil. Then a young boy dies and he's buried in the same place and...'

Lukas held up his hand to stop me. 'It's just a story. And you're not evil.'

'Every time I come back,' I said, 'I'm a little bit different. I'm stronger. I feel more powerful.'

'It's only a book.'

'Yeah.' I shrugged. 'I guess so.' I turned to replace it on the shelf. As I did so, a piece of paper fluttered from its pages onto the floor. I frowned, picked it up and unfolded it. If I wasn't mistaken, it was a printout from a computer screen – a screenshot from an anonymous Darknet forum.

'They cleared the place out,' I said. 'But they forgot this.' I passed it to Lukas. My pulse rate was accelerating.

He read it aloud. '*Required. Small group with experience testing boundaries and taking risks. Must be familiar with biscuits and unafraid of bluebottles. Substantial compensation for the right applicant.*' He looked up.

'In some circles,' I said, '"Biscuit" is slang for gun.'

'And "bluebottles"?'

I set my mouth into a thin line. 'Police.' I stared hard at the piece of paper. 'This gang didn't come up with the idea to rob the Talismanic Bank on their own – they were hired.' I folded my arms, feeling my heart race. 'And that,' I said, 'changes everything.'

CHAPTER TWENTY-ONE

By the time we left AAA Locksmiths, there were only two hours to go before midnight struck and my day was re-set. I was fresh out of ideas and tired of going round in circles. I'd done all I could for now. I had no clue who might have hired the gang. The only thing left was to wait for the day to re-start itself one final time and cross my fingers that I could control what happened.

I'd learned a great deal through the re-sets but only time would tell if I'd learned enough. As long as I could avoid any loss of life, whether it be Lukas's or a Talismanic bank employee's or Margaret Wick's or Adam Jones' or anyone else who deserved better, I'd count it as successful. If I could bring down the gang and find their mysterious employer at the same time, I'd host a damned party. With champagne. And those silly string poppers. And posh canapés that I'd cook myself, if I had to.

'How's your shoulder?' Lukas asked.

I'd barely given it a thought for hours. It continued to ache but there had been no more bleeding. Frankly, it was the least of my worries. 'It's alright, I guess.'

'We have some decent medical equipment at Heart,' he told me, referring to his nightclub. 'If we head there, I can get someone who's properly trained to look it over and do what they can to help along the healing. With or without the aid of vampire saliva. You don't want it to hold you back when everything re-starts again.'

I considered his words. 'I don't want to go to Heart,' I said finally. The thought of the sweaty crowds and thumping music was more than I could handle.

Lukas's expression shuttered. 'Very well. I can follow you to Supe Squad to make sure you get back safely. Or to your own flat, if you prefer.'

I licked my lips. 'I don't want to go to Supe Squad. I don't want to go home either.'

His eyes flicked to mine.

'Do you have any medical supplies at your house?' I asked.

'I do.'

'Perhaps,' I said, 'we can go there instead.'

'We could do that,' Lukas murmured carefully.

I kept my gaze steady. 'Then you can check my shoulder.'

'Uh-huh.'

'You can use your own saliva to help it heal.'

'Mmmm.'

The rest of my words came out in a rush. 'And then there'll still be enough time for me to rip off your clothes and for us to have wild, passionate sex.'

I didn't miss the sudden flare of intense triumph in Lukas's black eyes although he quashed it quickly. 'Are you doing this,' he asked slowly, 'because I won't remember it? Because in a few hours, for me, it will have never happened?'

'No,' I answered simply. 'I'm doing it because I want to feel your body next to mine. I want to feel your body inside mine.' I swallowed, suddenly worried I'd misjudged the situation. 'But I understand if this is too much for you, or if you feel like I'm taking advantage and you need to say no.'

'Believe me,' he muttered. I could feel the heat emanating from his body, although our skin was not touching. 'I would never say no. Not to you.'

WE TOOK TALLULAH. Every molecule in my body was bitingly conscious of Lukas's proximity. It was almost painful to breathe. I felt hyper-aware of him; every time he shifted his weight or moved, no matter how slightly, I felt it.

Anticipation clung to the air and I knew that the goose bumps on my skin had nothing to do with the cold. I'd never quite understood it when I'd heard people talk about electricity between partners. Now I did. It was as if the very oxygen around us snapped and spun of its own accord. My chest was tight and there was an odd tremor in my hands that I couldn't seem to control. I kept my eyes on the road, unable to look at him. Neither of us said a single word.

I pulled up outside his grand house, ignoring the double-yellow lines. I clambered out of the car and joined him on the pavement just as he straightened up. We turned to each other, toe to toe. His Adam's apple dipped as he swallowed before he extended his hand. I reached to take it. Our fingers touched and I felt the familiar flare of heat spark between us—

A harsh voice called from the other side of the road.

I turned my head. Collier. He was sitting in an unmarked police car with the window wound down and a derisive expression on his face. 'I might have known.' He opened the door and stepped out. 'I might have known that the two of you were screwing. It explains a lot.'

Lukas growled. I shook my head. 'I've got this,' I

murmured. I walked into the middle of the road to address DI Collier face to face. 'What exactly does it explain?' I demanded.

'You can't stay in Supe Squad and be unbiased. Not when you're fucking a supe.' The sneering edge to his voice matched the nasty glint in his eyes. 'Especially not that supe.'

I'd used the same excuse when I'd told myself that I had good reason to avoid Lukas. That's why I knew it was bullshit. 'Really? So what you're saying is that no police officer in the rest of the Met can ever have a relationship. If your department deals with humans and arrests humans, but you also sleep with humans, then you can't possibly be fair and even-handed. We should all take a vow of celibacy.'

'You're twisting my words,' he spat.

'Am I? Are you married, DI Collier? When you sleep with your wife, does that mean you're sleeping with the enemy?'

'That's completely different! And you know it.'

I kept my arms by my sides, forcing myself to look relaxed. I wasn't going to get defensive. I had nothing to get defensive about, not where Lukas was concerned. Not any more.

'No,' I said. 'It's not. My personal relationships have no bearing on my professional life.' I was aware that I was echoing words that Lukas had said to me not too long ago. 'I'm more than capable of separating the two. As I assume you are.'

'Does he suck your blood?' Collier's lip curled. 'Does he bleed you dry? Does he use slick words and wrong power to get you to do what he wants? Because there's at least one terrorist running about this city, and all you seem to be interested in is getting your leg over.'

'There is no terrorist. There are criminals who I'm going to catch. I'll ensure they're put away for a very long time. But there's no terror plot, and deep down you know it as well as I do. You're spinning your wheels and swinging your big dick and you've gone nowhere. I've seen enough to know that you can be good at your job, but you're letting your prejudices get the better of you, DI Collier. You can't see the wood for the trees. And you know what I think?'

His lips drew back across his teeth in a snarl more convincing than any I'd ever seen from a vampire.

'I think,' I whispered, 'that you're much better than this and you know it.' I raised my eyes to his so he could see the truth of my words. And then, without any warning, I curled my fingers into a fist and punched him on the nose.

'Aaaaaargh!' He staggered, his hands clutching his face. I watched. I hadn't thrown my full weight behind the blow. That wouldn't have been fair, even to Collier.

'Go home, DI Collier,' I said. 'And tomorrow, be better than you are today.' I pivoted and re-joined Lukas, slipping my hand into his and flashing him a smile. 'Alright,' I conceded softly, 'I did that because I know he won't remember it and it felt damned good.'

Lukas dipped his head to my ear. 'Violence usually leaves me cold,' he said. 'Despite the fact that I'm a vampire, blood doesn't turn me on. But I have to say, that now I'm even more aroused than I was before.'

I squeezed his hand, then I tugged him up the steps and through the door of his house.

I'D ALREADY PULLED off my T-shirt by the time we reached his kitchen. Lukas opened a cupboard and drew out a large first-aid kit while I jumped onto the marble-topped kitchen island and carefully unpeeled the makeshift bandages from my shoulder. My flesh felt tender, and the bullet hole was ragged around the edges, but the wound looked clean and there was no sign of infection. Dr Yara had done a good job.

Lukas dampened a cloth and gently wiped away the crusted blood. He looked up at me with a question in his eyes.

'You don't have to,' I said. 'I know my blood doesn't taste nice.'

'I want to,' he replied. 'I just want to know that you want it too.'

'I wouldn't be here if I didn't.'

Something gleamed in his expression then he fixed his attention on my shoulder, his tongue darting out delicately to lick my skin. My fingers curled round the cool marble edge and I closed my eyes. The wound tingled and the dull ache that had persisted throughout the day eased immediately. Vampires were truly impressive creatures.

Lukas tied a new bandage round my shoulder, his touch so gentle that I barely felt the brush of his fingers. He fastened it carefully and planted a single feather-light kiss on my collarbone. I shivered. He brushed another kiss and then another, his lips making a trail from one side to the other. Each touch of his lips was agonising. I groaned.

'I want to please you,' Lukas muttered. 'Tell me what you like.'

I opened my eyes and gazed down. 'I like you.' And then to prove it, I reached for his belt and undid it, my fingers grazing his skin.

Lukas drew in a shuddering breath. Without warning, something in his body language altered. He carefully removed my hands from his waist, stepped back and shook his head. 'Wait.'

Wait? I swallowed. If Lukas wanted space, I'd give it to him. 'What is it?' I asked.

He took a moment or two. It was clear that he was

selecting his words with care. 'It's not that long since your ex did what he did to you. I know you're still experiencing trauma from both times that he killed you. I imagine dying at the hands of the person you trust most in the world must be truly terrible. If I could erase what happened, I would. Believe me, Emma,' he said with soft insistence, 'I really would. I can understand that opening yourself up to someone else must feel impossible.'

His expression was sober. 'It's why I've tried to keep my distance and not pressure you too much. It's why I didn't pursue matters when you kept avoiding me. And I know you have concerns about some of my practices as Lord. You know my stance on the police. But this can't be just about sex for me. I want it but, if that's all this is, I won't allow it. I'm not Scarlett and you're not Fred.'

He sighed heavily and I saw the troubled glimmer in the dark depths of his eyes. 'Don't do this now if it's because you feel guilty that I died. I know I won't remember any of this but you will. The last thing I want is more barriers between us in the future, especially when I won't be able to understand why.'

It was a few seconds before I could respond. 'I didn't know,' I whispered. 'I didn't know that you were thinking all that.'

There was tenderness in his gaze. 'How could I not? You do a good job with your tough police detective image, but it's obvious to anyone with eyes that there's a whole lot more to you than that. Layers upon layers of Emma. Any time I think I've unpeeled one, I find another.'

My tongue wetted my lips. 'I've struggled with this,' I admitted. 'I don't know if I can trust you – and I don't know if that's because of me or because of you. And your death certainly has a lot to do with me being here right now. Not because I feel sorry for you, but because it made me realise how stupid I'd been to deny my feelings. I don't know what the future will bring – I don't even know what tomorrow will bring, and I've lived it three times already. But I know that I want this now because I want you. Not sex,' I smiled faintly, 'although that would be good, but you. Lord Lukas Horvath.'

He gazed at me before his lips descended on mine.

All coherent thought fled as the dull ache in my groin increased. Lukas's hands moved to my waist, tightening their grip as the kiss deepened. I pressed my body against his and, when that wasn't enough, hooked my legs round his waist.

He lifted me off the marble top, holding me against him. I leaned back slightly and looked into his eyes. They glittered black, with an intensity I'd never seen before. His chest was rapidly rising and falling, his short breaths matching mine. 'Upstairs,' he growled.

I couldn't speak; all I could do was nod. I wrapped my arms round his neck and he moved quickly, carrying me upstairs. It still seemed to take an age. When we finally reached his bedroom and he laid me gently on the bed, I remembered to breathe.

I glanced round the sumptuous room. The bed was a heavy mahogany four poster, complete with dark satin sheets. The wallpaper was a rich red brocade and, when I caught a glimpse of myself in the mirrored ceiling, I barked out a laugh and found my voice. 'I feel like I've wandered into a Victorian bordello.'

Two high points of red coloured Lukas's cheeks. 'I haven't re-decorated for quite a while. But I'll change it to whatever you want.'

I smiled at him. 'I like it. It suits you.' I placed a hand on the mattress beneath me and tested it. 'It's not water.'

'Even I have limits.'

My smile grew to a saucy smirk. I pointed at the chair opposite. 'Sit,' I commanded.

Lukas did as he was told. I pushed myself up onto my knees. With slow fingers, more because I was trembling than trying to be sexy, I undid the top button of my jeans and started to push them down my hips. I glanced down, belatedly realising that my underwear was of the greying kind rather than lacy lingerie. Now it was my turn to be embarrassed but, from the way that Lukas's breath caught, he didn't seem to care.

I wriggled the rest of the way out my jeans and pushed them aside before turning round so my back was to Lukas. I reached for the hook on my bra and unclipped it, sliding the straps down my shoulders. I flicked a look over my shoulder.

Lukas groaned. He sprang out of the chair and reached me in a second, lifting me so that I was facing him yet again.

'I thought,' I murmured, 'that I told you to sit.'

I felt his hot breath on my skin. 'I'm done being a good boy.' He kissed me again.

This time our movements were more urgent. I scrabbled at Lukas's trousers, undoing the zip and pushing them down while he discarded my bra. His hands cupped my breasts, the base of his thumbs caressing my taut nipples. His head dropped, his tongue lapping a trail from my mouth downwards. I moaned, unable to help myself. My hands fumbled, reaching for his hot, hard cock. My fingers encircled it briefly before stroking down towards the tip.

'Witch,' he muttered. He hooked his thumbs round my panties and yanked them off. I released my grip on him. A moment later he was inside me, all the way to the hilt. I gasped and fell back. Lukas looked at me, his expression one of delight, triumph and deep satisfaction. And then, inch by inch, he slowly slid out. His control was absolute.

With a ragged breath I reached for his body again, trying

to pull him back. But he was taking his time. He waited, with only the tip of his penis still inside me. 'Tell me, Emma.' He licked his lips. 'Tell me you want me.'

My answer was little more than a croak. 'I want you.'

'Only me.'

I nodded. 'Lukas…'

'Say it.'

I swallowed. 'Only you.'

He smiled, then he thrust again. Our sweat-slick bodies rose to meet each other. I flung back my head, catching a brief glimpse in the mirrored ceiling of his muscled body on top of mine before I let myself go altogether, shuddering uncontrollably.

I LAY ON MY SIDE, one arm draped across Lukas's chest and my legs entwined with his. His fingers toyed with my hair but his eyes were on the clock by the bedside table. 'There are only a few minutes to go. You'll remember all this.' He paused. 'I won't. Will you tell me what happened?'

'Will you believe me if I do?'

His gaze dropped to mine. 'Always.'

'Then, yes,' I whispered. 'I'll tell you.'

The corners of his mouth lifted slightly and I felt him relax. 'Good.' His thumb stroked my cheek. 'No matter what happens when you start the day again,' he said, 'and no matter what the outcome is, you'll have done your best. Even if things don't work out as they should, I know you well enough to appreciate that once you make a decision about something, you throw yourself into it with every inch of your heart.' His hand moved to the centre of my chest. 'And, Emma, you have such a beautiful heart. I don't want you to be frightened of me or what this might become. I would never hurt you.'

'I know.' And I did. Lukas wasn't Jeremy. And whether he was a vampire or not, and whether I truly trusted him or not, he felt like a part of me.

I smiled at him, allowing my eyes to drift closed. I could lie here for ever. I didn't want to think about what was going to happen next, or whether I'd finally manage to succeed in bringing down the bank robbers. There were still too many unanswered questions about them. Who had hired them? Who was the sniper? How had they known which safety deposit boxes to steal? I sighed and nestled deeper against Lukas's hard body, unsure if I'd ever find the answers.

A moment later, my eyes flew open and I sat bolt upright.

'What?' Lukas asked. 'What is it?'

'Pralk's office.' Goddamnit. I could have smacked myself on the head for not thinking of it sooner. I cursed loudly. Out of the corner of my eye, the red glow of the digital clock taunted me. It was 11.59pm. My time was almost up.

'What about it?'

'He had photos on his walls. Employees of the year. There were several of an older goblin with glasses. I saw it during my first episode, when I was speaking to you about what was inside your safety deposit boxes.' I stared down at my feet. A curl of smoke was already starting to rise up.

'So?'

'I interviewed the bank employees today. *All* of them. But the guy with glasses wasn't there.'

The smoke was starting to coil round my legs and stretch up towards the ceiling. I knew that Lukas couldn't see it. And I knew I had only seconds left.

'Maybe he was on holiday. Maybe he doesn't work there any more.'

'Maybe.' I turned and looked at him. 'But my gut is telling me that's not it. I can't explain it. Lukas…'

A wisp of smoke appeared from nowhere, creating a barrier between us. I gripped his hand and squeezed it tight. Shit. 'Lukas,' I whispered again.

'Don't go, Emma.'

'I…'

I didn't get the chance to finish my sentence.

CHAPTER TWENTY-TWO

THE RADIO CRACKLED AND THE SUNLIGHT GLEAMED. AS A COLD wash of clarity hit me, I slammed my foot on the brake, jerking forward but stopping an inch from the rear of the taxi in front of Tallulah. The taxi driver's hand shot out of the window and he extended his middle finger in my direction. I stared at it for a brief second. I could still taste Lukas. Then I pulled Tallulah out and swerved round the taxi, grabbing the radio with one hand.

'DC Bellamy, this is Dispatch. Please acknowledge.'

'This is DC Bellamy.'

'What is your current location? Your presence is required at the London Eye.'

I pressed down on the accelerator and drove off the bridge, already veering towards the large observation wheel. 'I'm less than ten minutes' away. I'll deal with the suicidal vampire.'

'How did you know...?'

I clicked off the radio. I didn't need any unnecessary conversations. Every second counted and I couldn't waste a single one. My plans for today already involved an incredible amount of risk and very real danger. I had to stay focused or disaster might ensue.

With one hand on the steering wheel, I dug out my phone and found the first number I needed. Fortunately Fred answered on the second ring. 'What's up, boss?'

'You have to head to Tower Bridge,' I told him. 'I've had a tip-off that there's about to be an incident there.'

I knew from his voice that he was instantly on the alert. 'What sort of incident?'

'Some drama students are going to pretend to be were-wolves and hijack a tour bus. I need you to get to the scene and do what you can to manage it. The clan alphas will appear at some point. Keep them there for as long as you can. The students are harmless – as far as they're concerned, it's nothing more than a daft prank. But I need the alphas kept out of the way for as long as possible. It's for their own good.'

'I don't understand.'

'You don't have to. I'll explain later.'

'Um, okay.' He sounded doubtful but he'd do as he was told.

It felt strange to be condoning the bank robbers' diversion to keep the werewolves out of the way, but I couldn't leave anything to chance. This was my last opportunity to get everything right.

'Thanks. I'll see you at Supe Squad later this afternoon.' I hung up and called Liza.

'You're supposed to be taking the day off to visit family,' she said when she answered, clearly suspicious.

I almost snorted. My visit to my uncle now seemed like it had taken place a lifetime ago. 'It took less time than I thought it would,' I said. I tried to sound cheerful to throw off her balance and make it easier to get her to agree to my next request. Unsurprisingly, it didn't work.

'What's wrong? Is this to do with what's happening at the

London Eye? I've already had about five calls about that. Horvath is at the scene, so it'll probably be alright. Goodness knows why any vamp would want to make such a spectacle of themselves. The mind boggles.'

'Mmm.' I reached a set of traffic lights and pulled up Tallulah, drumming my fingers on the steering wheel and peering ahead. I had a good view of the London Eye from here and I glimpsed the black-clad figure of Adam Jones as he ascended. 'What's going on at the Eye isn't important,' I lied. 'I have a job for you. It's going to involve leaving the office.'

'I'm supposed to stay here and man the desk.'

'I'm aware of that. But it's a beautiful day outside and you'll like this task.'

'I doubt that very much.'

I smiled slightly. The traffic lights changed to green and I drove forward yet again. 'It's very important you get the timing right,' I said. 'So listen carefully. How much money is in the petty-cash tin?'

'A few hundred quid.'

'Great. Empty it out. I'll replace it later.' I outlined what I wanted her to do. 'Can you manage that?'

'Of course I can manage that. What I don't understand is why.'

'I don't have time to explain, but it's really important.'

'If it's so important, why can't you do it?'

I parked Tallulah and jumped out onto the pavement. 'I've got somewhere else I need to be. Promise me you'll do this, Liza. And that you won't be late.'

Her response was grudging. 'I'll do it.' She paused. 'But you'll owe me.'

I grinned and started crossing the road. 'I will. Thank you.'

She muttered something under her breath that might

have been to do with the idiocy of detectives like me. I grinned some more, then made one last call. This was the one I was least looking forward to.

'You've reached the Criminal Investigations Department,' a bored switchboard operator said.

With my free hand, I reached for my warrant card and waved it at the familiar face of the young police officer manning the cordon. He nodded at me. Ignoring the gawking crowds, I trotted past him and headed for the foot of the London Eye, where Hannigan, Paige – and Lukas – were waiting.

'I need to speak to DI Collier as a matter of extreme urgency,' I said. 'My name is Emma Bellamy.'

'One moment please.'

I gripped the phone tightly.

'This is Collier,' said a gruff voice.

'DI Collier, you don't know me. I'm Detective Constable Emma Bellamy. I work out of Supe Squad.'

'I've heard of you.' He already sounded like he hated me. 'What do you want?'

'I'm at the London Eye. There's an incident here involving a member of the public who's impersonating a vampire. I'm about to take him into custody. The thing is...' I sounded appropriately hesitant and thanked my lucky stars that I'd heard Molly's insights about Collier.

'Yes?'

'I might be mistaken, but I'm sure I heard him shout something about Timothy Barratt. I recall that you did superlative work in investigating Barratt's murder last year and bringing his killer to justice. It might be nothing but I wondered...'

'I'm on my way.'

I smiled. I'd just taken out two birds with one stone.

Maybe things would go my way after all. I pocketed the phone while Hannigan started to flap his arms and yell.

'You have to get that idiot down!' he shouted. 'There are news crews here already. This isn't the sort of publicity we need right now!'

'Are you suggesting, Mr Hannigan,' Lukas enquired, 'that the pages of tomorrow's newspapers are more important than a person's life? Perhaps we should hope for a gust of wind to knock the poor fellow off his perch? Then you can clean up the bloodied mess of brains and splattered internal organs while the tourists get back on board for their selfies.'

I strode up. 'I am Detective Constable Emma Bellamy. I'm with Supe Squad.' I gave both Hannigan and Paige a breezy smile. 'Don't worry. We'll get all this sorted out in a jiffy.'

I glanced at Lukas. I couldn't stop my gaze from softening. I looked him up and down, enjoying the opportunity to see him in his ridiculous ruffled shirt yet again. Then I thought about what it had been like to have his lips on mine and to feel his body next to me.

As Lukas registered my expression, a tiny crease appeared in his brow. 'Hello, Emma. If I didn't know better,' he murmured, 'I'd say you were thinking of something very interesting indeed.'

I licked my lips. 'I am.'

'How are you? You've been avoiding my calls.'

I didn't look away. 'I'm sorry about that. I should have spoken to you but I felt a lot confused and a little scared. You deserved better. I won't avoid you again, I promise.'

Lukas tilted his head, a lock of jet-black hair falling across his forehead. 'Something's happened,' he said. 'Something's changed.'

'Yes.' I nodded. 'It has.'

His eyes narrowed. Then his nostrils flared and he

glanced at my shoulder. He stiffened. 'Are you bleeding? Have you been hurt?'

'It's an old wound. I'm fine.'

'You look more than fine,' Lukas muttered. 'In fact, scent of blood aside, you look as if you're glowing.'

I couldn't prevent the grin that spread across my face. 'Do you know,' I said softly, 'I feel like I am glowing.'

'What the hell is going on?' Hannigan screeched, while Paige stared at us both, her mouth hanging open. 'This isn't the time for some bizarre flirting session! There's a damned vampire halfway up my wheel! Get that freak down from there!'

'Don't worry, sir,' I murmured, my eyes still on Lukas. 'We'll sort this out.' I pulled myself away and walked over to the Eye. Adam Jones was already about halfway up. I tilted my head and stared at him as he climbed. The poor kid thought he was immortal.

A second later, Lukas joined me. 'Who is he?' he growled.

I yanked my attention away from Adam. 'Pardon?'

'Who's the guy? Who made you glow? You can't tell me that there's not a man involved. It's written all over your face.' He looked furious.

I felt a jerk of astonishment. I must have been far easier to read than I thought. I considered my answer before opting for the simple truth. 'You,' I said. 'You're the guy.'

'What?' he bit out.

'It's taken me a while,' I said, 'but I've finally seen the light.'

His eyes glittered, searching my face. 'Are you teasing me, Emma?'

'No.' I drew in a breath. 'But this isn't the time for this conversation.' I nodded upwards. 'Can you climb up there and try to encourage the … vampire down? I have a feeling he doesn't want to jump and this is all some sort of show. I'm afraid he'll run off at the first opportunity. If I can position myself to stop that, perhaps we can find out what's going on here.'

'Believe me,' Lukas said. 'I want to know exactly what's going on here.' A muscle ticked in his jaw.

I felt a rush of anxiety that I'd played this all wrong and he would delay his climb. I shouldn't have worried; Lukas turned to the wheel and started to scale the observation wheel without a backward glance. I released the air in my lungs before jogging to the spot beyond the security barrier where I knew Adam Jones would end up.

I didn't have to wait long. 'Left!' I heard Lukas yell. 'Go left!'

I tensed. Moments later, a black-hooded figure scrambled over the barrier, intent on escape. He didn't notice me until I grabbed him. In one swift movement, I cuffed him with a plastic tie and hauled him to his feet. 'Adam Jones,' I said. 'You are under arrest.'

He blinked before his face went slack with astonishment. 'How the fuck do you know my name?'

I smiled at him. 'I hope you're not planning on helping anyone rob any banks later today, Adam.'

His shock swiftly transformed to panic. 'What? What are you talking about? No! No way! I wouldn't do that. What bank? I wouldn't rob a bank! I'm not that kind of person!'

Someone ought to have told him that the more you denied something, the more culpable you appeared. I sighed and patted him on the shoulder as I heard a new set of sirens. DI Collier. Right on time.

I half led, half dragged Adam Jones to the front of the Eye. The crowd goggled at him and so did half the assembled police officers. Lukas, down from his own climb, appeared. He took one look at Adam and his face darkened. 'You're not a vampire.'

'He was wearing fake fangs,' I said cheerfully. 'They fell off when he was halfway up the wheel.'

Lukas frowned. 'Why?' he asked. 'Why do this?'

DI Collier was already striding towards us. 'Get back from that suspect!'

I clicked my tongue. 'You'd better do as the man says, Lukas. This guy is human. He should be taken into police custody for further questioning.'

'He pretended to be a vampire,' Lukas said through gritted teeth. 'That means I'm involved too.'

I shook my head. 'Not according to the law.'

Collier sent me an approving look that didn't warm me to him in the slightest. 'Here you go, sir,' I said. 'It's probably best if you take him to CID headquarters at Curtis Green and question him there. I'm not sure what he knows about Timothy Barratt but—'

'Who the fuck is Timothy Barratt?' Adam Jones burst out.

Lukas folded his arms. I gave him a quick look, hoping he would interpret it.

'I'll take charge from here.' Collier reached for Adam.

'Good,' I said briskly. I checked my watch. Time to vamoose. I swivelled and started marching back to Tallulah. Both Collier and Lukas called after me. I sent a silent apology in Lukas's direction and gave Collier not a second thought. Then I turned off my phone to avoid the inevitable calls from DSI Barnes. The Talismanic Bank, here we come.

CHAPTER TWENTY-THREE

Tallulah was on her best behaviour as I zipped through the bustling London city streets. I slowed when I spotted the happy family with their colourful bunch of balloons. Moments later, I drove round the corner onto the main road in time to see Liza stride up to the woman on the pavement. The small dungaree-clad boy goggled at her, his attention transfixed by the gooey chocolate cake she was carrying. I nodded, satisfied, as Liza pulled out a thin wad of cash and handed it to the woman before kneeling down to the boy and offering him some cake. Then I put them all out of my mind. The easy part was done; now I was slipping into less-charted territory. Time was still on my side – but only just. And only if I were fast.

Rather than turn onto the same street as the Talismanic Bank, I swerved Tallulah round to the road that ran parallel to it. I wanted to get as close to the rear of the bank as I could. Fortunately, my luck held and I managed to drive into the single available parking space outside the doctor's surgery.

I leapt out and jogged round, scrambling easily onto the

flat roof. I eyed the empty courtyard of the bank. Pralk had been right: from this distance, vaulting across the gap while avoiding the sensors on top of the wall appeared all but impossible. Then again, I was a phoenix so I didn't have wings. But if I were careful, I might just be able to fly.

I would only get one chance. If I set off the alarm by accident, all my plans would fail. The trick would be to aim for a specific point in the courtyard and focus on it. I wasn't especially aerodynamic but I'd learned one or two things from witnessing Adam Jones's controlled tumble from the Eye.

I drew back, allowing myself several metres for a run up. My heart thumped against my chest. Run, I told myself. Jump. Roll. I repeated the words in my head like a mantra. Run. Jump. Roll. Run. Jump. Roll. I pushed my hair out of my eyes. And then I went for it.

Loose gravel on the surgery roof flew up around my feet as I gave it everything I had and sprinted towards the edge. I had to gain enough momentum to spring upwards and clear the wall. I might not be an Olympic long jumper, but I had to believe I could do it.

My toes hit the roof's edge and I pushed off, pumping my arms and legs as if I were running through the very air itself. Up, up, over and ... the ground rushed up to meet me.

I folded myself into a ball, bent my knees and prepared for impact. It was jarring and I gasped with pain when I smacked into the hard concrete of the courtyard. Despite my best efforts, I hadn't landed well and spears of agony shot through my left ankle. The force of my landing also sent waves of pain radiating through the wound in my shoulder. I grimaced and blinked back involuntary tears, but I couldn't allow myself the luxury of feeling pathetic.

I heaved myself upwards, glanced at the wall and gave it the finger. Then I limped over to the bank's rear door. It was already 1.21pm.

I put the numbers into the keypad, suddenly doubting my memory and praying that I wouldn't set off the alarm by getting the code wrong. When I heard the lock click open, relief flooded through me.

I pushed open the door and stepped across the threshold. I'd made it this far. I straightened my back and, ignoring the screeching jolts of pain from my shoulder and my ankle, strode along the corridor, past the messy staffroom, the computer server room and the chillingly familiar safety deposit box room.

I reached the final door and shoved it open into the main hall of the Talismanic Bank. Part of me had been expecting one of the bank employees to spot me and demand to know what I was doing in the bowels of their building, but my entrance was obscured by one of the large marble pillars. Not a single person glanced in my direction.

I counted three bank tellers and five customers. There was the pixie, staring at her phone with intense concentration as she waited for her turn. The two werewolves, whose blood had previously leaked all over the shiny floor, were deep in conversation, chuckling at some shared joke. There was the human who'd wandered in off the street to goggle at the architecture.

For a moment I watched them all. They had no idea what was about to happen unless I could stop it. An invisible hand wrapped round my chest and squeezed it tight.

I squared my shoulders and marched over to Lord Fairfax's beta. She was next in line. I hooked my arm round hers. She stiffened and turned to throw me off. I was ready for that and tightened my grip. 'Hello, Toffee,' I murmured. 'I need you to come with me. Lord Fairfax asked me to find you.'

'He doesn't know I'm here.' Her eyes narrowed. 'And I'm not going anywhere with you.'

This was the riskiest part of the operation, and I tried not to let my fear show on my face. I knew from the brief CCTV report Liza had given me that the trio of robbers hadn't started shooting until Toffee challenged them. All my plans hinged on getting her out of the way before they arrived. I didn't have her real name, so I couldn't use it to compel her; even if I'd had it I doubted I would have succeeded – She was a beta – and that meant she was strong. My powers over high-ranking supes were patchy at the best of times.

'Okay,' I muttered, keeping my voice low. 'You caught me out. I've not spoken to Fairfax – but I need to talk to you urgently. It's part of a Supe Squad investigation that's incredibly time sensitive.' I hoped my vagueness would snag her interest. Unfortunately, it didn't.

'I don't care what you're doing. I'm not saying anything to you until I've spoken to my alpha.' Her lip curled and I saw the challenge in her eyes. 'If you want to wait until I'm done here, we can go to Lisson Grove together and speak to him.' She laughed coldly. 'But you don't want to do that, do you? Because it's Fairfax himself you're investigating.' I blinked and Toffee laughed again. 'I'm not stupid, detective. Why else would you want to talk to me?'

'I can't tell you here – it's too public. And your lord isn't at Lisson Grove. There's an incident occurring on Tower Bridge. He'll be heading there.'

That caught her attention. 'What incident?'

'A group of werewolves have hijacked a bus and they're holding the people inside hostage.'

She stared at me. 'Bullshit.'

'It's true.'

'If it's true, why aren't you there?' she sneered.

'My colleague is there in my place,' I said. Toffee yanked her arm back. I let her go, unwilling to antagonise her too much and lose control of the situation. 'Listen, Toffee, you…'

I didn't get a chance to finish my sentence. She pulled out her phone and jabbed in a number, then she stepped further back. Eyeing me as if I were some kind of rabid dog, she held the phone to her ear. I didn't take her attitude personally; she wasn't any friendlier to the person on the other end of the line. 'Where the fuck are you?' she barked.

I strained my ears to hear the answer but I could only make out a few words. Then her eyes widened and her expression altered.

'What? What do you mean there's been a hijacking at Tower Bridge? Why didn't you call me?' She was already backing away. 'Goddamnit!' Toffee whirled round and sprinted out of the bank at full speed.

Everyone in the bank stared after her, except the pixie who glanced at me with open curiosity. I shrugged. It hadn't happened quite the way I'd expected but I'd achieved my goal: Toffee was out of the way and, with any luck, her speedy exit wouldn't have alarmed whoever was spying for the gang.

It made sense that she'd hear about Tower Bridge and would hotfoot it over there. Just in case, however, I drew out my own phone and pretended to call someone. 'What's happening at Tower Bridge?' I demanded loudly. 'Why would werewolves hijack a bus?'

Several mouths dropped open. The pixie gasped and the two McGuigan wolves looked at each other nervously.

And, at that very moment, the three masked robbers came in. 'Everyone down on the floor, now!'

Nobody moved a muscle. The woman raised the muzzle of her gun to the ceiling and fired a shot. That was more than enough; every single person, me included, dropped.

Even though I was expecting it, the cold marble floor against my skin was a shock. I couldn't prevent the swirl of nausea in the pit of my belly either; I was gambling a lot on Toffee's absence. I prayed I'd made the right choice.

I turned my head so I could watch the robbers. They marched forward confidently. The woman headed straight for the bank tellers, whilst the man by her side diverted through the door. A moment later, I heard the sound of crunching metal as he smashed open the stainless-steel box that controlled the bank's power. Almost immediately the overhead lights flickered off. Now Mosburn Pralk and the other staff were trapped upstairs while the rest of us were trapped down here.

The third robber faced the rest of us, moving his gun from bowed head to bowed head. I noticed one of the werewolves twitch as claws started to emerge from his right hand. The stress was forcing him into lupine transformation – either that or he was consciously planning an attack. Whatever it was, I had to stop him.

'Safety deposit boxes,' the woman barked, pointing her gun at one of the bank tellers. The middle-aged goblin behind the screen stared at her, her face slack with terror.

I slid a few inches along the floor, hoping that the robber wouldn't notice.

'I want the safety deposit boxes. Get me all the keys,' the woman ordered.

I slid forward another five inches.

The werewolf's leg was in spasm. He was trying to hide what was happening but it wouldn't be long before the robber noticed and opened fire.

'Nobody will be hurt,' the woman said, 'as long as you all cooperate.'

I saw fur springing up across the werewolf's cheekbone. I had to act. I swung my head towards the bank's front door. Come on. I held my breath. He should be here by now.

The bank teller fumbled with something and I heard the

masked woman hiss irritably. Much more of this and she'd lose patience. Then I heard footsteps and I breathed more easily. Finally.

'Hello?' There was a pause from the poor McGuigan werewolf who'd chosen this moment to wander inside to deposit his cheque. 'Uh…'

There was a flurry of movement. Two of the robbers spun round, as the third loosed off a single shot that thudded into one of the marble pillars. I was already on my feet. I threw myself not at the robbers but into the path of the confused, McGuigan werewolf, my hands raised in surrender.

'Don't shoot him!' I yelled. 'We're behaving! We're doing as you said!' I waved frantically at the incomer. He belatedly realised what was happening and lowered himself to the floor. I did the same, directly in front of him.

'I'm Detective Constable Emma Bellamy,' I continued. 'I'm with Supe Squad. I guarantee that nobody here will do anything to stop you, myself included.' I forced as much authority as I could into my tone. 'I take full responsibility for everyone here. If you shoot anyone, shoot me first. But we'll do whatever you tell us. We're not moving.'

The robbers stood absolutely still. I saw the black muzzle of the nearest gun waver and my stomach tightened further. Be sensible. Please. This time, be sensible.

There was a loud clinking sound and the bank teller's voice rang out. 'I've got the keys! Here! Here are the safety deposit box keys!' She held up a narrow box and rattled it.

For another half second nobody moved a muscle. Then the female robber spun round. 'Pass them through.'

The bank teller did as she was told. Some of the tension in my body eased.

The woman took the box and double-checked the contents. She nodded to her colleagues. 'I don't care whether she's with the police or whether she's the Queen of fucking Sheba,' she said in her fake Cockney accent. 'She'll bleed as red as the rest of you. We're in charge here. Stay where you are for another few minutes and you all might live to see another day. Make any moves and you won't.'

She and the nearest male robber, probably the one Adam Jones had labelled the Professor, strode to the door and the corridor beyond, leaving their gun-toting companion to keep an eye on us.

I glanced at the werewolf lying a mere three metres away from me. His body was flat and there was no sign of further spasms or fur. Even his claws had disappeared, smoothing into human skin and neatly trimmed fingernails. My ploy had worked. Praise be.

The first time the masked gang had entered the bank, Toffee had seen herself as the highest ranking and most powerful creature in there. It had been her responsibility to act. I'd removed her from the equation. In her absence, the other werewolves, particularly the one who'd begun to change, had taken up that baton. By speaking out, I'd positioned myself as the highest ranking hostage so the responsibility for what happened next passed to me. The onus of attempting an attack on the robbers had been stripped from the other werewolves now that I was at the top of the hierarchy. And that meant that the lives of everyone in here might be saved.

It took three minutes and twelve seconds. It felt like a lifetime as each second dragged by. The robber in front of me kept his gun trained on the back of my skull but I knew he was aware of everyone else in the bank too. Everyone behaved. I could see the small pixie, her eyes tightly squeezed shut. The only human was mumbling to himself in terror, an incessant litany that was the only sound in the hall. None of the werewolves moved. Then the other two robbers marched out, each holding a small tower of locked safety deposit boxes.

The woman nodded to the third gunman. He swung his gun from me to the werewolves to the still cowering bank tellers, covering his colleagues' escape. Their shiny shoes trod past me as they left with maximum efficiency. Seconds later I heard the brief rumble of an engine firing up outside. The last robber turned and ran out of the door at top speed. The bank's heavy front door banged shut behind him.

They'd gone.

CHAPTER TWENTY-FOUR

IT WAS SEVERAL SECONDS BEFORE I MOVED. WHEN I RAISED myself up and slowly climbed to my feet, it was as if a dam had burst.

The werewolves sprang up, rage and anxiety written on their faces. 'So much for fucking Supe Squad!' one of them yelled. He was in my face, his fists clenched. His ears were already sprouting fur and he was struggling to control himself. 'Aren't you supposed to stop crime? You just let those fuckers do what they wanted!' He spat on the ground. 'You're a waste of space!'

I didn't react. His fury was borne out of fear and adrenaline. Besides, from where he was standing, he had a good point. He hadn't seen himself lying on this very spot in a pool of his own blood.

'It might have escaped your notice,' I said calmly, 'but they were carrying very large guns.'

'So? I know who you are and I know what you're capable of. You're immortal, ain't you? You can't die. Why would you be afraid of getting shot?'

'Because,' I answered, 'if they'd shot me, they'd have shot you too. And everyone else in here.'

'You…' He faltered and his expression fell as he absorbed the possibility that he might not have made it out of the bank alive. 'You don't know that.'

Unfortunately, I did. I gave him a crooked smile and turned, just in time to see Mosburn Pralk burst through the door. 'Is anyone injured? Did anyone get hurt?'

The bank teller who'd handed over the box of keys emerged from her booth. From the interviews I'd conducted, I knew her name was Mista Tio. She was married, with three children, loved her job and took great pride in it. She brought home-made cakes in at the end of every month for her colleagues. The thought of the bank being robbed had genuinely never occurred to her. Now it was something she'd never forget.

'We're fine,' she said shakily. She was very pale beneath her golden skin and her green eyes looked enormous. 'They let off a shot but no one was hit.'

'Thank God.' Pralk sagged in relief. 'When they shut off the power, all the doors upstairs locked automatically. It took far too long to over-ride the system. You're all safe, though, and that's what matters. We can replace money. We can't replace you.'

The bank teller swallowed. She didn't appear mollified by his concern. 'They didn't take money,' she whispered. 'That's not what they were after.'

Pralk's brow creased. 'Then what…?'

'The safety deposit boxes,' I said, striding forward. I stuck out my hand. 'Good to meet you, Mr Pralk. I'm DC Bellamy.'

He blinked at me. 'Goodness. I've heard stories about your prowess, detective, but I didn't realise you were this good. You got here faster than I did – and I was in the building.'

'I was already here,' I explained.

'What?'

'I was already in the building when the robbers arrived.'

Pralk narrowed his eyes. 'Wait. If you were here, why didn't you stop them?'

The antsy werewolf snorted. 'That's exactly what I said.'

'Because if I'd intervened, innocent lives would have been lost.' I refused to apologise for my perceived lack of action. I knew exactly what I was doing.

Pralk's bottom lip curled in the faintest moue of disgust. Then he thought of something else and turned back to Mista Tio. 'The safety deposit boxes?' he asked.

She nodded, her fingers twisting together. Pralk's body went rigid. Uh-oh. I guessed the real penny had just dropped. 'Which ones? Which ones did they take?'

Her skin turned even paler. Rather than wait for her to gather her wits and think of an answer, Pralk whirled round and headed back the way he'd come. He moved remarkably quickly for someone so tall. I followed; I already knew where he was going and I knew what he would find there.

The safety deposit room looked exactly the same as it had the first time I'd been there. The same boxes had been targeted. I gazed round, unsurprised. Pralk, however, let out a low moan. He obviously didn't require a list to tell him who owned the missing boxes. And of course he recognised that the bank's own safety deposit box had been attacked.

I allowed him a moment or two, then I closed the door to afford us some privacy. 'Mr Pralk,' I said. 'You won't remember, but this isn't the first time we've met.'

He barely heard me. He continued to stare round the room, a desolate expression darkening his face. Then his gaze abruptly snapped to mine. 'What do you mean? If our paths had crossed, DC Bellamy, I certainly would have remembered.'

'Carpe Diem,' I said softly.

'Pardon?'

'I know you've heard of it because you told me you had. I've taken the Carpe Diem potion. As far as I'm concerned, this is the fourth time your bank has been targeted for robbery.'

He looked at me for one very long, very heavy moment as my words sank in. 'So,' he said finally, 'not only were you present during the robbery, but you also knew it was going to happen.' His hands dropped to his sides. 'In which case, DC Bellamy,' he bit out, 'I would love to know what the *fuck* you are playing at.'

This was the first time I'd heard Mosburn Pralk swear. Until now, I wouldn't have believed that a swear word could ever cross his lips. I acknowledged his anger with a nod but I didn't drop my gaze. 'Believe me, I've been trying to find the best way to deal with it. This is my last chance to get things right. Nobody has died this time around, which I count as a win. I know where the gang will be this evening, and I know how to stop them in their tracks. What I don't yet know is who they all are. At least one of the gang members has eluded my efforts so far.'

'Nobody has died this time?' He didn't move. 'So on other occasions…'

'There were deaths, including your own employees.'

He swallowed. 'Oh.'

I pointed at the empty lockers. 'Lord Horvath. Lady Carr. Lady Sullivan. Lord McGuigan. Lord Fairfax.' I paused. 'And the Talismanic Bank. The robbers knew exactly which boxes to go after.'

'You're suggesting someone from this bank is involved?' He shook his head vigorously. 'No. Carpe Diem potion or not, I won't believe that anyone who works here had anything to do with this.'

I allowed myself a small smile. 'That's what you've said every time.'

'Because it's true!'

'It's not.' I licked my lips. 'It can't be. The gang knew exactly what to take.'

'There is not a single employee here who would pass on that sort of information.'

'How about,' I asked softly, 'the employees who aren't here?'

Pralk frowned. 'What do you mean?'

'Can we go to your office?'

'Now?'

'There's something there I need to check.'

His unhappiness deepened. 'I have to inform the Board of Governors about what's happened. I have to make sure my staff are alright. I have to…'

'Please. It won't take long.'

He passed a hand across his forehead and sighed heavily. 'Very well then.'

We walked up the staircase in silence. Pralk's desperate gloom was palpable and there was nothing I could say that would ease his anxiety. He was thinking about all the information that had been lost and the ramifications if it fell into the wrong hands. I couldn't guarantee that I could stop that from happening. I was doing the best that I could, and I was certain I'd thought through all the possibilities, but it wasn't a foolproof plan. There wasn't one.

Pralk's office door was open. I walked in, ignoring the desk and the pile of files on top of it. Instead, I focused on the far wall and the array of smiling photos. I found the one I needed in seconds. 'This one.' I tapped my fingernail against the bespectacled goblin with the cravat. 'According to this photo, he was employee of the year in 2019 but when I interviewed your staff he wasn't here. Is he here today?'

Pralk stared at the photograph. 'That's Boswell Strom.'

'Where is Mr Strom? Did he call in sick? Is he on holiday?'

'Neither.' Pralk folded his arms and looked at me defiantly.

'He's the only member of your staff I've not spoken to. I've cleared all the others, but Strom…'

'I can assure you that he had nothing to do with the robbery and he certainly hasn't been passing on privileged information to anyone.'

'You can't be sure of that.'

The bank manager sniffed. 'I can. Boswell Strom is dead. He passed away after a stroke.'

My stomach dropped. 'When?'

'November. Almost seven months ago.' Pralk's voice was flat. 'He is not your man.'

I sank down into a chair. Damn it. When I'd thought of the photograph before the smoke had reappeared to reset my day, I'd been so sure this man had to be involved. He was the missing link who would lead me to the last member of the gang, not to mention the missing safety deposit boxes. But if Boswell Strom was already dead and had been for several months… I cursed loudly.

'Were you pinning all your hopes on him?' Pralk asked. 'Was this old photograph your only lead?'

Not the only lead, it had been the best one. I grimaced and cursed again.

'Frankly,' Pralk continued, 'the idea that Boswell would have betrayed this bank is laughable. He dedicated his life to it. He'd been here for decades. He even risked his own marriage because of his job here. His wife was none too happy – she wanted him to retire and frequently told me so. She was a pixie, though, not a goblin. She didn't understand what this place means to people like us.' A fond light crossed

Pralk's eyes. 'Boswell always said that this place was his second wife.'

I nodded distractedly. Then my head shot up. 'His wife. Is her name Esmeralda?'

Pralk seemed surprised. 'It is.'

'I've met her,' I said slowly. 'Outside the bank.'

'She lives across the road. I don't know why she doesn't move away and give herself some peace of mind. Maybe she still holds a grudge against us. Boswell worked until the day he dropped dead, and she refuses to cross our threshold or to talk to anyone who works here. Quite a few of us have reached out to her but she won't respond. She sees his death as our fault, even though it was Boswell who wanted to stay on. I suggested to him several times that it was time to retire but he wasn't interested. His wife is quite different in temperament but I suppose opposites attract.' He shrugged, as if the vagaries of married life were a mystery to him.

'When I spoke to her,' I said, 'she told me that the Talismanic Bank was a wonderful institution.'

Pralk snorted. 'She was being sarcastic. She keeps an account here, but only because she has no choice. She hates us and she always sends in a proxy when she has any business to attend to. I told Lord Fairfax as much when I visited him a few weeks ago and he asked me about my staff and their families. And I'll tell you what else I told him. Just because someone like Boswell's wife despises us doesn't mean that most of the supe community doesn't hold us in high esteem. To think that someone like her could pull off a bank robbery on this scale is ridiculous.'

Perhaps it was. But I'd spoken to this pixie; I'd looked into her eyes and I knew what she'd said. 'She wasn't being sarcastic,' I murmured. However, she might have been lying about her opinions of the bank to put me off the scent. She hadn't told me that Margaret Wick had been taken hostage when she must have known. And Adam Jones had mentioned that the fourth gang member was an older woman – an older woman with blue eyes. My skin tingled at the thought.

There was a knock on the door. Mista Tio appeared, looking more pale and worried than ever. 'Mr Pralk,' she whispered.

He smiled at her. 'What is it?'

She swallowed nervously. 'The clan alphas are here. And Lord Horvath.'

Pralk closed his eyes briefly in dismay. 'Very well,' he said. 'Thank you, Mista. I'll come down and speak to them.'

She nodded and withdrew. Pralk glanced at me. 'Tell me, detective. You know what's going to happen next. How will the supe leaders take the news that their most precious valuables have been stolen?'

I grimaced in sympathy. 'You don't need me to tell you that. You already know.'

CHAPTER TWENTY-FIVE

AFTER THE FIRST ROBBERY, THE ATMOSPHERE HAD BEEN sombre. The absence of any dead bodies on this occasion allowed the small assembly of high-powered supes to be far more vocal.

'How can this bank have been robbed?' Lady Carr demanded. Her petite body was shaking with rage. 'This is beyond the pale! This institution is supposed to be safe. It's supposed to be protected!'

'I agree,' Fairfax growled. He fixed Pralk with narrowed yellow eyes. 'How could you have allowed this to happen?'

'It's fine,' Lady Sullivan said dismissively. 'The Talismanic Bank has insurance. We will incur no real losses. Right?'

Pralk swallowed. 'Er…'

I sneaked a look at Lord McGuigan. He was pale and obviously shaken, but he remained silent. My gaze drifted to Lukas in the corner; he was watching me carefully, his expression inscrutable. He knew there was more to this situation than I was letting on. No doubt he was aware it was tied to what had happened at both the London Eye and Tower Bridge.

Lord McGuigan cleared his throat. 'What did these robbers steal?'

'I'm afraid that it wasn't money they were after,' Pralk said. 'Not in the first instance, anyway. The vaults are on a timer and you are correct that our insurance would have more than covered any financial loss.'

'They went after the safety deposit room,' Lukas murmured. He raised his eyebrows towards me in a dark question.

I nodded. 'Yes,' I said. 'That was their target. They deliberately arranged for diversions to ensure you couldn't intervene.'

'You were here.' Lady Sullivan spoke quietly but her eyes pierced me. 'You could have intervened.'

Fairfax's head snapped towards me.

'I'm on the case,' I said. I gestured to Pralk. 'Perhaps you should show everyone the safety deposit room.'

He didn't appear happy about the prospect but he knew it was inevitable. 'If you'd all like to follow me,' he said.

I ignored Lady Sullivan's glower and Lord Fairfax's continued stare and turned away. Events at the bank could continue without me. I headed out of the building with Lukas on my heels.

It was clear from the crowd gathered outside that word of the robbery had spread like wildfire across the supe community. I scanned the faces but I couldn't see any sign of Esmeralda Strom. My gaze hardened.

'What's going on, Emma?' Lukas asked.

I pushed up onto my tiptoes and shielded my eyes from the sun's glare. There was a group of women towards the back, short enough to be pixies. I squinted and then grimaced. None of them was Boswell Strom's widow.

'It's complicated,' I replied. I glanced at him and smiled reassuringly. 'But don't worry. I have things under control.'

'You didn't seem particularly shocked by what happened at the London Eye with that ridiculous fake vampire. And you don't seem particularly shocked by this robbery.'

'Mmmm.' I turned my head. There was the front door that Esmeralda Strom had told me was hers. I wondered if she was in. She had to be around here somewhere. When Adam Jones was killed on this very spot during the second robbery, she'd been here. She couldn't be far away.

'Emma.' Lukas reached for my arm. 'You must have left the London Eye and come straight here. How did you know to do that?'

I paused in my search for the older pixie and met his eyes. 'I can't explain it right now. But I will, Lukas. I promise.' I raised my hand to his cheek. He jerked in surprise at my touch. 'I meant what I said before. You're my guy, and I will tell you everything as soon as I can. But now I'm on a clock and lives are at stake if I don't do this properly.' I leaned in and brushed my lips against his. He stood stock still. 'I'm not playing a game. I need you to trust me.'

Part of me expected him to argue. His hand went to his mouth and he touched his lips. A dark light flickered in his eyes. Then he nodded very slightly. 'Very well. But I'm going wherever you go, and you can't stop me.'

'You don't want to check what's been stolen from the bank?'

'I think I already know what's been stolen. And so do you.' He tilted his head, still watching me.

'Yes,' I admitted. 'I do.' I smiled slightly. 'At least if you're with me, I'll be able to protect you.'

I was gratified to see that I'd shocked him. 'Protect me?'

I smiled again. 'Just stay away from ransom demands and bridges.' I pointed towards Esmeralda's front door. 'This way,' I murmured. 'There's a particular pixie I need to find.'

We crossed the road, skirting round the still-growing

crowd. Lacy net curtains hung at the windows of Esmeralda's little home, preventing me from peering inside for any signs of life. I rapped hard on the door. Don't jump to conclusions, Emma, I told myself. Wait to see what she has to say for herself first.

I dropped my hand and allowed my knuckles to graze against the back of Lukas's hand. An electric shiver ran through me at the searing heat of his skin and he glanced towards me. Then the door swung open.

Esmeralda Strom's lined face gazed out at me. I was short but she was at least a foot shorter. She was wearing the same tent-like dress that she'd been wearing when Adam Jones had earned himself a bullet in the face directly outside here – but on that occasion she'd been out on the street. So why had she stayed inside this time?

I looked into her eyes and didn't smile. 'Mrs Strom?'

'Yes.' She blinked at me.

'I'm Detective Constable Emma Bellamy. This is…'

'Lord Horvath,' Esmeralda Strom said. She glanced at Lukas. 'I know. We've met a few times, although I doubt you'd remember. I saw that there was a terrible commotion at the bank across the road. Is that what you're here about?' She leaned forward, the hem of her dress flapping in the breeze that blew in from the road. Her eyes widened and her voice grew breathy. 'Was it robbed?'

'Unfortunately, it was.' I watched her carefully. 'Did you see anything that might help us track down the robbers? There's still a chance we might catch up to them.'

'Oh goodness.' Her hand went to her throat. 'Was anyone hurt?'

She was delaying her answer; I knew it in the very marrow of my bones. 'No, but the robbers were heavily armed. It's a miracle nobody was shot.' I didn't take my eyes from her. 'What did you see? You must have an excellent view of the bank from here.'

'I'm afraid,' she said, her words quavering slightly, 'that I was at the back of the house pottering in the kitchen with the wireless on. I didn't see anything at all. I heard shouts and I came to see what the noise was. But the only thing I saw was a small van speeding down the street.' She pointed. 'It went that way.'

I followed her finger. 'It turned right at the end of the street?'

Esmeralda nodded. 'I believe so.'

Except it hadn't turned right; I knew it hadn't. The florist's van turned left – because the left turn led to the road for Wormwood Scrubs and beyond. The left turn led to the disused tunnel where the gang swapped vehicles.

'That's very helpful, Mrs Strom. Thank you.' Lukas nodded and drew out his phone. 'I'll get cars sent off in that direction straight away. The robbers have probably already gone to ground, but it's worth checking. There may be witnesses who've seen them.'

I placed my hand on his arm. 'Don't bother,' I said. 'It's a waste of time.'

He frowned at me. Esmeralda's eyes suddenly grew sharp. 'Well,' she said, 'the police know best, I suppose.' She started to close the door. 'I'm sorry I couldn't be more help.'

I wedged my foot next to the door frame, preventing her from slamming the door in our faces. 'Actually,' I said, 'I think you can still help. In fact, I need you to come down to the Supe Squad building with me and answer some more questions so you can assist with our enquiries.'

I felt Lukas stiffen. No doubt he was baffled as to why I was so focused on one old lady when a trio of bank robbers was escaping through the city with a haul of stolen goods in their greasy mitts.

'Of course,' Esmeralda told me. 'I'll do anything I can. But I didn't see anything.' She glanced at the slender golden watch on her wrist. 'Why don't I meet you there later today? What time would suit you?'

'You can come now.' For the first time I smiled. 'I'm parked right around the corner. I'll give you a lift.'

'You don't have to do that, detective.'

My smile widened. 'It would be my pleasure.'

I DEPOSITED Esmeralda Strom in the same interview room that Adam Jones had occupied on another time line, then I checked in with Liza. I could feel Lukas's black eyes burning into me the entire time. He remained glued to my side, as if he were afraid I'd turn tail and sprint away. That was okay. As long as he was next to me, he wasn't listening to any ransom demands or making life-threatening plans that I didn't know about.

'DSI Barnes had been calling non-stop,' Liza said. 'She's demanding to talk to you. She said she'll come down in person if you don't get in touch with her soon.' She paused. 'Was the Talismanic Bank really robbed?'

'Unfortunately it was.' I grinned cheerfully. 'But I have a feeling I'll solve this crime before the day is out, and that everyone involved will be brought to justice.'

Liza appeared startled. 'Uh, that's good.'

'It is. If Barnes calls again, tell her that I'll meet her and DI Collier at Curtis Green later. Try and stop them from coming here. We could do without the interference.' Then my voice softened. 'And thank you for what you did earlier. With the money and the chocolate cake. You don't know what a difference that made.'

'It was just a cake.'

'It's never just a cake, Liza.'

Like Lukas, Liza wasn't stupid. She gave me a long look that suggested I had a lot of explaining to do. 'True,' she conceded finally. 'This one had chocolate curls on it that I made myself.'

The Supe Squad front door banged open and Fred stomped in. 'Bloody drama students!' he yelled. 'It wasn't werewolves at all. It was drama students! They thought they were doing some kind of performance. I can't believe the stupidity of people!'

He marched up to me, his hands waving. 'But here's what I think. I heard about the robbery at the Talismanic Bank on my radio. Hear me out. I think that whoever is behind the robbery hired the students to create a diversion.' He flicked a look at Lukas. 'And the same thing happened at the London Eye. This is all about the robbery. It's not about terrorism or suicide or anything like that, it's about money.'

'Money,' I agreed, 'with a good dose of power thrown in.' I turned to the closed door that led to the interview room. 'And perhaps revenge, too.'

'Huh?'

'What's going on here, Emma?' Lukas asked.

'You're about to find out.' I hoped. 'Can you do me a favour first though?'

He folded his arms. 'Go on.'

'Get some of your vamps out here to sweep the nearby streets. And perhaps the rooftops opposite as well.'

'Emma…'

'Please?'

His eyes searched my face. 'Very well,' he said finally. 'The detective's wish is my command.'

I kissed him quickly on the cheek. It was highly inappropriate – the expressions on Liza and Fred's faces confirmed that. Lukas, however, curled a hand round my waist and squeezed it tight. 'I'm looking forward to finding out what's really going on here,' he murmured in my ear.

'Believe me,' I replied, feeling the beat of his heart as his body connected with mine, 'it's quite a story.'

CHAPTER TWENTY-SIX

FRED AND I TOOK UP OUR POSITIONS IN THE INTERVIEW ROOM and set up the preliminaries. Esmeralda Strom sat opposite us, her spine stiff and unyielding.

'I don't know why I'm here. I'm starting to feel like you think I'm some sort of criminal,' she said. She gave a high-pitched titter, as if to suggest that the very idea was preposterous. She wasn't nervous, not yet. But she was worried.

'This won't take long,' I said. 'We only have a few questions. You're an important witness to what happened at the bank.'

'I already told you. I didn't see anything.'

I nodded. 'Mmm-hmm.' I gazed at her. And then I remembered what my uncle had said, and his complaint about the way he was treated because of his age. I looked at Esmeralda more closely. She wasn't as old as she'd appeared at first glance, but adopting a patronising edge might work.

I raised my voice, implying that she was slightly hard of hearing, and tried to look sympathetic. 'I don't suppose you have very good eyesight at your age,' I said.

She bristled. 'There's nothing wrong with my eyesight!'

'That's good to know,' I soothed. I paused, and then, as if it had only just occurred to me, said, 'Are you comfortable there? Would you like a cushion?'

Her brows snapped together. 'Do you offer everyone you question a cushion?'

'I'm not sure what you mean, Mrs Strom,' I said. 'I'm merely trying to ensure that we meet your needs.'

She couldn't prevent an irritated scowl flashing across her face. A flicker of satisfaction ran through me. As long as I could force her emotions to the fore, she'd be off-balance. I might even provoke her into telling me the whole truth.

'So,' I leaned forward, 'I understand that your husband worked at the Talismanic Bank until his death in November of last year. Is that correct?'

She nodded abruptly.

'If you could speak aloud,' I said. 'For the purposes of the tape.'

'Yes.'

'I'm very sorry to hear about his passing. Is it unusual for a goblin and a pixie to maintain a long-term relationship?'

'It was more than a relationship,' she snapped. 'We were married. And, yes, I suppose it's unusual, but only because there aren't that many goblins or pixies.' Her lip curled. 'As a member of Supernatural Squad, I'd have expected you to know that already.'

I gave a gentle smile to indicate that I was both patient and kind despite her cantankerous nature, and I looked at her as you might look at a new-born baby. Or a puppy. It worked, and she glowered even more.

'I'm quite new to this position,' I told her. 'And I'm only young. I still have a lot to learn.'

She folded her arms and the sleeves of her dress rode up. 'Clearly. Why are you asking about Boswell? I thought this was about the bank robbery.'

'All in good time, Mrs Strom.' I glanced at her bare arms, noting the red marks on her elbows. 'Have you injured yourself recently?'

'What? No.' She looked down and, realising what I was looking at, immediately dropped her arms so that her sleeves covered her elbows again. 'I have eczema.'

I didn't know a lot about eczema but it seemed highly unlikely that it only affected elbows. Then again, if someone were to spend a lot of time lying down with their elbows propped up on the ground or the floor while they gazed through a sniper's scope, they might well get those sorts of marks.

'Mrs Strom,' I said, 'do you have any experience with guns?' Even Fred jerked at that question.

Esmeralda stared at me. 'Don't be ridiculous,' she sniffed. 'What would I want with guns?'

I made a mark on the clipboard in front of me. 'So if we contacted local gun clubs, they would have no record of you making any visits?'

She didn't answer but her skin paled.

'Mrs Strom?'

'No comment.'

'I see.' I made another mark. 'And if we search your house, we'll find no evidence of any guns inside it?'

She pinned her mouth closed.

'No high-powered rifles with scopes?'

She didn't move.

'No ammunition that a skilled sniper might use?'

Her mouth twitched but she stayed silent.

Very well. I tried another tack. 'You don't like the Talismanic Bank, do you?'

This time she spoke, tension layering every word. 'I don't see what that has to do with anything. At this particular moment I don't like you very much, either. It doesn't mean

I'm about to attack you.'

'Mmm.' I looked up from the clipboard. 'Why don't you like the bank?'

'Because they worked my husband to the bone. He was there right up until the day he died. He should have retired long ago.'

'They didn't prevent him from retiring, though, did they? Didn't Mosburn Pralk encourage your husband to retire and he refused?'

Esmeralda looked away.

'Mrs Strom,' I persisted, 'were you jealous of the bank?'

She rolled her tongue around her mouth. Her lips were thin and pursed and I sensed a deep rage simmering within her. 'I would like legal representation now,' she said, enunciating her words very clearly.

I shrugged. 'Very well.' I turned my head to Fred but kept my eyes on Esmeralda to gauge her reaction. 'Can you make all the necessary arrangements while I prep for the interview with Adam Jones?'

Fred knew that Jones wasn't anywhere near here. He was, however, smart enough to play along. 'Yes, ma'am.' Esmeralda remained mute but I was sure that her body had stiffened slightly at the mention of Adam's name.

I tapped my mouth. 'While we wait for your solicitor to arrive, Mrs Strom, I wonder if I might prevail upon you to take part in an identification parade?'

She didn't say anything.

I sighed and stood up, walked to the door and placed my hand on the handle. 'You know,' I said aloud, 'leniency is more likely when criminals admit to what they've done. There are always deals to be made.'

Esmeralda Strom still didn't speak. I cursed inwardly and left.

I TOOK a sip of my lukewarm coffee, aware that everyone's eyes were on me. 'She might not be admitting to anything yet,' I said, 'but I'm convinced that she's the fourth member of the gang. She's probably the one who hired the others. And she's definitely the most dangerous of them all. We have her, though. And we have Adam Jones, who can identify her.'

'Except,' Lukas pointed out, his arms folded across his broad chest, 'we don't have the three humans who carried out the heist. Nor do we have the safety deposit boxes which were stolen.'

I gazed at him briefly then my eyes slid away. 'No. We don't have any of that,' I admitted. I put my mug on the table as the doorbell rang.

Liza got to her feet and went to answer it.

I sucked on my bottom lip. 'Something else is going on here,' I muttered. 'Something's not right.' I frowned as I tried to connect the dots. The same nebulous unease that had bothered me in the bank and led me to Esmeralda was still bothering me now.

Liza's heels clicked as she returned. 'Esmeralda Strom's solicitor is here. I've shown him into the interview room so they can talk.'

I frowned. 'That was fast.'

Fred, who had been quiet up to that point, widened his eyes. 'Er...' He scratched his head and looked awkward.

'What is it?'

He flushed. 'I've not actually called the duty solicitor yet. Unless Mrs Strom has called someone herself, then...'

My blood chilled. What if that wasn't a solicitor in there at all? What if ...? I sprang up and sprinted out of the room and down the corridor, flinging open the interview room door. Esmeralda and the small figure seated opposite her looked up.

'This is outrageous!'

I stared at the gremlin. He stalked toward me and placed his hands on his hips. He barely reached my tummy button but that didn't mean he wasn't intimidating. His sharp grey eyes, furious voice and aggressive stance more than made up for his short stature. I looked him up and down, taking in his pointed ears, folds of skin and neatly tailored suit. On the table behind him sat an open briefcase full of papers. The only weapon he appeared to have on him was an old-fashioned fountain pen – but I wasn't taking any chances.

'Any conversations I have with my client are confidential!' he spat. 'You have no right to barge in here like this.'

Maybe I was in the wrong but I wasn't going to back down. Not yet. 'I want to see some identification.'

The gremlin rolled his eyes melodramatically. 'Phileas Carmichael, Esquire.' He reached into his pocket and I tensed, but all he drew out was a slim wallet. He produced an ID card with his name and profession on it.

'Who called you here?' I demanded.

'I don't have to tell you that.' He sniffed. 'I've been hired on Mrs Strom's behalf. I have a legal right to speak to her alone.' The challenge in his stormy gaze was obvious. 'You are breaking the law, detective.'

I glanced at Esmeralda. She appeared vaguely amused and raised an eyebrow at me. Clearly, her imminent safety wasn't being compromised in any way. I grimaced and stepped back. 'I apologise. I'll leave you in peace,' I bit out.

'Next time,' Carmichael hissed, 'knock and wait!'

I left without saying another word.

Lukas was standing in the corridor, watching me.

'Phileas Carmicheal,' I said. 'A gremlin. Do you know him?'

He tensed. 'I do. He's expensive – and very skilled. He represents clients in private supe matters, as well as humans in the human courts. He knows his stuff. And he's no ambulance chaser.'

'Someone called him here on Esmeralda Strom's behalf but he won't say who.' The niggling worry that had been bothering me began to coalesce. I sucked in a breath then strode into the main office and pulled out my phone. By now, I knew the number off by heart.

'You've reached the Talismanic Bank. I understand that you may be concerned after today's events but—'

I interrupted Mista Tio. 'I'm not an angry account holder. This is DC Bellamy. I need to speak to Mosburn Pralk right away.'

She didn't hesitate. 'One moment, detective.'

Lukas, Fred and Liza were watching me. Fred opened his mouth to say something but I put my finger to my lips and hushed him. Pralk's voice filled the line. 'What is it? What have you found?'

'There's something I need to know, Mr Pralk.'

'Go on.'

I ran my tongue across my teeth. 'Boswell Strom,' I said.

'What about him?'

'Would he have had access to the safety deposit box records?'

He didn't answer.

'Mr Pralk—'

'I don't like what you're implying. Besides, the man is dead. I fail to see…'

'We're investigating a theory that Boswell Strom might have told his wife about the boxes, or she might have got information from him without him realising.'

The goblin sucked in a breath. 'I suppose it's possible.'

245

'Boswell could have seen the records? He might have known which box belonged to whom?'

'Yes.' Pralk's response was grudging.

I thought of something else and hung up without saying farewell. My eyes snapped to Lukas.

'What?' he asked softly. 'What is it?'

'You had three boxes at the Talismanic Bank. You must have had two of them for some time, but the third one is new. You must have opened it recently because it contains information about me. You were planning to give me the key.'

Lukas didn't blink. 'How do you know that, Emma?' He pushed himself off the desk he was leaning against and walked towards me. 'How on earth do you know that?'

'When did you open the third safety deposit box, Lukas?' I pressed.

He gazed at me. 'Three months ago. I opened it at the beginning of March, not long after I met you.'

'Boswell Strom died in November. Even if he told Esmeralda who owned which box, he wouldn't have known about that last one.' I moved to the window and looked at the rooftops on the opposite side of the street. 'Esmeralda Strom must have shot Adam Jones outside the Talismanic Bank,' I said to myself.

'Adam Jones is in custody at CID,' Lukas said. 'Alive and kicking.'

'Yes.' I nodded. 'He is. She must have been the one who shot you from the hotel as well.'

'You've been shot, Lord Hovarth?' Fred exclaimed.

'Emma,' Liza said nervously, 'perhaps you ought to go and lie down for a while.'

I tapped at the glass. 'She's not as old as she looks but she's pushing seventy,' I murmured. 'Could she really have clambered up to those rooftops to kill Adam Jones the third time around? The first shot from there missed – it hit the wall. It was the second shot that hit Adam. On Westminster Bridge, she shot three people dead with three shots from an even greater distance – but here she missed when she was much nearer. It took two shots to kill one person. The only explanation is that on that occasion it wasn't her. Esmeralda Strom is in league with the bank robbers and she might have hired them, but there's someone else – and that someone else has hired Phileas Carmicheal on her behalf. They're terrified she'll spill the beans.'

Lukas moved up beside me. 'You're babbling, Emma. You're not making any sense.'

I tilted my head up to his. 'You have a birthmark,' I told him. 'On the inside of your thigh.' I smiled. 'It's shaped like a heart.'

His jaw slackened.

I headed for the door. 'I have to talk to Adam Jones again. He might know more about the fifth person. I can get him to confirm Esmeralda's identity at the same time.'

'Boss...' Fred looked at me as if he were afraid he'd have to call a hospital and get me committed. So did Liza.

I waved at them reassuringly. 'Don't worry. I've got this. And I'm not crazy!'

As I left, I heard Liza's mutter, 'Emma, you're completely stone-cold nuts.'

CHAPTER TWENTY-SEVEN

Lukas folded himself into Tallulah's passenger seat, obviously unwilling to let me go anywhere on my own. I didn't argue; I preferred to have him by my side. I turned on the engine and put the car into gear while Max doffed his hat. I acknowledged the doorman with a wave and pulled away from the pavement.

'I understand you have a lot of questions,' I said. I kept my eyes on the road but I could feel Lukas's eyes burning into me.

'D'Artagnan,' he said, 'you have no idea.'

'Okay.' I drew in a breath. 'In a nutshell, I've been re-living the same twelve-hour period. This is my fourth time dealing with the bank robbery, so obviously I know things that no one else does. I won't get another chance to solve it after today. This will be the last re-set.'

He didn't say anything.

'Groundhog Day,' I told him. 'I took a weird potion on a desperate whim and now I'm living Groundhog Day.' And then I said, 'Last time you believed me.'

'Last time.' He took a deep breath. 'Okay. I'm not saying I

don't believe you. I'm simply trying to … get my head around the idea.' He continued to watch me. 'Is that why you're holding your shoulder awkwardly? You've obviously injured it.'

'I got shot the second time around. It's not serious, just … a bit sore. Unlike when I die, any wounds I receive don't re-set themselves.'

He was silent for a moment, then he exploded. 'God-damnit. You have no sense of self-preservation, Emma!'

'Pffft. It's fine.' I glanced at him before adding quietly, 'Worse things happened to you.'

His fingers drummed angrily against his thigh. He didn't seem to care about what might have happened to him. 'And my birthmark? How do you know about that?'

I licked my lips. 'You already know the answer.'

There was a long silence. When he spoke, his voice was stiff. 'Did we make love because you knew I wouldn't remember it?'

'No. We made love because we both wanted to.' I cleared my throat awkwardly. 'Or at least I did. I'm pretty certain you did too.'

'I can guarantee that,' he muttered.

A tiny smile flickered across my face.

'Was it good?' he bit out.

I knew that he wasn't asking because of male pride; he was asking whether it was something I'd like to repeat. 'Yes.'

Another beat passed. 'The last thing I remember is you avoiding my calls. Is that avoidance something you now regret?' he asked silkily.

'I was avoiding your calls because deep down I knew this was inevitable and I'm afraid of what it might become. I have no illusions as to where your priorities lie, Lukas. I fully expect you to break my heart sooner or later – but I've decided that I no longer care. I have to stop worrying about what happens tomorrow and enjoy today.'

'I won't break your heart.' Each word rippled with tension.

I didn't disagree with him; there was no point. But when I finally parked by the Curtis Green police building where Adam Jones was being held, it occurred to me that he hadn't asked a single question about the bank robbery or its perpetrators. It was as if he couldn't care less about them.

Liza had called ahead and informed DSI Barnes that we were coming. She was already standing in front of the imposing granite façade – and DI Collier was beside her. When I strode up, with Lukas by my side, Barnes offered me an icy glower. I knew she was furious that I'd not been in touch. She didn't call me out in front of Collier – she was too good for that – but her expression left me in no doubt as to how she felt. I'd find a way to make it up to her. And to explain.

'Good afternoon, DC Bellamy,' she said. She sniffed at Lukas. 'Lord Horvath.' She pointed to Collier. 'This is Detective Inspector Alistair Collier. I believe you've spoken already on the phone.'

Collier folded his arms across his chest. Unsurprisingly, he wasn't jumping for joy at the sight of a vampire on the hallowed steps of his building. Lukas smiled pleasantly but Collier wasn't mollified. 'Lord or not,' he growled, 'he can't come in here.'

'Yes, he can,' Barnes said. She flicked her wrist to indicate that was the end of the matter then looked at me. 'I understand you're here to speak to Adam Jones again.'

I nodded. 'I have a couple of urgent questions for him.'

'Is this related to the robbery at the Talismanic Bank? Are all these events tied together?'

'Yes.'

'DI Collier is going to—'

I interrupted her. 'I have everything under control.'

'I'm sure you do, but you can't investigate a crime of this magnitude on your own. It's not up for argument. DI Collier is going to take point.'

'Forgive me if I'm mistaken,' Lukas interjected, 'but this crime, regardless of its magnitude, took place at a supernatural institution. DC Bellamy has already established that at least one of the criminals is a supe.'

Barnes's eyebrows rose slowly upwards.

'A pixie,' I supplied helpfully.

'Indeed.' Lukas smiled. 'Therefore the investigation should be run by Supe Squad.'

'Adam Jones isn't a damned supe,' Collier growled. 'Although he doesn't seem to know a thing about Timothy Barratt, despite your suggestions to the contrary, DC Bellamy.'

'I might have misheard him,' I replied smoothly. 'And as for him being human, that's why I placed him in your custody. Mr Jones is a peripheral character in this particular drama but he might have information that will help with my investigation of the bank robbery. And the bank robbery is a supernatural crime. I don't require outside help.' I looked at Collier and then at Barnes. 'I guarantee that if we need more support, I'll ask for it.'

'We?' Collier sniped, glaring at Lukas. 'You and this … this … this … creature…'

'Oh, do be quiet.' DSI Barnes tutted. She jabbed her finger at me. 'Very well, DC Bellamy. You will report to me every two hours with full updates. You will not turn off your phone. And before you leave here, you will give me a detailed report.'

I breathed out. Finally she'd seen the light. 'Thank you.'

'Don't thank me,' she snapped. 'Just find the bastards who

did this before every supe in the city starts rioting. I've got half the politicians in the city breathing down my neck. I don't need any more hassle.'

'You don't need to worry about any supes,' Lukas interjected smoothly.

'Yeah, yeah. Follow me. I'll take you to Jones.'

Collier coughed. 'DSI Barnes—'

'You can stand down for now.'

DI Collier's cheeks turned a mottled purple. I resisted the temptation to stick my tongue out at him; after all, I was a grown woman not a child. But it was a close-run thing. I dipped my head instead to mask my expression and trotted after DSI Barnes into the building.

The Supe Squad building was beautiful, if rather dilapidated. In terms of atmosphere and technology, it was also a million miles away from the edifice here at Curtis Green. For one thing, our security system consisted of disapproving looks from Liza and a heady mixture of verbena and wolfsbane, which any non-supe wouldn't register. The reality was that anyone could wander in and poke around if they really wanted to. In contrast, Curtis Green possessed metal detectors, security guards, CCTV cameras and the distinct sensation that you were being watched at all moments. It was like being at an airport, except I hadn't packed my suntan lotion and I wasn't expecting any fruity cocktails at a beach-side bar in the near future.

Nobody was exempt from security, not even Barnes. The three of us queued up behind a cluster of uniformed officers with all our metal objects and bags placed onto the rolling belt for X-ray. I dug into my pockets and tossed my phone and keys into one of the small grey trays. Lukas did the same. I glanced down while DSI Barnes strolled through the metal detector without pausing. I barely registered Lukas's wallet and the heavy bunch of keys he'd put beside it – but then I took a closer look and froze.

'You can come forward now,' the security officer said. I didn't hear him. I was still staring at the tray. 'Ma'am…'

'DC Bellamy,' Barnes barked. 'Get a move on.'

I reached down and scooped up my belongings.

'DC Bellamy!' Barnes called. 'What is going on?'

I raised my chin. 'Sorry to waste your time. We don't need to speak to Adam Jones at all. I'll talk to you later and explain everything.' I picked up Lukas's keys and wallet.

'What is it, Emma?' he asked.

Barnes stomped past security and glared at me. 'I'd like to ask the same question. What on earth is going on?'

I picked out the three little golden keys on Lukas's chain and held them up. 'Sometimes,' I said, 'you need to take a step back to see the bigger picture. This is the key to understanding everything.'

DSI Barnes shook her head. 'I don't get it.'

'You will.' I grinned and spun round for the door. 'I'll explain everything later.'

'DC Bellamy!'

I waved at her. But I didn't pause.

CHAPTER TWENTY-EIGHT

It was clear from the array of sleek cars sitting outside Supe Squad with their engines ticking over that all four clan alphas had decided to make an appearance. No prizes for guessing why.

I spotted Toffee leaning against the Fairfax limousine and jerked my head in her direction. 'You should join us,' I said.

Surprise flashed across her face and her eyes narrowed slightly. 'It's not my place.'

'Up to you.' I nodded at Max, who seemed fascinated by the goings-on, then I headed inside with Lukas by my side.

I glanced at the interview room where Esmeralda Strom had been the last time I'd seen her. The door was firmly closed. I swept past into the main office. It appeared that the clan alphas were only just getting warmed up.

'I demand to speak to her,' Lady Sullivan said, her voice edged with steel. 'I'll find out where my fucking things have gone before the rest of you can so much as blink.'

'That's not how things work around here,' Fred said.

'Indeed.' I folded my arms and gazed around coolly. The

four alphas, Lady Sullivan, Lady Carr, Lord Fairfax and Lord McGuigan, were spread across the room. Mosburn Pralk was beside them. Both female alphas displayed expressions that suggested the simmering threat of violence. Pralk's face was a mask and Fairfax looked equally inscrutable. Mmm. Lord McGuigan simply looked defeated.

'Where the hell have you been?' Lady Sullivan snapped. 'What does that fucking pixie have to say for herself? I demand to know!'

Someone cleared their throat behind me and I glanced back, jerking in surprise when I saw Phileas Carmichael. 'My client has considered the matter,' he said loudly, 'and would like the opportunity to address you all.'

Everyone in the room stared at him except me. My attention was on somebody else. 'Sure,' I said. 'What's the harm?'

Fred and Liza frowned at me but I pretended not to notice. 'Bring her through,' I said to Carmichael.

'Is that a good idea?' Lukas murmured *sotto-voce*.

'Actually,' I said, 'it might work in our favour.'

We waited while Carmichael brought Esmeralda. Her pleasure at seeing the small – but extraordinarily powerful – assembly was obvious. She reserved a specially delighted and nasty grin for Mosburn Pralk. He didn't blanch but held her gaze.

Lady Carr stepped forward. The diminutive werewolf alpha looked ready to tear Esmeralda from limb to limb. 'Well? What do you have to say for yourself?' She tapped her foot impatiently. 'And where the fuck are my things?'

If the stern alpha's tone was supposed to cow Esmeralda Strom into submission, it didn't work. She lifted her chin, her blue eyes cold and piercing.

'Look at you,' she murmured. 'Look at all of you. All that power, and you still let a little old pixie like me get the better of you. Not just me, either. Three humans with the combined intelligence of a soggy paper bag have bested you. Your bank,' she sneered at Pralk, 'was the easiest place in the world to rob. Your security is a joke. You thought that because you were the grand Talismanic Bank, with the protection of all these fuckers, you were safe.' She sniffed. 'You couldn't have been more wrong. I've proved that.' She tried to point to herself despite her bound wrists. 'Me.'

I sucked in a breath. She'd admitted it. She'd admitted she was involved.

'Are you looking for applause?' Lord McGuigan asked icily. 'Do you want adulation for turning against your own kind?'

Esmeralda laughed. 'My own kind? You're not my kind. We couldn't be further apart. Do you think that because we're both supes we're the same? You lot look down on the rest of us. You always have. Just because you've got the numbers and you happen to have sharper teeth, you think you're better than we are. I've proved that you're not. Even at my age, I could run rings around you.'

Lady Sullivan glanced at me. 'Either she gets talking,' she snapped, 'or I get walking.'

'You're not going anywhere,' Esmeralda said. 'You want your valuables too much to walk away.' A smile played around her lips. She was enjoying the power she held over all of us. I sneaked a look at Phileas Carmichael. If he was disturbed by his new client's declarations, he wasn't showing it.

Lord Fairfax folded his arms. 'You're the mastermind of this operation, are you?'

I froze, watching them like a hawk. Esmeralda turned her head. For a long moment she didn't speak. Her eyes held his as she smiled. I shifted my weight and prepared to intervene if necessary. Then she answered. 'I am. I'm a pension-drawing pixie and I almost brought you to your knees. Remember that when you're safely tucked up at home tonight.' She smirked.

'Where are the other three members of your pathetic little gang?' Carr enquired. 'And where are our belongings?'

Fairfax stepped forward. 'Give her to me,' he growled. 'I'll get her to talk.'

No way. That was not happening. 'Not a chance,' I said. 'Mrs Strom, if you have something to say, you'd better get on with it.' I was waiting for her to get to the truth, either by accident or design, but I didn't possess infinite patience. Esmeralda Strom was on a very short rope.

'Boswell loved our bank,' Pralk said. 'Why attack the one place that your husband dedicated his life to?'

'Because he should have dedicated his life to *me*. He should have loved *me*!' Her face twisted.

Pralk stared at her. 'He did love you.'

'Not as much as he loved your fucking bank.'

'So you did this for revenge?' Lady Carr questioned. 'To get your own back on the Talismanic Bank and to stick the knife in your dead husband's back?' She rolled her eyes.

'And to prove to you that you're not as powerful or invincible as you think you are,' Esmeralda said. 'I very nearly won.'

'But you didn't win,' Lukas said. 'What were you planning to do with the boxes? You can't have believed that you could sell the contents without getting caught.'

'They were going to be ransomed back to you. For a good price.'

'So where are the boxes now?' he asked. 'And where is the rest of the gang?'

'I'll tell you,' Esmeralda murmured, 'if the deal I receive in return is good enough.'

Fairfax exploded. 'This is a waste of time! She's obviously not planning to tell us a fucking thing! She's toying with us.'

When I turned to him, my expression was ice cold. 'Lord Fairfax,' I said, 'you—'

Unfortunately I didn't get the chance to finish my sentence. Liza interrupted, her eyes wide and her voice quivering. 'What the hell is that?' She was staring out of the window with a look of horror. One by one, the others followed her gaze, their mouths dropping open. Even Lukas looked taken aback.

It was no wonder. Standing outside the window was the largest werewolf I'd ever seen. Even on all four paws, it had to be over a metre tall. It had gold-tipped fur that did nothing to conceal its taut muscles. The wolf swung its head towards us and I caught a glimpse of gleaming green eyes and lethally sharp teeth. Then it raised a front paw and tapped its claws against the glass.

'Who is that?' Lukas's voice was tight. 'Who the fuck is that?'

There was genuine fear on Lady Sullivan's face. 'I have no idea.'

Esmeralda threw back her head and laughed. I muttered a curse under my breath and looked at Fred. 'Get her to safety,' I said. 'You, Liza and Mrs Strom. Don't leave this building under any circumstances.' I glared at Esmeralda. 'Do not let her out of your sight.'

Fred swallowed, his Adam's apple bobbing nervously. 'What if that thing tries to get in here?'

I shook my head. 'He won't.'

I stormed out of the Supe Squad front door onto the street. Any passers-by had made themselves scarce and run for safety. The only other living being, besides me and the wolf, was Toffee. Scraps of her clothing lay in tatters on the road, and Toffee herself was lying on her back with her furry belly presented in total submission.

A cool breeze picked up, ruffling the large wolf's fur. The gigantic creature turned towards me, his tongue lolling out of his mouth. He drew back his lips and snarled.

I rolled my eyes. 'Well,' I drawled, 'you certainly know how to make an entrance.'

Lukas burst out of the door and advanced, prepared to attack. I swung an arm out to hold him back. 'Don't.'

His eyes flashed but he knew me well enough to obey. I took another step forward. I could hear the other alphas coming out; from their growls, at least one of them had transformed. I ignored their aggressive snarls and took another step towards the werewolf. He took another step towards me.

'Emma.' Lukas was worried.

I waved a hand dismissively. This was fine. It was all fine. The werewolf's slitted green gaze was fixed on me with the absolute focus of a predator. Then, without warning, he lunged. Instinctively I put my hands up in front of my face – but the wolf didn't touch me. He stopped an inch away. I stared into his face without flinching. 'You have shitty timing, Mr Webb.'

The wolf opened its mouth. And then he licked me.

'Wh–what?' Lady Sullivan pushed her way through. She hadn't yet transformed into lupine form but, from the way fur was springing out in patches across her face, she was on the verge of it. 'Webb? Devereau Webb?' She shook her head. 'But you were only bitten once. I don't understand.'

'He's been bitten more than once,' I said. 'In fact, three times.'

Webb sat back on his haunches looking very pleased with himself. Oh.

'Four times?' I asked.

I hadn't thought it was possible for a werewolf to grin, but grin he did.

'That's not possible,' Lady Carr breathed from behind me. 'There are strict protocols in place. He could never have been bitten that many times without us knowing about it. Four times? That's impossible.'

Lukas remained by my side. 'A potion. You said you drank a potion, Emma. And that potion...' He didn't finish his sentence.

I nodded. 'Mr Webb gave it to me. After he'd taken it himself.'

'You knew about this?' he demanded. 'You knew what he'd done?'

'By the time I realised,' I said softly, 'it was far too late to do anything about it. And I had more pressing concerns to worry about. Devereau Webb's transformation was a *fait accompli*.'

There was a loud snapping noise, like the sickening sound of bones breaking. Devereau Webb moaned slightly. His golden fur turned into human skin, revealing a smooth tan that was marred only by the faint bruises and puncture wounds from his werewolf bites. He slowly pulled himself upright onto two feet. I ignored his lack of clothes and focused on his face.

'That's a very strange sensation,' he murmured. 'Very strange indeed.' He rubbed the back of his neck, then he raised his head and looked over my shoulder. 'Hello, cousins,' he said. He ran his tongue over his teeth. A tiny crease lit his brow. 'Where's the other one gone?'

I looked round. Lady Carr and Lady Sullivan were standing side by side, staring at Devereau Webb with a mixture of horror and astonishment. In Lady Carr's case. there appeared to be a sprinkling of lust as well. Lord

McGuigan was in wolf form, his hackles raised. Toffee was still on the ground. But Fairfax was missing.

I clenched my teeth and glanced at the sleek black cars parked neatly nearby. Before I could move towards them, an engine roared and the nearest car swerved out before accelerating down the street at top speed.

CHAPTER 29

I ROARED. THEN I PICKED UP MY FEET AND SPRINTED FOR Tallulah, wrenching open the door and throwing myself into the driver's seat. I should have acted sooner. I shouldn't have allowed Devereau Webb to distract me from what was right in front of my nose.

Esmeralda Strom wasn't the boss of the gang; she hadn't orchestrated the bank robbery. Lord Fairfax had. I'd known it as soon as I stared at Lukas's keys lying in the plastic tray in front of the metal detector at Curtis Green.

Scarlett had told me that Fairfax had installed metal detectors at his properties. Lukas had told me that he'd been forced to visit Fairfax instead of meeting me for dinner. The others had probably all done the same recently – Mosburn Pralk certainly had. And if they'd removed their keys to pass through Fairfax's detectors, all it would have taken was someone to note down the numbers etched into the metal to know which safety deposit boxes to target.

Not only that, Fairfax had known that Esmeralda Strom held a grudge against the Talismanic Bank because Pralk had told him all about it. Even Toffee had seemed to think that I was investigating her own alpha. She'd doubted him – and she was one of his top beta wolves.

The evidence was circumstantial but there was enough to damn him. I'd been trying to give Fairfax enough rope to hang himself and confess what he'd done. Instead, I'd given him the opportunity to escape. I'd allowed a power-hungry alpha werewolf with a propensity for violence to run away and rampage through the streets of London. Anything could happen.

I heard Lukas shout but I didn't pause. It was safer for him if he stayed away. Bringing down one of the supe leaders was something for Supe Squad – and that meant me. I revved Tallulah's engine and took off in pursuit as Fairfax's car reached the end of the road and turned right.

Tallulah seemed to recognise the urgency and let me accelerate with surprising ease. I paused briefly at the cross-roads to avoid being hit by oncoming vehicles. When I reached the end of the road, I spun the steering wheel right and strained my eyes for Fairfax's tail lights. Darkness was already falling and it was difficult to be sure what vehicles were up ahead. I accelerated again, hoping that the car a hundred metres in front was the one that I wanted.

'Come on, Tallulah,' I muttered aloud. I changed gears and pressed my foot down harder.

A motorbike pulled out in front of me from a side street. I cursed and swerved, narrowly avoiding it. Tallulah's tyres screeched in complaint; her engine didn't have anything like the same horsepower as Fairfax's expensive car. But in these narrow streets, she had greater traction. There was still hope.

The car ahead reached a roundabout and turned left. I held my breath while the shops and buildings around me became a blur of colour. Three seconds later I reached the same roundabout – and so did a lorry making late-night deliveries. It pulled out from my right and blocked my path. I had no chance; I slammed on the brakes and jerked forward with enough force to send a bolt of pain through my wounded shoulder. Tallulah's engine stalled. I hissed and hastily re-started it. I turned as soon as the lorry had passed but it was no use; the car had vanished. It could have turned down any of the streets to either my left or my right.

I drove down the road, trying to glimpse the vehicle, but there was no sign of it. I made an educated guess, took one of the roads to the right and headed onto a main city artery. There were more cars here, but none of them was the one I was looking for.

I continued for another minute before I pulled over. Fairfax could have gone in any direction. Chasing him like this was never going to work; I had to think strategically.

I sucked on my bottom lip and considered, and then it came to me. I knew exactly where Lord Fairfax would be going. He'd obviously realised that the gig was up so he wouldn't dare stay in the city. He wouldn't be afraid of me, but he would be terrified of the other alphas, Lukas and the Talismanic Bank. They were the ones he'd stolen from, and quite possibly planned to kill at the same time.

I couldn't imagine what he'd been thinking. I thought of Toffee's corpse from the first time I had gone through the robbery. Fairfax hadn't expected her to be at the bank and he'd been genuinely shocked by her death. But when you play with fire, you must expect to be burnt – and that others might be immolated in the process.

'It's alright, Tallulah.' My voice echoed round the small car. 'I know where to go.'

LONDON IS SERVED by six airports. In theory Heathrow, as the largest, was the most likely choice for Fairfax's getaway. But the alpha werewolf was on the run and his best chance of escaping was to get away as quickly as possible – and that meant going to the closest airport. London City wasn't far away. It only covered short haul destinations but that was all Lord Fairfax needed. He could hop on a plane to a European city and disappear, or continue his journey to a more far-flung place.

I crossed my fingers that my instincts were correct and set off. At the same time, I grabbed my police radio. 'Dispatch,' I said as clearly as possible, 'this is DC Bellamy of Supernatural Squad requiring urgent assistance.'

The response was immediate. 'This is Dispatch. Go ahead, detective.'

'I have a dangerous suspect on the loose. I believe he's attempting to fly out of the country. I need all flights out of London City Airport checked.'

'What name are we looking for?'

I ran my tongue across my lips. 'There are three possibilities. He has three fake passports in the names of Johannes Muller, Michael Hatt and Arnold Steenkamp.' Fairfax had made a major error when he told me about the contents of his safety deposit boxes. At the time, he probably thought that being truthful would keep him in the clear – but he'd told me about the passports and the names on each one.

'I'll pass your request on to the relevant team and get back to you.'

'Quickly, please.'

'Noted.'

The radio crackled and the disembodied voice disappeared. I concentrated on the road ahead, maintaining a good speed. By the time I was turning into the first London City Airport car park and haphazardly parking in the nearest space, I had my answer. This time it was a different voice. 'DC Bellamy, this is Control.'

'Go ahead.'

'A South African citizen by the name of Arnold Steenkamp has just checked in for a flight to Zurich.'

'Alert the airport police. He won't risk carrying a weapon through an airport, but he is very dangerous. They should locate him but not approach under any circumstances.'

'They are highly trained and very experienced. They can deal with all manner of people.'

'I bet they've never dealt with an alpha werewolf on the run before,' I said.

The voice on the other end of the radio hesitated. 'Werewolf?'

'*Alpha* werewolf.'

There was another pause. 'I'll inform airport police immediately. When can they expect you?'

I glanced up, estimating the distance between the car park and the main terminal. 'Three minutes.'

'Very well.' The radio clicked off. I dropped it, jumped out of Tallulah and slammed her door closed. And then, yet again, I began to run.

My feet smacked against the bare concrete. A family heaving large suitcases out of the boot of their car froze to stare at me. I ignored them – and the couple arguing about whose responsibility it had been to pack their passports – and swung towards the door, taking the steps three at a time.

Inside the terminal I discounted the travelator as too slow, given the numbers of travellers ambling along it, and sprinted down the corridor towards the check-in gates. Spotting two fluorescent-jacketed security officials, I headed straight for them.

'I'm DC Bellamy!' I yelled. 'Where...?' I didn't have to finish my sentence. They were ready and they knew who I was.

'ID?'

I dug out my warrant card and held it up. The nearest one examined it quickly before nodding and pointing at a door. 'This way. We can bypass security. Your wolf has cleared immigration. We can stop him ourselves and—'

'No.' I was adamant, not because I wanted the glory for myself but because there was a real danger that Fairfax would turn furry and go crazy. A bus being hijacked by fake werewolves and the London Eye being brought to a standstill by a fake vampire had caused chaos, but that would be nothing compared to a werewolf transforming in the centre of an airport. I knew supes and I knew Lord Fairfax. This was my responsibility.

The three of us ran for the door. We swung first one way, then another, emerging into a bustling crowd of weary travellers, duty-free shoppers and excited holidaymakers.

'Which way?' I demanded. 'Where is he?'

The shorter of the two officials pressed a finger to his ear and listened to his earpiece. 'Left,' he grunted. 'In front of the café by Gate Nine.'

I took off and the officials followed in my wake. There were people everywhere and I was forced to weave in and out to get through them. Fortunately, this wasn't a large airport and, after dodging round a group of drunk businessmen on their way home after a long meeting in the city, I saw Fairfax. He was standing stiffly, a taut expression on his face. And he wasn't alone.

I came to a halt. An armed guard strode up to me, one hand on his gun, more than ready to intervene. I hoped it wouldn't come to that. 'Should we evacuate the airport?' he asked.

I shook my head, hoping I was making the right call. 'No. He'll come quietly now he knows we've got him.' I gestured at the three people standing beside him. 'The others are humans. They need to be arrested as well.'

Guards and police were appearing from all sides. Airport threats were taken very seriously indeed. 'Stay back,' I ordered. 'I'll call you if I need you.'

Like all werewolves, Fairfax possessed supernatural senses. Although the blonde woman was jabbering at him furiously, he looked up and glanced round. He noted the sudden increase in security personnel. Then his gaze swung to me. Well, hello.

Lord Fairfax went white as a sheet. He stepped away from the trio of irate humans but Moustache Man was having none of it. He reached forward to grab Fairfax's collar and haul him back, but the werewolf muttered something and the man stalled. His head whipped round, but it was too late. I was already stalking towards them.

'DC Bellamy.' A yellow sheen rolled over Fairfax's irises. 'You followed me here.'

'Not exactly.' I smiled nastily. 'Let's just say I had an inside track on what you were up to.'

'Bastards,' the woman hissed. 'She's with the police?'

The bespectacled man, who Adam Jones had dubbed 'the professor', shuffled to the side. 'I don't know any of these people,' he declared loudly.

Yeah, yeah. 'Take a look around,' I murmured. 'There are a lot of guys here with a lot of guns. This is an airport. There's no chance you'll walk away from this. If you try anything – if *any* of you try anything – you'll be shot dead instantly. Your only chance is to come quietly.'

'Why?' the blonde spat. 'Why should we? We've not done anything wrong!'

'You robbed the Talismanic Bank.' I spoke calmly but implacably. None of them were getting away, not from here, not now. The best-case scenario was that they'd allow themselves to be arrested without making a scene.

I pointed at their bags. 'I'll take a wild guess that you've got more in there than a trashy novel and a toothbrush.'

'You ... you ... you...'

Moustache Man made a break for it as panic got the better of him. He spun round and sprinted to his right but there was nowhere for him to go. Within ten feet, three plain-clothed officers had leapt at him and brought him down to the floor. He didn't even have time to call out.

There were a few shouts and screams from the people around us but, as shock gave way to self-preservation, the other travellers scattered as they made the sensible decision to get the hell out of the way.

I didn't flinch. I simply looked at the other two. 'You should be pleased,' I said quietly. 'This could have ended far worse for you. At least this way you'll still be breathing when tomorrow comes. Drop the bags. Put your hands up, and lower yourselves to the ground.'

The blonde and the professor exchanged looks then did as they were told. I jerked my head at the security officers who swarmed towards us and hauled away the hapless pair. I still didn't know their names but it didn't matter; they were merely puppets in this affair.

I licked my lips before turning to their master. 'Did you think,' I questioned softly, 'that you'd actually get away with a crime of this magnitude?'

Lord Fairfax regarded me without blinking. Now that he'd recovered from his initial shock at my appearance and understood the inevitability of arrest, he'd recovered some of his equilibrium. With deliberately slow movements, he dropped his bag. He managed a small smile. 'Of course I did. Otherwise why do you think I'd go to all this trouble?'

'Why?' I pressed. 'Why steal from your own?'

'You wouldn't understand.'

'Try me.'

Fairfax sighed. 'It wasn't about money – I'm not that

crass. The truth, detective, is that we've been losing ground for years. What the wolves need is someone like Lord Horvath, someone who can rise above the others and take charge. I knew that if I could weaken the clans I could make them stronger in the long run. It would show the others that we need to work together more closely. Disaster unites rather than divides. All the werewolf clans need to do to grow stronger is to join together, but that won't happen unless there is a reason. The right leader can provide that reason.'

I stared at him in disbelief. 'So you thought that you'd steal from your own kind then, when chaos ensued, you'd step up to lead all the clans?'

'You look sceptical, but history is full of examples. The UN was formed after the horrors of World War II. The United States of America came into being after the thirteen revolted against the British.'

'You're hardly George Washington.'

Fairfax shrugged. 'Scoff all you like. It could have worked.' A trace of sadness flashed across his face but I suspected he felt sorry for himself, not for the loss of what he thought the werewolves could have become. He sniffed. 'It *would* have worked. I don't see why you're so upset. It's not as if anyone died.'

I almost laughed aloud. 'But you wanted them to die. You wanted several people to die.' I stared at him. 'Your plan was to sell the contents of the safety deposit boxes back to their owners. You were going to begin with Lord Horvath. You would arrange for him to meet the robbers somewhere quiet – Westminster Bridge in the middle of the night, perhaps.'

Fairfax started.

'You wouldn't show up yourself. No – you'd get others to do your dirty work. That way, you'd have deniability. You'd arrange for the others to sell Lord Horvath's things back to him. Except,' I smiled grimly, 'you also knew that he would never agree to such a thing. He'd never negotiate in that way. He'd try to bring down the robbers rather than hand over a ransom. So you'd make sure that you had Esmeralda Strom positioned at a distance to kill not just Horvath but the robbers as well. There would be no blame apportioned to any supes because the bank robbers would be identified as human. They'd be dead, so they couldn't answer any questions. Lord Horvath would be dead and the vampires in chaos. The safety deposit boxes would be supposedly lost forever. Including, the box belonging to the Talismanic Bank with the names of unregistered supes inside it.' I raised my eyebrows. 'I wonder what you'd have done with that list. More blackmail and bribery, perhaps?'

'This is bullshit,' Fairfax bit out. 'There's no blood staining my hands.'

I ignored his pathetic attempt at denial. 'And then, so you could be absolutely sure of your own success, you'd locate Esmeralda and kill her. After that, you could take all the glory at having solved the greatest heist and biggest murder the supernatural community had ever seen.'

His voice dripped with hatred. 'You'll never prove any of that.'

I didn't take my eyes off him. 'Probably not, but I won't have to. You've already given me all the evidence I need by trying to run.' I nudged his bag with my toe. 'What's in there? The real Hope Diamond? A couple of contradictory copies of *Love's Labours Won*?'

Fairfax stared. 'You're very well informed.'

'Yes,' I said. 'I am.' I could feel the security officials and police around me growing impatient. It was time to bring this to an end. 'You still have a small chance of redemption.'

'What do you mean?'

'Hand yourself in. The world at large won't find out that

one of the werewolf alphas tried to be a criminal master-mind, and the supes' reputation will remain intact. Or,' I continued, 'resist arrest and damn all the werewolves. Every clan and every wolf will be tainted by your deeds for decades to come. This is your last chance to be the werewolf alpha your clan believes you to be.'

A tiny muscle throbbed in Fairfax's jaw but other than that he was inscrutable. I had no clue what he was thinking. 'The others will kill me for what I've done. You know that.'

I thought about Lukas's dead body lying on Westminster Bridge. Fairfax hadn't pulled the trigger on that occasion but he might as well have. 'I have no control over supe law,' I said quietly. And then, because I remained a damned fool despite everything, 'However, I will speak for you. As you say, nobody died.' This time.

Fairfax's shoulders slumped and, in that instant, I was sure it was going to be alright. 'Okay then,' he whispered. 'Okay.'

FLANKED by police officers and airport officials, I walked Lord Fairfax out of the airport. I couldn't bundle him into Tallulah – it would have been highly inappropriate, not to mention dangerous – so I arranged via DSI Barnes for more suitable transport. A sealed prisoner transport van was already waiting for us in a quiet corner away from the public. Two grim-faced men opened the back doors and I handed over Fairfax.

My phone buzzed. I dug it out from my pocket, expecting to see numerous missed calls from Lukas, Liza and Fred amongst others. The calls were there, listed on the glowing screen, but there was also an anonymous text message: *The Talismanic Bank sends its regards.*

I stared at the message. Then I opened my mouth to yell – but it was already too late. There was a single, loud crack that rent the air like an explosion. Fairfax didn't have time to look surprised. His body slumped, hitting the van door before falling backwards in a shower of blood and bone.

The police around me sprang into action, preparing for more shots. No more came.

I didn't need to check what was left of Fairfax's skull to know that he'd been hit by a single silver bullet. Apparently supe justice had been served.

CHAPTER 30

'WELL,' DSI BARNES SAID. 'WELL.' UNDERNEATH HER MAKE-up, her skin looked faintly green.

'We recovered the stolen items,' I told her. 'Fairfax was carrying them in his bag. He paid off the bank robbers with cash and kept the valuables for himself. The hand-off must have taken place moments before I arrived at London City and confronted them. They were all planning to travel their separate ways. It's fortunate we caught up with them before they boarded a plane.'

'Indeed.'

'I think it's best,' I said carefully, 'that we return everything that was stolen and don't ask too many questions.'

Barnes gave me a sharp glance but she didn't disagree. Interrogating the provenance of the recovered items could open up a Pandora's box of trouble that none of us truly wanted.

'You should know that Adam Jones has been charged with public affray and trespassing,' she said. 'He's made a deal. He'll spend the best part of a year inside prison but he'll be out before too long.'

'And the bank robbers?'

'Their sentences will be much longer.'

I nodded. I'd expected as much – and I didn't feel a trace of sympathy for them. The three humans had shot a lot of people inside that bank. The fact that I was the only person who remembered it was neither here nor there.

DSI Barnes linked her fingers together. 'All that brings us to Devereau Webb. We've been trying to pin charges on him for years. Now that he's a werewolf he's beyond our reach. He seems to like you. Do you know what he's planning now that he's a supe?'

'No,' I answered honestly. 'I don't have a clue.'

'The fact that he managed to bypass every safeguard and law and get himself turned into a werewolf will cause problems. We can't advertise what he did because the ramifications could be massive. Every Tom, Dick and Harry with a criminal record will try the same thing.' She sighed. 'You'll need to keep a close eye on him.'

'I'll do my best.' What I hadn't mentioned to anyone was that Devereau Webb had said that he'd been bitten four times before he'd turned. That meant he had the potential to become very powerful indeed. I wasn't going to mention it now, either; his transformation was already causing enough problems. 'Although I suspect that every supe in the city will be doing the same. Mr Webb will be under many watchful eyes.'

Barnes grunted. 'That will be a good thing. We already know that supe justice doesn't allow much room for manoeuvre.'

I swallowed. She could say that again.

'What about the rest of the Fairfax clan?' Barnes asked. 'Are there any obvious contenders for their new alpha?'

I shrugged. There was Toffee, I supposed, but whether she'd want the position was another matter. 'I guess we'll have to see after the next full moon, when the ranking Fairfax wolves challenge each other.'

Barnes pinched off a headache. 'Everything about this is a shit show,' she muttered, as much to herself as to me. She raised her eyes to mine. 'I'm under pressure to add more police detectives and officers to Supe Squad. You won't be alone for much longer.'

'The supes won't like that.'

'They'll have to deal with it. If there's one thing the last day has proved, it's that you need more support.' She held up her hands before I could protest. 'You did a good job, Emma, I'm not denying that. But the winds of change are afoot. You can't continue alone, not in the long run.'

I was silent for a moment. Then I spoke up. 'If I can make one request?'

'Go on.'

'Don't assign anyone like DS Collier. The wrong person will only cause more problems.'

Barnes raised an eyebrow. 'Do you want to tell me more about what happened during your … re-sets?'

I glanced down at my knuckles. There was a faint bruise from where I'd punched Collier. It was still remarkably satisfying. 'I've already told you everything that's relevant.'

She watched me. 'Very well,' she said finally. She stood up. 'I'll expect your full written report by the end of the week. Do me a favour, though, and leave out any mention of magic potions.'

I nodded dutifully and walked her to the door before returning to the main office where Fred and Liza were waiting.

'Is she pissed off?' Fred asked.

'Let's say she's … resigned herself to what's happened.' My mouth flattened. 'I think we'll have some new Supe Squad recruits before too long.'

'Great.' Liza folded her arms unhappily. 'I can hardly wait.'

I flicked on the kettle. 'Is there any news about Esmeralda Strom?'

'She's going to be locked up. The Talismanic Bank offered to *"look after her"*,' Fred drew quotation marks in the air, 'but the werewolves have decided that she's their responsibility. I doubt we'll hear of her again. She's headed to Clink.'

I grunted. Clink was the supes' own gaol. I'd never visited – and I never wanted to. I put a teabag in my mug and added hot water, gazing absently down as the colour of the liquid darkened.

'I almost forgot,' Liza said. She waved an envelope. 'This came for you earlier. One of the Sullivan wolves dropped it off.'

I stiffened, abandoning my tea in favour of taking the envelope. It was unmarked. Using the tip of my index finger, I opened it up, drawing the two sheets of paper from within. The first was a handwritten note, produced with looping calligraphy from an artistic hand. There were only two words. *As Promised.*

I frowned and glanced at the second sheet of paper. Ah. My DNA results. I scanned it and snorted at the typed conclusion. *Human: negative. Supernatural: Inconclusive.* Story of my life.

'What is it?' Liza asked.

I shrugged. 'Just Lady Sullivan trying to pretend that she's my friend and reminding me that most werewolves are good guys.' I balled up the paper and tossed it into the nearest wastepaper basket before returning my attention to my tea. I extracted the tea bag then poured in a splash of milk and stirred. Before I could take a sip, however, my phone rang. When I saw the caller display, I started.

'Hello?' I answered cautiously.

'Is that a question?' my uncle barked down the line. I

didn't get the chance to answer. 'Never mind. I saw your name mentioned on the news this morning. I suppose I should be impressed. You solved a bank robbery in half a day and destroyed an entire werewolf clan.'

I sighed. 'I didn't destroy anything. One werewolf alpha was killed. The clan will be fine.'

He sniffed. 'If you say so. You clearly did good work. Your parents would have been proud.'

From my uncle, this was effusive praise indeed. Something was up. 'Thank you,' I managed.

'I thought I would let you know,' he continued briskly, 'I managed to find that box of things relating to your mother and father. I've packaged it up. It's already on its way to you. I have no idea whether any of it will be useful, but I'd hate to think that you'd send a swarm of vampires and werewolves after me if I didn't keep my word.'

'I wouldn't…' My voice faltered as I realised that this was my uncle's way of making a joke. 'Thank you,' I said again.

'Take care, Emma,' he grunted. Then he clicked off.

'Are you alright, boss?' Fred asked.

I nodded. For all I knew, there was nothing in my uncle's box beyond a few old photographs. I wasn't going to get excited. Yet.

Liza lifted her head and glanced out of the window. She smiled. 'I didn't think it would be long before he showed up again.' There was a teasing edge to her voice. I followed her gaze, noting Lukas as he emerged from the car. He stood on the pavement for several seconds, looking as if he were deep in thought. A small breeze toyed with his hair. Then he lifted up his chin and put his hands in his pockets. A moment later the Supe Squad doorbell rang.

'I'll get it,' I said.

Liza smirked. 'Are you sure? I can always send Lord Horvath on his way or pass on a message for you. You don't have to talk to him in person.' She paused. 'Unless you really want to.' Her smirk grew.

I took a deep breath. 'I really want to.' I raised a hand to my hair as if to smooth it down. A moment later I realised what I was doing and dropped it again. Then I walked out to open the door.

'Hi Emma.' Lukas angled his face up towards mine.

'Hi.' I felt stupidly awkward.

His black eyes searched my face. 'How's your shoulder?' he asked finally.

'A bit sore still. It's healing nicely though.'

'Good.'

We both continued to look at each other.

'Nice weather we're having,' I said. Then I winced. My small-talk skills definitely required work.

The tiniest smile lit the corners of his mouth. 'Yes. It's very summery.'

I bit my lip. 'Are you here about something in particular?'

'I am.'

I waited.

Lukas extended his palm in my direction. 'I know it's a bit late but I thought you might like to come for lunch. I came in person so you couldn't avoid me. And so you have to look me in the eye when you make up an excuse as to why you're too busy.'

'I'm not that busy.' I tilted my head. 'I can spare an hour or two.'

Lukas's eyes suddenly gleamed. 'Are you hungry?'

'No.' I leaned forward and took his hand. 'Shall we go to your place?'

He looked at me. I stepped away from the Supe Squad porch towards his car. A heartbeat later, Lukas followed.

ABOUT THE AUTHOR

After teaching English literature in the UK, Japan and Malaysia, Helen Harper left behind the world of education following the worldwide success of her Blood Destiny series of books. She is a professional member of the Alliance of Independent Authors and writes full time, thanking her lucky stars every day that's she lucky enough to do so!

Helen has always been a book lover, devouring science fiction and fantasy tales when she was a child growing up in Scotland.

She currently lives in Edinburgh in the UK with far too many cats – not to mention the dragons, fairies, demons, wizards and vampires that seem to keep appearing from nowhere.

OTHER TITLES

The complete *FireBrand* series

A werewolf killer. A paranormal murder. How many times can Emma Bellamy cheat death?

I'm one placement away from becoming a fully fledged London detective. It's bad enough that my last assignment before I qualify is with Supernatural Squad. But that's nothing compared to what happens next.

Brutally murdered by an unknown assailant, I wake up twelve hours later in the morgue – and I'm very much alive. I don't know how or why it happened. I don't know who killed me. All I know is that they might try again.

Werewolves are disappearing right, left and centre.

A mysterious vampire seems intent on following me everywhere I go.

And I have to solve my own vicious killing. Preferably before death comes for me again.

A Charade of Magic complete series

The best way to live in the Mage ruled city of Glasgow is to keep your head down and your mouth closed.

That's not usually a problem for Mairi Wallace. By day she works at a small shop selling tartan and by night she studies to become an apothecary. She knows her place and her limitations. All that changes, however, when her old childhood friend sends her a desperate message seeking her help - and the Mages themselves cross Mairi's path. Suddenly, remaining unnoticed is no longer an option.

There's more to Mairi than she realises but, if she wants to fulfil her full potential, she's going to have to fight to stay alive - and only time will tell if she can beat the Mages at their own game.

From twisted wynds and tartan shops to a dangerous daemon and the magic infused City Chambers, the future of a nation might lie with one solitary woman.

Book One – Hummingbird
Book Two – Nightingale
Book Three – Red Hawk

The complete *Blood Destiny* series

"A spectacular and addictive series."

Mackenzie Smith has always known that she was different. Growing up as the only human in a pack of rural shapeshifters will do that to you, but then couple it with some mean fighting skills and a fiery temper and you end up with a woman that few will dare to cross. However, when the only father figure in her life is brutally murdered, and the dangerous Brethren with their predatory Lord Alpha come to investigate, Mack has to not only ensure the physical safety of her adopted family by hiding her apparent humanity, she also has to seek the blood-soaked vengeance that she craves.

Book One - Bloodfire

Book Two - Bloodmagic

Book Three - Bloodrage

Book Four - Blood Politics

Book Five - Bloodlust

Also

Corrigan Fire

Corrigan Magic

Corrigan Rage

Corrigan Politics

Corrigan Lust

The complete *Bo Blackman* series

A half-dead daemon, a massacre at her London based PI firm and evidence that suggests she's the main suspect for both ... Bo Blackman is having a very bad week.

She might be naive and inexperienced but she's determined to get to the bottom of the crimes, even if it means involving herself with one of London's most powerful vampire Families and their enigmatic leader.

It's pretty much going to be impossible for Bo to ever escape unscathed.

Book One - Dire Straits

Book Two - New Order

Book Three - High Stakes

Book Four - Red Angel

Book Five - Vigilante Vampire

Book Six - Dark Tomorrow

The complete *Highland Magic* series

Integrity Taylor walked away from the Sidhe when she was a child. Orphaned and bullied, she simply had no reason to stay, especially not when the sins of her father were going to remain on her shoulders. She found a new family - a group of thieves who proved that blood was less important than loyalty and love.

But the Sidhe aren't going to let Integrity stay away forever. They need her more than anyone realises - besides, there are prophecies to be fulfilled, people to be saved and hearts to be won over. If anyone can do it, Integrity can.

Book One - Gifted Thief

Book Two - Honour Bound

Book Three - Veiled Threat

Book Four - Last Wish

The complete *Dreamweaver* series

"I have special coping mechanisms for the times I need to open the front door. They're even often successful..."

Zoe Lydon knows there's often nothing logical or rational about fear. It doesn't change the fact that she's too terrified to step outside her own house, however.

What Zoe doesn't realise is that she's also a dreamweaver - able to access other people's subconscious minds. When she finds herself in the Dreamlands and up against its sinister Mayor, she'll need to use all of her wits - and overcome all of her fears - if she's ever going to come out alive.

Book One - Night Shade

Book Two - Night Terrors

Book Three - Night Lights

Stand alone novels

Eros

William Shakespeare once wrote that, "Cupid is a knavish lad, thus to make poor females mad." The trouble is that Cupid himself would probably agree...

As probably the last person in the world who'd appreciate hearts, flowers and romance, Coop is convinced that true love doesn't exist – which is rather unfortunate considering he's also known as Cupid, the God of Love. He'd rather spend his days drinking, womanising and generally having as much fun as he possible can. As far as he's concerned, shooting people with bolts of pure love is a waste of his time...but then his path crosses with that of shy and retiring Skye Sawyer and nothing will ever be quite the same again.

Wraith

Magic. Shadows. Adventure. Romance.

Saiya Buchanan is a wraith, able to detach her shadow from her body and send it off to do her bidding. But, unlike most of her kin, Saiya doesn't deal in death. Instead, she trades secrets - and in the goblin besieged city of Stirling in Scotland, they're a highly prized commodity. It might just be, however, that the goblins have been hiding the greatest secret of them all. When Gabriel de Florinville, a Dark Elf, is sent as royal envoy into Stirling and takes her prisoner, Saiya is not only going to uncover the sinister truth. She's also going to realise that sometimes the deepest secrets are the ones locked within your own heart.

The complete *Lazy Girl's Guide To Magic* series

Hard Work Will Pay Off Later. Laziness Pays Off Now.

Let's get one thing straight - Ivy Wilde is not a heroine. In fact, she's probably the last witch in the world who you'd call if you needed a magical helping hand. If it were down to Ivy, she'd spend all day every day on her sofa where she could watch TV, munch junk food and talk to her feline familiar to her heart's content.

However, when a bureaucratic disaster ends up with Ivy as the victim of a case of mistaken identity, she's yanked very unwillingly into Arcane Branch, the investigative department of the Hallowed Order of Magical Enlightenment. Her problems are quadrupled when a valuable object is stolen right from under the Order's noses.

It doesn't exactly help that she's been magically bound to Adeptus Exemptus Raphael Winter. He might have piercing sapphire eyes and a body which a cover model would be proud of but, as far as

Ivy's concerned, he's a walking advertisement for the joyless perils of too much witch-work.

And if he makes her go to the gym again, she's definitely going to turn him into a frog.

Book One - Slouch Witch

Book Two - Star Witch

Book Three - Spirit Witch

Sparkle Witch (Christmas novella)

The complete *Fractured Faery* series

One corpse. Several bizarre looking attackers. Some very strange magical powers. And a severe bout of amnesia.

It's one thing to wake up outside in the middle of the night with a decapitated man for company. It's another to have no memory of how you got there - or who you are.

She might not know her own name but she knows that several people are out to get her. It could be because she has strange magical powers seemingly at her fingertips and is some kind of fabulous hero. But then why does she appear to inspire fear in so many? And who on earth is the sexy, green-eyed barman who apparently despises her? So many questions ... and so few answers.

At least one thing is for sure - the streets of Manchester have never met someone quite as mad as Madrona...

Book One - Box of Frogs

SHORTLISTED FOR THE KINDLE STORYTELLER AWARD 2018

Book Two - Quiver of Cobras

Book Three - Skulk of Foxes

The complete *City Of Magic* series

Charley is a cleaner by day and a professional gambler by night. She might be haunted by her tragic past but she's never thought of herself as anything or anyone special. Until, that is, things start to go terribly wrong all across the city of Manchester. Between plagues of rats, firestorms and the gleaming blue eyes of a sexy Scottish werewolf, she might just have landed herself in the middle of a magical apocalypse. She might also be the only person who has the ability to bring order to an utterly chaotic new world.

Book One - Shrill Dusk

Book Two - Brittle Midnight

Book Three - Furtive Dawn

Made in United States
Orlando, FL
12 January 2024

42429029R00176